MW01273189

Cameo

Fritha Waters

Copyright © 2012 Fritha Waters
All rights reserved.

ISBN: 1-4699-3172-9
ISBN-13: 9781469931722

Dedication

For Carolyn and Mark

Prologue

She hated this room.

There wasn't one nice thing about it. No one had even tried to make it the slightest bit welcoming (homely would have been inappropriate at any rate, she thought). But they could have at least made the colour of the walls more pleasant, the nastiest shade of khaki had been chosen by some ill- advised or ill-willed individual, and by the condition of them, no one had apparently sought to right this wrong by painting over it in the last decade. The window was curtain-less and the battered Venetian blinds looked to her like heavily made up, broken eyelashes. There was no carpet on the floor, only what appeared to be the same kind of tiles as hospitals used; scuffed, yet still gleaming with a determined shine. It wasn't so much the room, she conceded with a sigh, but the feeling she got whenever she entered it. She gazed off through the viewless window; the room was on such a high floor that if she looked straight out from her seat, she was floating in a groundless sky.

'Associations' of course, as Gillian would have put it; the room could have been the most inviting place in the world, but her heart would still sink like a stone, a leaden cloud would descend on her lungs whenever she stepped through the swing-ing spring- shut door—the faint smell of bleach making her queasy. Within ten to fifteen minutes of her sitting there, the room would slowly fill with ghosts. Shipwrecks of bodies, empty and rotten within. They ran themselves aground here to anchor

for an hour and a half, before drifting off again, compass-less and without maps. These were shells of people, the light inside them having been blown out long ago—always extinguished (and this was a given) by another person.

Whenever she contemplated her attendance of the "Survivors of 'Childhood Abuse' group, the thought would come to her again; that it was all such a long time ago. In truth it wasn't just her for whom it was all so long ago for; Ellie, the overly large woman who walked with two sticks and wore thick glasses like the bottom of milk bottles was sixty-four. Maureen, who perpetually shook and had a habit of suddenly walking out of the room, was seventy if she was a day "Age doesn't come into it, Lillian," her daughter-in-law Gillian had said to her solemnly over the rim of the teacup. Gillian had always called her Lillian, and although it wasn't actually her name, Lily Maxwell had long since resigned herself to the fact that Gillian had never had her down as a Lily. 'Probably thinks it sounds too young,' she thought. Lily was a young-sounding name, fresh and spring-like, not suited to her scraggy neck and thin lips… Maybe it was simply because Lillian rhymed with Gillian, she mused…At forty-five Lily Maxwell could safely admit to herself that she was no longer young, although she quietly and stoically dismissed the thought that she was old. Still, there were quite a few things that were 'a long time ago' now…

"You never get over something like that," Gillian continued, her rounded vowels solemn "honestly Lillian, it doesn't matter how old you are; it still affects you."

"But I hardly ever think about it nowadays," interjected Lily, pouring herself more tea "really Gillian, it was just so long ago—I don't see what good it would do."

"Well, it's obviously still in your conscious mind," Gillian said, dipping a digestive into her cup, "this is exactly what we've been doing on my course at the moment 'suppressing unconscious trauma' it's called."

"I'm not exactly traumatized, Gillian–"

"But that's just it," Gillian went on earnestly, her small hazel eyes alight with excitement, "you might be traumatized and not even realise it—you might not even remember it fully—but your childhood mind could have stowed the trauma away, and you're damaging yourself by stamping down on it by not experiencing it fully," she continued enthusiastically, her hand still pressing the damp biscuit. "For instance, I suddenly remembered I was tremendously upset at the age of five when my baby brother was born and my parents were so pre-occupied with him they didn't even notice I'd learnt to spell my name, at the time I didn't say anything, but by discussing it now, in my course, I had to re-live it all—and I found it very distressing, but then afterwards it was this huge relief." Stopping for breath, Gillian finally bit into the biscuit, at the same time sighing and spraying crumbs, which Lily watched fall onto her lap. "Going to a group and sharing things with people who've had the same experience is tremendously helpful," she said, regurgitating the latest part of her course textbook

"Mmm," agreed Lily absently, at the same time wondering if she had any Dundee cake left in the pantry…or maybe some ginger snaps…

"Honestly Lillian," Gillian said firmly, "if someone more unstable had experienced what you've been through, they might not have even made it to your age."

Lily frowned momentarily, her mind streets away. "What's that then?"

Gillian stared incredulously at her, the half-eaten digestive poised above the near empty china cup "Well when you got snatched Lillian, of course—when you were kidnapped."

That night, in bed with John snoring quietly beside her, Lily thought of it for the first time in years. 'It' was how she always referred to it in her mind, having never been able to find the right words for what had happened. It was an event in her life, that much was true, but 'event' sounded too much like an enjoyable outing, to the pictures or the theatre. 'Incident' put Lily in mind of 'Crimewatch' and although, technically it had been a crime—it had never felt like that to her. It was just something that had happened in her childhood—like falling off a bike or skating on a frozen river.

She remembered the strained tight look of her mother's face, a second before she spotted Lily walking into the police station. She remembered the bone-crushing hug she received from both parents and the wide-eyed look from her sister, Barbara. Later, years later, Babs had confessed to her that she had wondered why such hell had broken loose when Lily had obviously been clear of danger, judging by the casual way she had drifted into the police station. Why had she, Barbara, had to miss out on the special lunch they had been promised when they had first got to Edinburgh, as well as ice creams and a trip to the castle? All because Lily had taken it upon herself to wander off and not tell anyone? Barbara didn't speak to her younger sister for the whole of the journey back to Manchester, their holiday cut short.

When they had arrived home to their surprised neighbours and no milk in the fridge, Lily's father had still stayed off work for the remainder of the week, Lily and Barbara feeling slightly off kilter with the sound of his moving round the house on a weekday. Edinburgh was never spoken of again within the family, and Lily was made to hold her mother's hand whenever they ventured out, up until the age of fifteen.

She had begun going to the Survivors group as a favour to Gillian, who after their conversation had gone to the extent of seeking out a support group for her under the misunderstanding that Lily had agreed to it. Lily never liked to hurt anyone's feelings and when she saw how much trouble Gillian had gone to; finding a group which was close to her house, making sure it took place in the evening so that Lily didn't have to miss work, she felt she couldn't say no. Finally, Gillian presented her with a time, a date and a light pink pamphlet on 'Survivors of Childhood Abuse' or S.O.C.A. (why did all these things have to have an acronym? Lily would ponder as she skimmed through the folded single page).

Was she really a survivor? Had she, in fact, ever been abused? As far she could recall, she and her 'abductor' had simply walked around Edinburgh taking in the sights—that was all she remembered…wasn't it? Every Wednesday evening Lily would check herself in the hall mirror before she went out of the front door. The smart little woman who looked back at her in her good black winter jacket, or dark green waterproof if it was raining, with all her own teeth and only a few grey hairs did not look like she was hiding some dark trauma under her neat exterior, no matter how much Gillian insisted she was.

This was one of the reasons why she disliked going to the Survivors of Childhood Abuse group; she had never felt like she had been abused, and so she felt like a fraud. She hadn't been torn up like these other poor women (and it mostly was women, the only man was eyed suspiciously and his utterances remained unanswered and unconsidered) Lily's life hadn't been dictated by that one 'episode' (which was the nearest word she could decide upon to describe 'it') she hadn't experienced some appalling violation which had obliterated her childhood like the women here, some had their lives ended before they had even begun. The man, Andrew, once shouted that he didn't want to be known as a survivor—he hadn't survived as far as he knew.

"It's only that I'm still fucking alive," he argued, "That's just coincidence."

The other members of the group were strangers to Lily, 'from a foreign field' as mother used to refer to people she had nothing in common with. Although they all lived within twenty miles of each other, districts meant nothing when it came to the disreputable streets which Lily would never dream of walking down, or shops and bars she had never known existed. These were the underground people, Lily thought. She wouldn't have looked at them twice on the street, only steadily ignored them and stared past their haunted expressions, instinctively knowing that theirs was a messy character and best avoided. There was nothing cruel in this, she conceded, having got to know them now, she would still never want to get directly involved in their lives; they were an alien race, one that Lily would never really associate with. She did feel guilty though, impossible not to. She likened it to seeing starving African children on the television and the feeling that she could do something if she tried, but really, when she thought about it, what could she actually do? These women were wrecks and Manchester was full of them. She could have seen them anywhere; Lynn might have sold her copy of the Evening News, or Kate could have served her the cappuccino in Morrison's.

The women's pasts too, were unknown landscapes to Lily. Ellie for instance had acquired adult behaviour by the age of twelve. Years ago, the judge who was dealing with the case against her father declared Ellie 'no angel', and in the trail of care homes and hostels she was known as a trouble-maker, a liar. It was a typical story by all accounts, although Lily had only come across this sort of thing in newspapers. Ellie had done the rounds of drugs and alcohol and having finally given them all up she now ate for comfort. But she had grown too heavy for her naturally slight frame. Recently, she had developed osteoarthritis and now she hardly moved from her small flat on a housing estate where the local kids threw rocks through her window.

In contrast, Lynn was a waif of a girl, reminding Lily of the pictures in her ancient copy of Hans Christian Anderson's 'Fairy Tales'; Lynn was the Little Mermaid or the Goose Girl; pale skin like alabaster, and wrists which looked as though they'd snap like sticks. She wouldn't talk in full sentences, limiting her tiny bird-like voice to a series of disjointed syllables. Lily had to force back tears and felt physically sick when Lynn described what had happened to her as a child. She had had to fight with all her might the thought of her own children at that age (or any child, of any age) meeting someone who might resemble Lynn's aggressor—the friend of the family and their neighbour of seven years. Lily felt as though her eyes had been *opened in the last few weeks, while attending the group; but in the worst possible way. Part of her felt compelled to keep them open; as though this were a horrific car crash that she felt it was her duty to watch.*

What broke her heart the most, what really wrenched her in half was that this room of crumbled people wouldn't exist if there hadn't been a few others in the world who had pummeled the light out of them. Because that's what they were, she would think, Lynn, Ellie, Kate, Maureen, Andrew and the rest…they were the results of a bunch of folk getting their kicks—those who had abusive tendencies which crippled bodies and scarred minds, which sucked the life out of people and left them ruined. The evening Lily had this revelation, she couldn't go home to John straight away, she left the group in the faded evening and walked the streets for an hour and a half, not really taking any notice of where she was going. Ending up in front of their green door, Lily wondered what the other women's doors looked like; what colour they were, did they have to type a code to get in? Was there even a front door at all? It was the first time she had taken the others from the group home with her, and Lily's head felt very crowded when she lay down beside John in their quiet neat bedroom that night. Lily sometimes daydreamed about what the women would have been like if others hadn't got to them first; Ellie might be married by now, with children—Lily could almost picture her in a hustling bustling house full of bouncing grandchildren, she'd be busy at the kitchen table with an apron on, flour on her cheek, making apple crumble. Or Lynn, who had the eyes and figure of a fashion model (if she would only put on some weight) she could be on the pages of magazines, travelling the world with an entourage of men falling at her small feet.

After three sessions Lily still could not really contribute to the circle's conversation, she was a confused and horrified fly on the wall. But she still went, dutifully, not wanting to let anyone down, was how she justified going to her husband, John.

"I told Gillian I'd go," she'd say as she put on her coat on Wednesday evenings, "It doesn't hurt anyway," and secretly, she felt compelled to go, almost on a selfish whim, the stories she couldn't bear to hear but felt drawn to, something within the nightmarish tales struck a chord, a horrific minor key which resonated with something deep down inside her.

She wanted to hear, she wanted to help these adult-children, but she didn't know how. What she did know was that she had to keep going each Wednesday evening. There was something else though, something that she wasn't admitting to John or really to herself, she didn't see it coming, she hadn't welcomed it but now that it was happening, she knew that she couldn't stop it.

She was remembering things, aspects of 'the episode' which she'd buried, either on purpose or simply forgotten—facts that had been swept away by the little gusts around the milestones of her life; her marriage, the birth of her children, the death of her father; events which were routine enough, but outweighed the memories stored from when she was six.

Her recollections were nothing spectacular at first, but little things like what flavour that ice cream was, and how big the hill was that they'd climbed that day—how her small legs had ached. But why was it, she wondered, that all the memories, few as they were, were tinged with a darkness? A vague menace, always in the background, quietly pulsing.

She had always remembered the mist that had covered the city that afternoon, but had never really believed it to be true. It had just added a dream-like quality to her memory. But one summer afternoon, sitting out in her sister Barbara's garden, she summoned up the courage to bring up the subject of that day in Edinburgh, so very long ago.

"Was there really all that mist, Babs?" Lily asked her big sister, leaning forward in her wicker seat, "or did I imagine that?"

"Oh yes, it was there, thick as pea soup it was," replied Barbara from behind a sun hat and large sunglasses. She now spoke with the clipped, well-polished accent of someone who lived much further south, thanks to a career as an elocution teacher. Lily, like her parents still retained her warm, rounded Manchester tone.

"That's what made Mum and Dad even more worried. I've never seen anything like it, couldn't see your hand in front of your face…and then you walked out of it, like a bedraggled fairy, babbling something about winning the lottery."

"It was her," Lily said, slowly unpicking memories in her mind, "she said she'd won it and that if I stayed with her that we could be rich and never have to worry again."

"You've never told me that," Barbara was studying her sister over the top of her huge sunglasses.

"I don't think I really remembered before," Lily murmured and wondered what else she'd forgotten. All these pieces of the jigsaw seemed innocuous enough but they paved a way for Lily to step onto, to visit the source of the void in her life that she'd always felt she'd been there.

1

Michael stepped out onto the pavement and held up his hand ready to shield his eyes from a glaring sun, so he was surprised when all he was met with was a faint prickling behind the eyebrows. All the same, he frowned involuntarily as he was faced with air that lay beyond brick walls for the first time in two years.

This natural light; although grey, opaque and mixed with a warm, slightly sweaty breeze, felt beautifully soft on Michael Lambert's skin. He breathed in the heavy traffic fumes, and the noise of the cars slapped him hard. He thought of films where rugged and ironic looking actors first stepped out of the prison gates—what did they do? They looked to the sky (Michael peered through his eyelashes at the dull, colourless cloud) they smiled ruefully (a grin spread across his face) and they coolly (he patted his top pocket for the familiar rectangular bulge) lit a cigarette. He shook one out, ducked low for the flame and puffing out smoke, started off along the street.

Taking his first steps, Michael was aware of the excitement that rose in his chest, but he tried to keep calm. He gazed around him, trying to spot any changes in the scenery, but was vaguely disappointed when he could see that there were no huge transformations, no new buildings; only the old ones made over, like women of a certain age wearing new lipstick.

Michael stopped and looked about, exhaling smoke. He was aware of the vast amount of space all around him, he felt tiny, the air wrapped around his body and flared outwards for miles. He could walk ten steps and not be next to a wall or another person; he could hear noises that he had only heard on television in the past two years; a dog barking, high heels on the pavement, shop doors opening. He could smoke without folding the cigarette away in his fingers, he could keep his head up, his back straight, (Inside 'A' Hall he would slope around, head to the floor, afraid he might meet an aggravated eye) he'd told himself then that when he got out, he would take in *everything*—he'd look all around him and absorb it into himself; the air, the street, the dirt, the litter, the people. The City. Edinburgh City. His City; the roads and buildings that had brought him up, his concrete parents that had led him up paths and alleyways, steering him round the map of his life. He had purposefully not told any of his real family that he was getting out today, in order to do just this—to savour the feeling of being alone, and being alone among strangers.

Michael realised he had stopped outside the pub, it was a different colour to the one Michael remembered—not that he had been in there more than once, but the building was lodged in his mind as one of the last sights of the outside that he had grasped through the police van's window. For the first month in prison he had associated the swinging faded sign of The Chesser with that of everything he missed and was denied to him. His father had mentioned once that he had slipped a visit to a bar into his routine whenever he came visit Michael. Derek Lambert Senior, known to all as Deek, would spend half an hour with his youngest son, not saying a lot. Glancing round at the other inmates and the other inmate's wives and sisters, he'd nervously turn over the change in his pockets—and then he'd push off.

"Right, I'll push off."

And one day he revealed that it was The Chesser that he pushed off to. Michael had asked what it was like.

"'Bout what you'd expect from a prison local," his father had shrugged.

"Grim-faced folk, pish lager…Wifies with faces like old slip- pers."

Since he had separated from Michael's mother fifteen years ago, Deek Lambert had been especially interested in women and their faces. Not that he had really gotten to know many new ones, apart from Debbie, his present girlfriend who, Michael suspected, had not exactly been new to his father, even when he was still married.

Michael ambled outside The Chesser, deliberating. It looked like a lousy pub that was true, did he really want to spend his first hour on the outside in a hole like this? He was tempted to go into the city centre and drop in on one of the bars he used to go to, he could go to Broughton Street and go to the Phoenix or the Barony—Doug or Pete might even be about—he'd give them the shock of their lives. But he was savouring his own company too much. Inside there had been loneliness and isolation, but Michael knew that that time was over. He knew now that he *could* see his friends, or ring his Ma—they were only steps away, there wasn't an indeterminably thick wall between them, or time stretching out like a river without banks. He had, as the song went *All The Time In The World.* A lorry trundled past and Michael sidestepped into the bar.

Inside was dark and dank. Dust swirled in front of a large TV screen that buzzed and flickered onto the dry faces of two old men who sat at the bar. They eyed Michael as he came in, but only for a second and then turned back to the screen. Michael strenuously ignored the television; he'd always hated it and had made a point not to watch it when he'd been inside. Films were different, he'd told himself (after his first week or two when the boredom was beginning to smother him) he would sit through videos, however crap they were, but he would not allow himself to be drawn into daytime television—it was there, Michael decreed, that lay apathy, and suicidal thoughts—if you found yourself feeling akin to Lorraine Kelly and her limp-faced guests, then really, you might as well top yourself then and there.

He walked to the bar, and again felt the fizzing in his belly that had accompanied him when he'd approached the door to the outside of the prison. He used to get it when he was a kid, that jingling in his guts, it felt as though he ought to jump up and down or else something might explode through the top of his head. He told himself that he almost didn't have the right to feel this excited after just two years—after all, there were lads inside who would still be there past their fortieth birthdays—what right had he to feel like a bairn at Christmas when folks like Kenny and Grant were still doing their time? But he still couldn't help but feel excited as he approached the bar and looked at the row of beer pumps, shining in the dour light of the overhead lamp.

There were footsteps, a crash and a bang and a dark head emerged from the floor. The girl behind the bar climbed out of the hole in the floor, stood on either side and let the trap door to the cellar thud down between her stilettoe'd ankles. Michael's eye- brows rose at the thought of climbing anything in those heels, and before he could whip his eyes away from the devil-horned shoes, the girl's voice brought him sharply up to her face level.

"Aye?"

Michael saw himself from her point of view—just another ex- con fresh out of Saughton, pale and rubber-faced, pissing his pants at the thought of a pint and dumbstruck at the sight of a woman. He tried to re-arrange his features into one of casualness and in- difference, and just as he was muttering, "Pint of Eighty, hen," the girl's face changed too.

"Mikey?" she said, peering at him under his lowered lashes, "Mikey Lambert? Derek Lambert's brother?"

Michael looked up sharply, frowning at her in the limbo land between ignorance and recognition. He studied her heavily made up face, the gelled stiff curls; she smiled at him eagerly.

"I'm Lauren McKee—I used to go about with Derek."

Michael nodded slowly, and as the penny dropped his eyes widened and his head nodded quicker. Of course, Lauren McKee, the object of many a fantasy of his thirteen-year-old self, but back then she had been younger too, pink cheeked and full of allure to his pubescent mind—her ringlets had been free of hair products and, as Michael recalled, she had had a habit of wearing very tiny skirts; in short she had been the typical Older Brother's Girlfriend; developed, exciting and completely beyond his reach. In Michael's memory Derek and Lauren had been together for the best part of a year, until she had abruptly stopped coming round the house, and a few weeks later was replaced by a Catriona Rogers. When Michael had asked Derek what had happened to Lauren, he had liked Lauren, Derek had told him to mind his own fuckin' business.

Looking at her now, pulling the pump fiercely with a well- practised arm, he had remembered that Lauren had once stepped into his bedroom; she had been waiting for Derek to get off the phone and had pushed the door open curiously. She had looked at his Hearts posters and poked at the spindly model airplanes hanging from invisible thread from the ceiling. Michael had spent the entire time in a furious blush, refusing to meet her eyes, although he had sneaked looks at her bum when she had her back to him.

"Aye, I remember you well," she was saying, "What've you been up to?" She shook her head in wonder, "Bloody hell, you look all grown up, how old are you now?" without waiting for an answer she pushed the foaming pint over to Michael who reached out for it quickly.

Relishing the familiar cold glass as his fingers wrapped round it, he raised the still-settling pint to his lips to suck off the foam—and then realised Lauren had stopped talking and was looking at him expectantly. He was about to explain his existence with a few mumbled sentences when she looked away, grabbed a dirty cloth and wiped the ring of beer from the bar. Deliberately not meeting Michael's eyes now, she asked with forced casualness, "How's Derek? What's he up to now?"

Michael suddenly felt sorry for her, he could see now that Derek had probably been a bastard to her but he marvelled at how she could still feel awkward over an ex-boyfriend of what, fourteen years ago?

"Good question," he said shortly, taking a gulp of beer and trying not to show just how nectar-like it was to his taste buds. "I haven't seen the prick for years either," it felt good to bad-mouth Derek, and to meet someone who at some point probably felt the same.

"Really? How come?" She looked puzzled.

"Well I wrote to him but er…" Michael paused, unsure of whether to continue, "He never answered the visitor's request."

Lauren glanced up. "Oh."

"Aye."

"But you're out now, right?"

"Aye," he repeated and looked at his watch, "for precisely thirty-six minutes."

Lauren looked at him; it was, Michael thought, the first real

look she had given him since he walked in. "Sorry to hear that."

"Well," he said with strained cheeriness, "It's all done with now." He could hear his voice rising in volume. "Done ma time an' all that shite!"

Lauren was still looking at him, disbelieving. "It's good to see you, Mikey," was all she said.

"Uh, it's Michael now," he corrected her, at the same time feeling foolish.

"Michael," she smiled, picked up the cloth again and worried it across the bar. He sunk his eyes to his pint and went to sit in a corner, with his back to the television.

When he left the bar it was nearly two 'o'clock. Michael's head swam as he let the heavy door swing shut behind him, unused as he was to downing three pints, let alone in the early afternoon. He had only spoken to Lauren once more to order the other two pints and then it was the end of her shift. She hadn't asked anymore about Derek but he could sense that she wanted to. He was glad to have seen her, it had knocked the corners off his nervousness of seeing a girl again and after the second pint he'd even toyed with the idea of asking her where she was going when she was finished, but he'd checked himself in fear of looking desperate. There was plenty of time for all of that.

Passing a phone box, Michael lurched into it on impulse; he fumbled in his pocket for twenty pence and looked for the slot.

Thirty pence?

In just two years?

Fuck. This discovery had knocked his dad's number completely out of his mind—dammit. Michael urgently wanted to ring someone, *needing* to ring someone, to have the novelty of using a phone on the outside, but the only number that sprang to his mind in sheer certainty was Derek's. Michael snorted derisively, shaking his head at the irony. Smiling to himself, he dialled the number, he would have the upper hand at least, if that fucker thought he could simply ignore him because he was inside...well, he was out now and, ach—he'd got the bloody answer machine. He listened to Derek Junior's flat voice, what Michael would call his yuppie voice, explaining that he wasn't in, though he might be at his office which was 0131 6634002, and if the caller wanted to ring him there, they could feel free to do so otherwise if they left a message he would be sure to get back to them as soon as possible. There were a lot of beeps after the message—maybe he was away? Michael almost put the receiver back again, when suddenly the long beep came on, he coughed,

"Hi, er Derek, it's Michael," he paused for the effect, and then made his voice casual and bright, "Yep, well...I'm out and, well..." he paused again, his eyes narrowed which he hoped would come through on the message, "it would be great to see you. I'll er...I'll give you a call later." He hung the phone up firmly, hoping the recording would end with a loud audible click like it did on all good gangster films.

Shafts of sunlight were piercing the cloud, the air was warming up around him and he could feel the slight balmy breeze on his forehead and under the arms of his t-shirt. Michael smiled widely as he lifted up his arms to catch the heat. This was it, he thought in wonder, it didn't get much better than this, not in Scotland anyway. Laughing at the tepid sky he drew a deep breath and looked around him—what next? Those pints had done him the world of good—the feeling he had now was one of normality; he had been like this so many times before he'd gone down; with mates at the Phoenix, after a match with his Da; the light head and heavy feet were as familiar as his own bedroom, drunkenness had slipped in as easily as an old friend, a comfortable coat. He found himself three strides from a bus stop, the buses that stopped at it were headed to the city centre and Michael thought that would be a fine place to go right now.

A bus was just lumbering up and Michael automatically stood in line behind the hunched back of an old woman, clutching a black bag on wheels. Michael revelled in the feeling of being ordinary; he was once again like everyone else; breathing in the actions of the everyday. Before he went inside, he remembered, he'd be impatiently shunting this old wifie onto the bus, muttering under his breath and cursing her slowness and frailty; now, she could take as long as she wanted, he would stand patiently back and even put forward a friendly arm to steady her on her way...she turned at his touch, her brow wrinkled in a frown.

"I'm fine," she snapped, snatching her arm away.

Michael stood back, holding his hands up in innocence, "Sorry love."

The old woman said nothing but scowled at him as she continued to shuffle up the bus. Her anger made Michael suddenly feel flustered and unsure as he stepped on, his exuberance gone and his tongue stuck to the roof of his mouth. He could feel the eyes of the other passengers fixed on him as he searched in his pockets for some change. The driver looked at him with a lifeless expression and as Michael's hand began to shake, the driver's eyes rolled in his head and he turned his face to the window.

"Sorry," Michael gabbled, sweat prickling his armpits, he felt the need to explain "I haven't been on a bus for a while, ken?" he shook the coins in his hands and the metallic smell floated up to his nostrils, "How much is it now anyway?" The driver; bored, still didn't speak as he tapped the coin box on which was a sticker that told him the fare would be a pound, and Michael gratefully slid the money in, a penny sticking to his palm. "Thanks pal," Michael breathed, another moment's panic when he didn't know where to grab the ticket, spat out from the machine but the driver ignored him and his shaking hands, pressed a button to close the doors with a hiss, and looked in his mirror to pull away. The lurching movement sent Michael stumbling down the aisle. The other passengers swayed in sync.

Michael found a seat next a girl with headphones, he felt too nervous even to look at her to see if she was attractive. He could hear her music soaking through the small pads on her ears, a heavy fast drumbeat and synthesisers. It did nothing for his mood but he forced himself to breathe deep; again reminding himself that if he had still been inside, he might well have told whatever numpty was playing this kind of crap to shut the fuck up.

In the corner at the front, where normally a wheelchair or buggy would be, sat a man hunched over a can of Tennents; occasionally he mumbled slushily to himself and the woman who had glared at Michael now glared at him, whispering in hushed, disgusted tones to her neighbour, who nodded gravely, both of them never taking their disapproving eyes from the slumped figure.

It seemed to take an age to crawl into town. Familiar streets were uncovering themselves to Michael, walls and corners, shops and houses. Memories came, tapping him on the back.

As they rumbled on past Haymarket Station, Michael kept seeing groups of people all walking in the same direction. He craned his head to try and catch more than glimpses of them. All of them seemed to be dressed in white; whether it was from head to toe; shirts, skirts or trousers or simply a nod towards the apparent uniform; a headband, a tie. Maybe it was festival time already, Michael thought, there were certainly a lot of people about—maybe it was the new thing this year to wear white, or there was some kind of church group on an outing.

None of the other passengers seemed to notice the phenomena; that the whole of Edinburgh seemed to be dressing identically. The bus stopped and a group of people got on, again, all of them were dressed in white, a family with two young children, a blonde girl and boy. Two teenage girls also got on, they carried sticks with bits of board stuck to them but whatever was on the other side was hidden from Michael's view. The girls looked like fairies, Michael thought, or cheap angels—the white cotton skirts hung limply over their striped tights; one of them wore big black boots. The other girl, the one with the three stray pink dreadlocks wore a pair of bedraggled wire wings, covered with stretched net curtain, in one side there was hole the size of a cigarette end. Tired Christmas tree fairies The father and mother of the family carried plastic bags and a wicker basket. Out of the top poked a thermos and a family-sized packet of crisps. The boy and girl sat together on the one seat available, picking at their white attire, waving sticks with white strips of material attached, like streamers. There was an excited air above the new passengers' heads; their chatter filled the bus. The man with his Tennents looked out from under his eyebrows, the two fairy girls stood self-consciously next to him and Michael smirkingly observed that his head was level with the taller girl's arse. She stood, stiffly aware of this whereas the man remained oblivious. His muttering lifted in volume as he blinked in the sight of the girls' signs.

"Aye, a caird on a stick hen, that'll do it," he chuckled to himself "A caird on a stick, that'll show them."

The girls looked witheringly at him and Michael smiled. He still hadn't a clue as to what was going on and was just thinking about summoning up the courage to ask his sullen earphoned neighbour when there was a crackle from above their heads and the driver's broad accent burst through the tannoy.

"Due to the march, Princes Street is closed, so if you're wanting Princes Street, get off at the next stop."

Like sheep, most of the passengers shuffled and trotted off the bus, baa-ing and wittering. Michael was enjoying the flow of the afternoon; evidently it wasn't a day like any other—for him or anyone else. It was one he knew he was going to remember; he pictured a big red 'record' button being depressed in his mind.

As he stepped off the bus Michael was hit by the atmosphere, the noise of people, drums and whistles, and many feet; he thought of the tribal roar of a football match; it was the same feeling.

Rounding the corner of the west end of Princes Street, Michael was confronted with an alien Edinburgh to the one that he left. There wasn't a car or a bus in sight; instead there were people. Thousands of people, all walking as if they were heading straight for him, all marching with purpose, laughing, shouting, blowing whistles, and all of them, without exception wore something white. Michael's brain drummed against his skull. He had not experienced crowds for a long time and his heart thudded in his chest. The beer had made his mouth dry and he felt the sun beating down on the crown of his head. He looked about him for a way out; he saw that there were more people at his elbows; all jostling forward and looping him along like a knitted stitch. Michael tried to squirm out but they held him fast and he was pushed along with them. He saw that he had no choice but to join the rest of the throng, as they turned the corner onto Lothian Road.

Michael was surrounded by white jerking figures that took no notice of him, he felt like he had gate-crashed a party where he knew no one at all, not even a friend-of-a-friend-like-who'd-definitely-invited-him-and-if-he-could-just-go-and-see-like...

A dancing boy in white dungarees, a bare chest and a black and red jester's hat with bells at the ends, blew a whistle in blasts, he carried a placard reading, *End Poverty Now,* next to him was an elderly man who Michael judged to be in his sixties, he wore a back to front red baseball cap and a white t-shirt reading, *Fuck the G8.* Michael wove his way towards the man in the cap and stooped down to be close to his ear.

"Who're the G8?"

"What?" The man cupped a liver-spotted hand around his ear and leant in towards Michael.

"WHAT IS THIS ALL ABOUT?" Michael raised his voice and tried not to yell down the old man's ear. The man jerked his head back and looked at Michael incredulously.

"Jesus—where have you been for the last year, son?" the old man shouted and shook his head mutter-ing "bloody stupid teenagers"

Michael opened his mouth to protest Protest that he was nearly twenty-eight when he caught the eye of the dancing dungeree'd boy who was shaking his arms after just finishing a bout of whooping and whistling.

"Dan't worry 'bout it man," the boy called to him in a strong

London accent "as long as you're here it dan't mat-ter."

"But what's it all about?" Michael was out of his depth, he thought he'd be returning to a place that he knew; where the changes were so gradual that Michael could change with it like a snake shedding its skin, moving through time.

At the side of the road, watching the procession like they were at a carnival, stood a family who Michael supposed to be Indian; they were brown-skinned at any rate, with large brown eyes. The tallest of the children, a girl, wore a bright, almost neon pink sari with a gold thread decorating the hem, the sun sparkling on the embroidery. She was smiling and pointing, looking up to her father who watched with stern amusement at the shouting crowds. His wife stood by his side holding a small bundle of baby in a white shawl, the woman looked confused and almost distressed by the noise and she shifted the baby uncomfortably closer to her breast. The other child, another smaller girl simply stared, an unreadable expression on her face.

"Woah! WHOOOOOAAAAAHHH!" Michael's neighbor, the bare-chested jester spotted the family and waved, shouting and whooping at the top of his voice, "FUCK Y EAH!" he shouted, "FUCK BUSH, FUCK BLAIR!"

Michael looked at him, bewildered, his eyebrows knitted into a frown. The jester turned to him.

"You know man," he said, his voice solemn as he weighted his words, "In an ideal world, we wouldn't have to do this." He grinned, jammed the whistle back into his mouth and emitted a shrill blast.

2

If the past is a foreign country, then he was a seasoned traveller. If he was honest with himself, the past was the place where he felt happiest. For Alistair Crick, life was empty now, he felt it held as much as a sieve in terms of fulfillment.

Some might say that he led a blessed existence, and years ago he might have agreed with them; after all, who wouldn't like to be earning the money he made, to have the choice of three houses and the world at his feet? Life had been easy for him, fame was a gentle leap, but now he was bored with it. Stifled. There had been no real effort on his part—and hence, he thought, no real accomplishment. Genetics had made up the ticket to his success; his father's Greek ancestry coupled with his mother's fine Scottish skin led to comparisons of Cary Grant and Bogart; and this had provided Alistair all sorts of favours in the acting world where looks were everything.

In the comfortable hindsight of his mid-thirties, and having finally managed to bring to a halt the rollercoaster that he boarded in his late teens, he had emerged dazed and not just a little confused. He had read somewhere that the Masai of Kenya believed having photographs taken of oneself depleted the soul—and having had thousands of flashbulbs go off in his face, he was now inclined to agree with them.

He no longer knew who he really was.

It was partly for this reason that he now sat in a first class train carriage, the changing landscape of Britain fluttering before him, journeying to Edinburgh, his homeland and the city that gave birth to him.

It had all began when Alistair had arrived in London to plug yet another film that he wasn't proud of. As he alighted at Heathrow, he stared stonily ahead as the hornets of the British press buzzed around him; wittering, clicking. Staring, but not seeing. A few shouts got through to him; how long was he going to be in the UK? Was it true about his recent split from his model girlfriend? Was he really back on the wagon?

She was sat in the third floor suite of the Doncaster Hotel, beaming white teeth. Suzanne was the third interviewer he'd had that day, another creosote-legged girl from another frothy and vicious magazine, and he doubted if she had even been born when his career was at its peak.

"So what made you become an actor?" she said, head tilted to one side.

How many times had he been asked this question, was anyone really that interested in the answer any more? Alistair couldn't even count the number of lazy smiles he'd given and said, "What can I say? I loved James Bond, doesn't every kid want to be James Bond?"

It was a line he could remember even when drunk (in the past it had sometimes been the only coherent sentence of whole interviews). But this time he answered differently, for there was something about the girl sitting opposite him, something in the mouth, the way the lips rode up to one side like a swing boat when she smiled. Then he was struck dumb as he suddenly remembered who she reminded him of. Someone he hadn't thought of in nearly twenty years.

"I was in love," he said softly and the girl hurriedly wrote in her pink notebook, aware that this might be her scoop of the year—'*Alistair Crick reveals all...*'

How could he have forgotten that? How could he have forgotten *her?* she had been the signpost that had directed him onto this path and led to everything else, his fame, his fortune, and then inevitably, his destruction and loss.

The interviewer was looking at him expectantly, that lopsided smile still lingering on her lips. Alistair saw the tip of her pink pen quiver slightly above the page. Leaning over to the squat table between them, he reached and pressed the 'stop' button on her tape recorder.

"What's your name again?" "Suzanne, Mr Crick."

His face cracking for the first time that day, he smiled warmly, "Alistair—please."

She giggled nervously and he leant back in his chair and held her gaze, fully aware of the power he had, how he owned the whole encounter.

"Would you have lunch with me, Suzanne?"

When he left her flat in the early haze of the London evening he felt excitement that he hadn't felt in years, and it had nothing to do with the long legs of Suzanne that he had left sleeping (the memory of her already fading). It was a natural high, not fuelled by drink, drugs or even money. He felt grounded, he had a purpose. He didn't even notice the few people doing double takes in his direction, an event which, however many times it happened, always managed to spark a thrill, but today, they went by, ignored. Alistair strode back towards the hotel, his head held high, the air smelling sweet. When he got there, he told the desk clerk to book him a ticket to Edinburgh.

Lauren McKee. The name so clouded in cobwebs that when he first grabbed hold of it again he thought he'd got it wrong. It was stamped with his childhood, where, on the streets of Oxgangs he had stood out for being middle-class (the reasons being that his parents had bookcases lining the walls and they sometimes employed a gardener).

Firrhill High School was harsh, but his parents refused to send him to one in Morningside, stating that it would be 'character building' to rough it with kids from the schemes.

And then there was her—Lauren. Her image swam into focus as soon as he'd conjured up the name from the packed cases of his past. *Lauren McKee.* She had been in his maths class at school, and Alistair would stare at her mass of black curls from the back of the room and inwardly howl. Was she any different to the others, he now wondered? At the time he would never have placed them in the same league, the rest of the girls being 'screeching harpies', according to his father. But even now, he thought that she could be distinguished; she'd had a way with her, a force that held onto you and didn't let go. And of course, that swing boat smile.

He had never been in love before. At least, he told himself aged sixteen, not like this. He had never felt such churnings in the pit of his stomach whenever he encountered her in the corridor, or suffered such sleepless nights. Other girls came and went, but Lauren was always there, holding court in his heart. He thought that she had an air of sophistication—and would have happily taken her home without worrying as to what his mother and father would think, something he would never have done with the girls he collided with on a Friday night.

Alistair had never been interested in drama until he saw the blue sheet of paper pinned to a notice board which called for students to act in the school play; *A Streetcar Named Desire.* And there amid all the other adolescent scribblings burned the only name he wanted to see, glowing among the rest. He auditioned for the part of Stanley and was awarded the part by the young Miss Driver who studied his fully developed arms and chest with great interest and simpered that she thought they had found their man. In the tradition of all good romances, Lauren was given the other leading role; Blanche Dubois, and to Alistair's joy, they not only spent most of the time on stage together, but those moments were sizzling with sexual energy, albeit slightly wooden and gangly with teenage self-consciousness. He was certain that by the end of the play Lauren would be his, but much as he tried to load all his predatory stares with other meanings, Lauren seemed immune. He couldn't understand it; he had never had this problem with a girl before, but it made him even more determined.

The acting came easily; Alistair simply exaggerated his natural extrovert into the character of Stanley, or to be specific, into the character of Stanley as played by Marlon Brando. The film was nearly thirty-five years old by that time, but with the help of a video procured from his mother's collection, he walked, talked and breathed Brando. His sneer, the way he smoked, his ugly glowering at Blanche's pettiness.

But it wasn't until he saw Lauren McKee up against the girl's dressing rooms passionately kissing someone who wasn't him, did he complete his character. The rage came behind his eyes and Alistair Crick burst onto the stage that first night with a ferocity that took the audience's breath away. Never had Blanche had so much disdain spat at her, and the actress who played Stella didn't know what had hit her, he literally swept her off her feet. Deep down he knew he had never performed better before or since.

Now, it so transpired that alongside the parents and families in the audience sat the brother of a talent spotter who worked for Scottish Television and unbeknownst to Alistair, his future was set. By the end of the *Streetcar* run he had a bit part in a television series, due to be broadcast that Hogmanay. From there he was plucked and flown to America, to star in a film which didn't do well, but was successful enough to place him on the gold plated road. But after a few years in the rat race of Hollywood, he discovered just what dirt lay beneath the shiny surface.

He was too young with too much money. There were the ubiquitous parties, the drugs and the fast living. Inevitably he crashed and burned. He made a string of terrible films. After the dreamlike entry into a rehabilitation clinic, and the nightmare exit out of it, Alistair found himself at thirty-five, a hollow shell, (though a taught skinned one with a dazzling American smile) not knowing what had gone before or what the future held. Until now.

The mission he had spontaneously given himself, that of finding and winning Lauren McKee, was like something out of the sugary romantic comedies he had starred in. Searching for Lauren felt like the first real thing he'd done in years. Finding her would tie up his loose ends; bring him back to a reality that he used to know—where things were *real;* raw and gritty, the people harsh but true. And Lauren was part of that, she was a diamond in the rough, unpolished but gleaming all the same. He admitted to himself that he did forget her in a sea of legs, breasts and hair, but thinking of her now, the pain of knowing she was never his, cut him to the quick.

Alistair emerged blinking onto Edinburgh's Waverley Station in the dusty sunlit evening, the smell of the breweries hitting him again. He'd forgotten the rich, savoury yeasty odour that swam around the streets of the city. He could hear the whispers begin among the other passengers, and two teenage girls ran up to ask for a photo; he wearily obliged.

Doggedly, he clambered up the steps from the station up onto a still busy Princes Street. The sun dipping down over the castle turned the sky a deeper shade of pink and he remembered just how beautiful Edinburgh looked to the outsider. And who knew? Maybe he was here to stay.

With thoughts of staying, Alistair realised that with both parents in the ground of Seafield Cemetery he had nowhere *to* stay. The Balmoral Hotel loomed over him and he found himself boyishly excited at the thought that he could go and book a room there. He had stayed in top hotels all over the world, however, the thought of staying at the Balmoral seemed to confirm that he had indeed reached the top. He smiled to think of Lauren's reaction when she saw him—the boy she spurned so many years ago, coming back as a man from across the world to claim her. Successful and famous, he would find her in this city, sweep her up from whatever dead-end job she was in, and bring her here, to the Balmoral where she would be overcome; because really, what girl wouldn't? The hotel would act like an expensive suit; it would speak of his good taste and affluence, yet as Lauren got to know him more, she'd also see his sensitivity, his vulnerability.

At the top of the steps, the doorman tipped his hat appreciatively and ushered him through the glass revolving doors. He approached the desk, behind which sat a young blonde girl, brushed and preened so she blended in with the polished floor. She didn't hesitate as she looked up immediately from her computer screen and bore down on him with a dazzling smile.

"Good evening sir and welcome to the Balmoral Hotel, how can I help you today?" Her accent was strong, he guessed Eastern European and he took the fact that her eyes didn't flicker recognition of his face, that his films probably hadn't made it to her country yet. Alistair booked the Deluxe suite instead of the Royal, as it seemed apt to be subtle and not draw too much attention to himself. As a porter was called to take his cases, he leaned over the desk.

"Incidentally, can I put in a request that any visitors looking for me, be turned away? I'm not expecting anyone."

He was thinking of the press, things would get much more complicated if the word got out that he was in Edinburgh. Again, the receptionist didn't bat a perfect eyelash, but nodded sincerely.

"Of course sir, I quite understand."

He thanked God for prudent staff. The girl's eyes were a beautiful shimmering blue, and on impulse he came back to the desk. "Unless of course you would like to join me for a drink when you finish?"

She smiled again, "I believe your room is 206, Sir."

Agneshka left at midnight, closing the door softly behind her. He got up from the huge messed bed and went to the window. The city lay spread out below him, a matrix of lights and noise. The castle sat precariously on its rock, perhaps ready to topple at any moment. He thought of Lauren and where she might be in this blanket of lights. In his mind's eye their meeting would be like the final scene of a film, *Across the Borders* perhaps, or *One More Time*. He had acted out so many emotional reunions he'd lost count; recited the fluffy lines to fluffy actresses and now here he was in the middle of his own romance, the story unfolding. The audience would be watching Lauren at this point, going about her everyday business, oblivious to what was about to happen to her. Inwardly he grinned excitedly, the lights of Edinburgh shone on his eyes.

That night he slept fitfully, in his scattered dreams he was chasing Lauren, but he could never quite see her face. He woke up sweatily, worried that he wouldn't recognise her when they eventually met again—but surely he would? A face so imprinted on the heart did not change so much.

The next morning his head was full and Alistair was too late for breakfast in the immaculate restaurant. He knew he must start searching, or at least get out of the room for a while and so he stepped out onto a crisp, gusty Edinburgh morning. He looked around, survey-ing the street. The cold air strengthened him a little and he asked the doorman to wave down a taxi.

"Do ah know you?" The taxi driver jerked his head back and forth to study Alistair's eyes. He wasn't really in the mood for the friendly cabbies banter so he put on his best Scottish accent.

"Ah dinnae ken, pal."

"Aye ah dae! You're that guy fae that film—what's it called…erm, no dinnae tell me."

"Ah tell ya, ah'm not," Alistair said loudly, his ac-cent disintegrating. "Just take me to Swanston Avenue." It was the first place he could think of to go, the house he grew up in was a natural destination when arriving in Edinburgh. And he could now make the connection of the house with his quest; how many hours did he lie on his bed, Tears for Fears and Deacon Blue thumping through his super-woofer speakers, staring at the ceiling, re-reading, *Lady Chatterley's Lover* for the tenth time and mooning over Lauren's lips…or he guessed he did anyway.

The cabbie drove all the way without saying a word, though Alistair could feel him shooting glares in the rear view mirror. To his astonishment he felt his eyes well up as they approached the old place, this was the soberest he'd been near the family home in years. Everything looked so small; the street looked impersonal with its identical houses, driveways and gardens. A row of pebble- dashed fifties style houses, impervious to personality, stating nothing except an old-fashioned dream of the lower middle class.

His old house looked dull and cloned, his parents having died and left it years ago; they had tried their hardest to make a faint mark on their indistinguishable suburban dwelling, but now there was nothing he recognised and he made the cabbie drive on.

Through the window he scrutinised the face of every passerby, wondering if he knew them and if he did, would they know Lauren? They drove up Lanark Road, towards where she used to live, and on instinct he told the driver to turn onto Inglis Green Road. He saw a girl waiting at a bus stop. She had the same hair as far as he could remember; long and dark down her back. Alistair called for the driver to slow down so that he could study the girl's face.

Lauren. It had to be her, a bit older, a bit more make-up but it was her, definitely her and Alistair couldn't believe his luck; surely they had to go through the travelling sequence of him searching the streets, showing strangers photos of the girl he left behind, running after similar dark-haired girls only to find he doesn't recognise them at all? But no, this was her all right, older obviously, but any wiser?

Alistair Crick. Alistair Prick he was known as at school, and within ten minutes of seeing him again I could see that nothing had changed. Oh I knew he had made his millions in shite films, but no one was really that impressed round our way. He was one of those lads who had grown up believing everything he had been told about himself—and a bit more which he'd invented along the way. When kids are wee, their parents will treat them like they're geniuses or something—then a brother or sister comes along, and the first kid is shunted off to the side for a bit—I should know, I was shunted off four times in all, but my point is that it's a good thing, all in all. Your corners get rounded off; you get to learn that the whole world doesn't revolve around you. Being an only child, Alistair never got all that, but it's probably the reason he's done so well; he still thinks we all live on Planet Alistair.

He was a good-looking lad I suppose, never my type though, it's like his face was too big for his head. All the girls in the year below fancied him, and that's where he got his reputation as a lady killer—whereas all the lassies in our year knew how much of an arsehole he was, and wouldn't touch him with a barge pole. I knew he was after me when we did that school play, he made it so obvious, trying to do the Marlon Brando thing, always prancing around backstage with his top off—I remember watching him through a door posing in front of the mirror and flicking his hair about—then he must have tripped on something because he suddenly went flying, he managed to stop himself by hanging onto a table but the look on his face when he stood up again, looking around him all in a panic, scared stiff *just in case* someone had seen him.

I'd seen one of his films but I hadn't really thought of him since school, then there he was, stepping out of a taxi on Inglis Green. He had on an expensive looking suit, and he was tanned (*no-one* is tanned in Edinburgh, unless it's the out-of-a-bottle kind). I looked at his face and he looked familiar, I even wondered if I'd slept with him at some point, especially when he started to walk quickly towards me, smiling.

"Lauren," he said, "Lauren McKee." It wasn't a question, it was a line out of a film. I suddenly thought he might be police, he had that look about him, and my mind flipped through anything I—or someone I knew—had done. I looked at him suspiciously but he was still smiling.

"Aye…?" I said.

"It's Alistair!" he cried, and held out his arms as if for a hug. My own arms tightened around my chest.

"Who?" I said, now a bit scared, wondering if I'd served this nutter ages ago.

"Alistair!" he said again, "Alistair Crick?"

I shrugged and he dropped his arms, disappointed.

"We went to school together?" he tried again, the penny dropped.

"*Streetcar?*" I asked. "Wow. Alistair–" I started, not really knowing what to say, having never particularly liked him and now he was looking at me as if this was the reunion between two long lost friends—or lovers. I couldn't resist a jibe, "What are you up to these days?" He looked a bit shocked.

"I…er…I make films"

"Oh right," I said nodding, "you kept on with the acting then?" He looked at me strangely, trying to work out if I was taking the piss.

"Yes, I did." he said, obviously not used to this type of reaction, he looked away as if surveying the land, "I work in Los Angeles now."

I managed to make myself look vaguely impressed, "Oh right," I said again. "What are you doing round here then?"

He didn't say anything for a bit, then he looked me dead in the eye—a trick I'm sure he learnt from one of his tacky films, it was one of those looks which the lead actor does before he delivers the Big Line.

"I'm here for you, Lauren," he said, all drama, "I came here for you."

It was not going as he planned, and he supposed he should have expected as much. Lauren had obviously never left Edinburgh, she hadn't *grown* as he had, hadn't experienced anything different from that which she grew up with. But he couldn't help feeling that she was mocking him, but he put it down to nervousness. All he could think, all he *knew* was that Lauren and he were supposed to be together. She was entwined with his life, and so he was with hers.

She was on her way to a friend's house, but he persuaded her to go and have lunch with him, he could see a glimmer of something in her eyes and he knew he could light the spark.

I felt sorry for him if I'm honest. I couldn't believe him when he said that he'd come to Edinburgh to see me—it was too cheesy to be true, but there was a part of me that was flattered—and I was a wee bit curious, even if it was Alistair Prick, but it was mad to think that someone who loads of girls would give their right arm for, was looking for *me*.

So I let him take me out to lunch at Tiger Lily on George Street—(poncy place I've never set foot in—the waiter had an earpiece for God's sake) people kept staring at us, well, him really. It was weird like, everywhere we went there were folk nudging each other, mainly teenagers who'd rented out his shite films from Blockbuster or seen his face in their teeny-bop mags. It made me feel nervous, like I was on display too—girls' eyes passed from him to me, and their lips curled up in a sneer; it was this sort of stuff that made me drink quickly and I was on my third large glass of Chardonnay when he stopped burbling on about places I'd never been and barely heard of, set down his own glass to look at me across the table (by this time I had a bit of trouble focusing straight).

"Lauren, I meant what I said about coming here for you."

I giggled but could feel myself blushing, if this had been your usual tosser off the street, I'd have told him where to get to, but something about the way he said it made me bite my tongue. He looked dead serious, but then, he might have been a better actor than I thought.

"I've never forgotten you," he said.

"Alistair, you hardly knew me at school," I snorted.

"But I did—you were different from all the other girls."

"What? The young lassies you mean?" the wine had put a gob on me, but he didn't smile.

"They meant nothing."

"Give me a break, Alistair, you lapped it up!" His face was still serious.

"They were nothing compared to you."

"Well…" I looked at him again, his face had grown onto his head a bit more, so that it fitted better and his hair looked nice, styled like, by someone who knew what they were doing. I blew out a sigh, the wine making me dizzy, "that was a long time ago."

We didn't say anything for a bit and I looked out down at my empty plate. He reached across the table and put his hand on mine. For some reason I didn't pull it away.

"Can I tell you something?"

I paused; again it felt like he was following a script, "Aye," I said slowly, "go on then."

"The reason I'm what I am today—you know famous, rich…" he suddenly sounded so high and mighty

(I thought of CJ from Reggie Perrin—'I didn't get where I am today...') the same old Alistair Prick.

"You don't have to go on about it, Alistair, I've seen your crap films."

He stopped, looked hurt, but didn't take his hand away, "But the reason I got into acting...the reason it all started—it's down to you."

"What do you mean?"

"*A Streetcar Named Desire.* I only auditioned because you put your name up as well."

"So?"

"That's where I was spotted—and then I went into TV and everything, and you know the reason I was spotted? The reason I was so good?"

I frowned at him, but decided to let that one go. "No."

"It was you—I saw you kissing that sixth former."

"What? Who?" I racked my brain to think who he meant.

"I didn't know his name, but when I saw you with him, on the opening night..."

"What—Ryan Matthews?" I was amazed, I hadn't thought of him in years, Alistair carried on regardless. "I just got so angry that I went on stage and acted my socks off, that's why the talent spotter approached me, that's why he gave me a part in *The Steamie.*"

"*The Steamie!* You were in *The Steamie?*" I shook my head, laughing. " I don't remember you in that."

"It doesn't matter!" he almost shouted, a few heads looked our way. "The point is, I started acting because of you, and I've got famous, and you're right, I've made some rubbish films, but I've got everything I could ever want—I've got a house in Hawaii…" He shrugged when he saw my unimpressed face. "I'll never really have to work again if I don't want to…but what I've realised since my parents died, and I stopped taking drugs is that I'm lonely—I've had girlfriends, obviously…but no one really significant, no one who means something to me, and that's why I've come for you, Lauren—its fate." He was breathless now, "You're the reason I started on this path, and now I've found you again I can tie up the ends…I can have some closure."

"Closure!" I almost spurted out my drink. "Fuckin' hell, Alistair, you've been in America too long."

He didn't say anything, just looked at me. "I could give you the world, Lauren, I could change your life, you won't ever get a chance like me."

"Oh, won't I just?"

"No, you won't." He stopped, looked down at our hands, mine was sweating under the weight of his. "I want us to be together, Lauren," he looked into my eyes "now, what do you say to that?"

There, he'd said it And even as he was saying these words, he knew that he was *right*. He was entering a new phase of his life, and although some might say he was going backwards—back to an old life of mundanity and dullness, he knew it was where he really belonged. Clichéd though it is, he thought, the longer one stayed in the film industry, the more personality one seemed to lose. It was like the fictional characters took over, and they were like a thick glossy syrup, coating the subtle nuances of what was real.

All I could think was, 'Who the hell do you think you are?' Then I thought, 'He's used to getting what he wants, well this time he's not getting it.'

But he looked sincere, and…but he's a bloody actor! What exactly did he want?

He thought he could sense something had changed within her. She was looking at him more seriously now. He knew the time was ripe, the restaurant was just beginning to dim its lights, ready for the evening service, the time had flown so quickly, and his head swam with the beauteous vision of Lauren in front of him, she looked so clean, so pure—so *unadulterated*. Impulsively he reached out and stroked her face.

"You're so much better than this, Lauren."

Inside I spat at him. So much better than what? Better than Scotland? Better than Edinburgh? Better than the 'boringness' of real life? Who the *fuck* did he think he was? A wee devil popped into my mind, fired an idea at me, it left me wondering if I could still have a shot at acting too…I forced a smile and looked up at him through my lashes.

"I never thought anyone would dare say that to me, Alistair," I said shyly and tried to look all bashful like, hiding a smirk. I held his hand against my cheek, my stomach lurched.

"Have you got a hotel here?" I asked him, all know-ing eyebrows. He nodded.

He could tell that she was impressed by the room, she almost bounced through the door, kept running her hands over things, going to the window and pointing to the view. He couldn't remember the last time he saw anyone this *excited*. This was him a lifetime ago, when money and big hotels were impressive, when his jaw would go slack over the price of a good cognac, and it would drop even more when he remembered he could afford it.

They emptied the mini bar, and then she phoned down for champagne. Alistair doesn't care; he tells him-self he has everything he's ever really wanted, here in this room. He wants this girl's innocence, lounging on the queen-sized bed with her shoes kicked off, laugh-ing like a hyena, her hair tumbling over the cover, she's dancing round the wine glasses, whooping. She was raw, she was *real*.

Ah fuck it, I remember thinking, *It won't hurt him, might teach him a thing or two about real life.* He probably wouldn't remember anyway, the state he was in—he kept saying that he didn't really drink anymore, and it showed, I could've drunk him under the table any day of the week. I was pissed myself, I admit it, but I could still find my way to making sure he passed out before;

1/ I did, and;

2/ before he could attempt anything resembling sex.

We were on the second glass of champagne, after a good four or five shots, when I could see his eyes rolling back and him slurring his words. I could see my chance (if I was behind the bar at the Chesser, I would've stopped serving him hours ago, the amount of crap he was talking.

"...You know Lauren, no one is real in Hollywood—now you take Scotland, everyone's so honest, no one suffers fools..." and "I've always thought of you... you know, even though I was screwing around and all, I never stopped thinking of you."

I'd never heard anyone try so hard. He definitely had it coming.

He woke up the next morning, cold and shivering. As he opened his eyes to the ceiling he realised he just had his underwear on. The room was bright and quiet with the dull noise of traffic drifting in. Alistair sat up, the pain in his head going off like a firework, he turned to apologise to Lauren who was asleep beside him but—there wasn't anyone there.

"Lauren?" he croaked, his voice reverberating around his skull. But no one appeared. The room was tidy; no clues as to what had gone on the night before—if anything *had* gone on...had it? Alistair got up off the bed and went to the bathroom for his robe, but as he swung back the bathroom door there was nothing but an empty hook. There were no towels, the bottles of shampoo and shower gel had gone. He crossed back into the main room of the suite and opened the wardrobe; the empty coat hangers jangled. There was nothing left, his three suits—two Armani, one Paul Smith had disappeared into thin air, he looked to the bedside table, fearing the worst and yanked open the drawer. Wallet, phone—both gone.

Even the champagne glasses, she'd taken them too.

The bitch. The cold-hearted, conniving, scheming, dirty bitch. How dare she? How *dare* she do this to him? Didn't she know what she could've had? What she could have been? He could have given her *everything*? Didn't she want that?

What was the matter with these people? Were they so *backward* that they couldn't tell when their boat had come in? They couldn't see beyond their small-minded, petty, foul and dirty little worlds, going to work in a dead-end, underpaid job five days a week and then on Friday night go and get pished in some grotty little bar, pull another small minded feral low-life and then go and have it away in some graveyard before one of them vomits...

The dirty bitch. What was he thinking? You couldn't change these people; they were all the same.

I couldn't stop laughing as I wobbled down the stairs with his stuff in his suitcase, I knew it was cruel but what I wouldn't give for the look on his face when he woke up...

"Scotland's so real, Lauren..." Yeah, well I'd show him some reality. Nearly pissing myself at the thought I shunted out of a fire exit on the ground floor, and walked out onto the street to the front entrance where a toffee-nosed git with a poncy top hat eyed me up and down.

"I'm just dropping off a case for someone," I said, "I won't be long." He said nothing but stood aside so I could go through. It was the same blonde girl at reception who had been there when we'd walked in. She looked at me strangely as I marched up to the desk. "Hiya, I'm just dropping off this stuff for Mr Crick—he's in 206?"

"I'm afraid Mr Crick is not expecting any visitors, Madam," she said, like a school teacher. I felt like a naughty kid, my hair all skew-whiff, probably my skirt up my arse.

"No!" I said, stifling a giggle. "No, that's fine, I can't stop anyway, could you just take it up to him around midday? That's when he said he would need it." A good five hours of panic should do him.

"Of course," she smiled smoothly, all professional like. "No problem at all."

No, I thought, there never is if you've got enough money

3

The young couple in black stared at her as she came through the door, obviously thinking she'd got the wrong house, or even worse, she was the police. Her slick make-up, polished hair and stern uniform didn't match up at all with the darkened smoky fug engulfing the flat. She smiled at them, enjoying their bewilderment. After all, who wouldn't be confused by the sight of her preened, glossy figure entering this formulaic den of iniquity?

She thought the girl and the boy looked too young to be there at any rate; the boy nervously hiding a joint behind his cupped hand and she could see now that they had the uniform of the graffiti artists that sometimes hung about the house, dressed all in black with streaks of silver or red hanging on their cuffs, still around them was a whiff of heady spray paint and she guessed that somewhere about the city there was now a new painting or slogan.

Agneshka was well aware of what her Balmoral uniform made her look like, an air-hostess or an estate agent, some superficial bimbo at any rate. She had learnt the term 'bimbo' quite early on in her arrival to Scotland, it was a funny word, and when she first learnt its meaning she could instantly imagine the type of girl the word referred to, which she knew was nothing like herself. Agneshka had refused to go the length of applying fake tan as many of her colleagues did; she liked the paleness of her skin and the fact that it didn't stand out from the pasty hue of the Scots, she was a foreigner true, a guest to the country, but that didn't mean she had to stand out. Her pastel skin gave her an ethereal look and the last thing she wanted was to cover it up with the colour of bottled browned tangerine.

She entered her bedroom, shutting the door to the thudding bass that shook the floorboards. She didn't really feel like a party, but knew that if there were coke floating around then she would get in the mood a bit quicker. One of the chefs at work had offered her some that afternoon and she'd fooled him at first by pretending to be shocked. He was a big man from Glasgow, with wild ginger hair that he'd unsuccessfully tried to tuck under his white chef's cap. The rolled five pound note looked tiny in his ruddy hand and his cheeks turned even redder as he lifted his head from the table and snorted loudly, (like a pig Agneshka thought, a husky wild boar) he then had handed the note to her. They had giggled for a while and he had tried to tell her a long and complicated joke that involved an Englishman and a horse, but his accent was so strong that she couldn't understand him and this made it even funnier. It was near the end of her shift which she was glad of as otherwise she'd be scratchy for the rest of the day, just biting down the time until she could get her hands on some more powder.

In her bedroom she shook her blonde hair out of its slickedback ponytail, running her fingers through it to tease out the hairspray. She pulled out the white silk cravat round her neck and threw it onto the bed. See-ing her reflection in the rust-spotted mirror, she raised an eyebrow at herself and dragged a hand across her mouth, leaving a slashed trail of red lipstick. Agneshka grinned. A receptionist gone mad. She loved finishing work, and now she had three glorious days off spread out in front of her like the yellow brick road. She unbut-toned her blouse and balled it up, throwing it into the corner to join the tumbling pile of dirty washing which lay in wait there.

Jigging to the music that swam in from the front room, Agneshka could feel herself relax and forget the hotel with all its swaggering guests, petty rules and the effort of trying to make others happy. She needed a drink—or something—to add to the party mood, and looking around her small room, dim in the glow of the fairy lights that hung above her bed, she spotted a Jack Daniels bottle with an inch left in the bottom, left over from another night of thumping bass and wide eyes. Putting the bottle to her lips, she sashayed over to the wardrobe and flicked through the hangers. She caught sight of herself again in the mirror, admiring how she looked in the half-light; the white of her bra highlight-ing the slight summer tan on her shoulders, her waist skinnily slipping into the pencil skirt without a ripple. She stood there, absently fingering her bellybutton. She liked her figure; liked the feel of her hipbones that jut-ted out of her skin, liked how her skin felt so smooth to the touch, though she would never have admitted any of this to anyone. She unzipped her skirt and stepped out of it, carefully folding it over a hanger. It made her smile at the thought that she was standing here in her underwear while next door there was a roomful of men oblivious to the fact. Girls too, but it was the thought of the men, with their stupid nicknames that the Scottish so insisted on giving each other—Welchie, Jamesey, Tam or Pilch—which made her want to laugh.

The men, or boys really, many of whom had tried at some point to talk her into bed (usually when they'd drunk enough or popped enough pills to pluck up the courage) none of them had succeeded but she had wondered in amazement at how humble they became, and how honest;

"Aggie, Ah just think you're an amazing lassie, ken? Ah know ah'm no much tae look at, an' ah'm no as smart as you like, but…well, ah think we could be good the 'gether, ken?"

Well, who could refuse an offer like that? It was funny, she was sure that she had a reputation for being picky in the group, as it seemed that at one time or another all the friends had partnered up with each other—Helen had been with Micky, Leanne had been with Joe and so on. The girls in the circle kept their distance from Agneshka, only really chatting to her when they were off their faces, but she didn't care. They probably thought she was just playing games with the lads, leading them on, being a tease, when really, Agneshka smugly thought, they knew that she just didn't fancy the look of any of them. When she wanted sex, she had it, just like anyone else; sleeping with someone fast-tracked you to their real personality, cutting out the middleman of small talk. Sometimes she didn't want 'deep meaningful conversations', she saw someone who interested her, and wanted to know them instantly—sex took care of all that, it cut through all the bullshit when they shed that layer of skin. Take that film star at the hotel last week, she had known who he was but pretended not to, which had made it all the more fun. He was charming, but a little screwed up, she thought. And there had been that other woman—the one who'd dumped his suitcase, Agneshka didn't really know what had happened there, but Alistair Crick had left the hotel quickly the next day, not even looking at her as he checked out...she didn't care, it was a good story to tell one day, but not to these people, the folk in the next room they were friends yes, but not like the ones she knew in Poland. These people didn't know her as well, but again she didn't mind that, she was happy to simply orbit around this circle for a while...

There was one guy, she had to admit that, and squinting in the mirror to flick more mascara onto her lashes, she wondered if he was in the living room right now.

The first time she had seen him was at four o'clock in the morning in an anonymous living room where the dawn light was filtering through the curtains, seeing out the enigmatic night with the commonplace of the new day. The remaining party-goers were assembled at the kitchen table, messily rolling joints and drinking vodka with anything they could mix it with; coffee, tomato juice, orange squash. Agneshka had been trying to find her way to the toilet and had stumbled into the living room where a man was lying alone on the floor. At first she thought he might be asleep, but as she passed he let out a deep contented sigh; one associated not with the pleasure of unconsciousness but of simply having one's eyes closed.

She stood above him, looking down at his upside-down face, wondering what it looked like the right way up but not daring to move round and see, when he slowly opened his eyes. A shaft of sunlight splashed across the left side of his face so he was partially blinded as he looked up at her. They didn't move for a minute and stood in the frozen tableau squinting at each other until Agneshka started giggling, her body was tired and her brain was fried and for a while she felt slightly hysterical, looking at this handsome upside-down face smiling and blinking up at her like a moving statue, she didn't want the moment to end, the warmth of the morning sun on her bare arm, the good face below her.

The man shifted himself up onto his elbows and she came round to face him.

"Have you always been there?" she asked, not recognising him from the party.

"What—on this floor?" his face was wide and kind.

She laughed again. "No, I mean have you been here all night, I didn't see your face."

"Well I came late on, I'm not sure what time it was, there were still a good few people here."

Agneshka said nothing but nodded, she sat down on the edge of the sofa, absently stroking her forearms with her sweating fingertips because it felt nice. She heard a roar of laughter coming from the kitchen and she was glad she was in here, away from them, with this man—whoever he was.

"Do you have a cigarette?" she asked.

"Aye, somewhere," he felt in his pockets awkwardly as he was still on the floor so he had to push his body up to get between the cloth at his sides. He pulled out a crumpled packet of Golden Virginia and a packet of Rizla and handed them to her.

"Would you roll it for me? My fingers are all sticky," she said,

splaying up her hands as if to show him the sweat. "They look clean to me," he said, smiling.

"I can't roll very well," she admitted, knowing they were flirting but it felt good and she was pleased.

"Here's a deal—why don't you get us a drink and I'll roll a cigarette for you."

"Ok, what do you want to drink?" "What's left?"

"Not much, I'll go to the kitchen and see." "Where are you from?"

"Poland."

"What's your name?"

"Agneshka," she paused and automatically added, "Aggie" knowing the difficulty the Scottish had for pronouncing her name,

"That's nice. Agneshka." His name was Stuart Moon—known as Moon, obviously. They had sat and drunk black sugary tea together because there was no alcohol left and no milk. Agneshka couldn't remember what they talked about but she knew that at some point Stuart had gone to the CD collection and put on a Billie Holiday album so the whole encounter had a vivid soundtrack in her head.

They didn't go to bed together that morning after the night before, or even kiss, and afterwards she had been thankful for that. The following days they carried each other around within themselves, neither particularly remembering what they talked about but knowing that it had meant something. Stuart kept thinking that he saw her in the street, nearly running up to a bobbing blonde head or tapping a slim shoulder at the bar. He played his own Billie Holiday album constantly. Every time she lit a cigarette, Agneshka would think of what he had said,

"When you first meet someone, a cigarette's a good thing to have. Probably the best thing you can do is put a bit of fire between you and a stranger."

In her room now, Agneshka looked at her reflection again, she was ready; scruffy blue jeans and her slashed red top, the stretchy material clinging to the outline of her small figure. Her teased blonde hair pinned up in a strategic mess to the top of her head, a few strands pulled down to frame her face. Her work lipstick wiped off and lip gloss applied so they wouldn't crack—would her lips be needed tonight? She didn't know, but the anticipation and excitement surged through her as she opened her bedroom door, strode on through to the living room and called out in a loud voice, "Ok, who's got the coke?"

And a cheer erupted on her arrival.

Aggie.

Aggie Aggie Aggie Aggie Aggie, Aggie, Aggie Aggie, Agneshka…

That's how I like to say it…Ag-nesh…ka. Not Aggie, like some old woman's name, an old woman with wrinkled flesh that is oceans away from her perfect skin…Agneshka—she's been sitting on my shoulder all week, staring at the same stars. She's now so present in my mind that I know that when I actually see her in the flesh (the oh so smooth flesh) it won't be quite real…it'll be like she's a celebrity, a film star who I know but I've never met, someone whose face changes, a mask for a thousand personalities…she'll be too short or her hair isn't the colour I've been seeing in my mind's eye for hours on end.

Is this the beginning of a love story? Can this message on my phone from Jimmy be the domino that kick starts the rest into action? A party. A gathering of people in a house. Gathered to take illegal and legal substances. To get high, to get blotto-d, pished, oot yer face, scoobied…whatever. Is this the place where I want a love story to start? In the middle of grinding jaws and goggling eyes, red-rimmed with insomnia and amphetamine, where anything that's drinkable can be drunk, anything snortable is pushed up the nostril and anything dry enough rolled into a Rizla and lit…

It feels an unwholesome scene to be approaching her with propositions of love. Purity within the grime.

Love. Is this what I'm talking about now? Real Love? Deduced from one meeting, a few shy smiles—or not so shy on her part; the way her eyes found mine and lay there, waiting like a lioness ready to pounce. I did my best to sit with her in that place, but that locked glance was terrible, and irresistible. I have to look and yet I cannot. The addiction of expectation—I know something can happen. I know a story is in the making.

From this new window I look out onto a setting sun above the city's skyline, the traffic dimming, the dust settling—for now.

The Noise has gone home for the day, but they will come out again in a few hours—they've spent their money in the shops; spending their workday pennies on objects of want. Now they're having their tea, the all important tea, the mantra of the grease-wiped mothers who shuffle them to their table with trays of chips and sausages.

The man-boys will take a shower, spraying fine hot water onto their smooth hairless lives. Dolling up for the night ahead. Flapping out their best pants and squidging gel on their hair. They bathe in a sea of chemical sky. Perfumed and lacquered, spots squeezed and eyes large, they jeer and goad their reflections in the mirror.

The cocktail and lager girls will be fluttering lashes at themselves as they pour scent on their chests, praying to the God of stilettos that theirs keep on tonight and that their knickers stay present until the right moment. The chattering parrot lassies, bellies already swilling with glasses of Lambrusco and cigarettes. Their ironing-board hair slipping sliding around their orange shoulders. Tits and Teeth. Nails and arse.

This new house, this new room is still a blank canvas for me...I've slept here for two nights and I think we're getting on all right...I could invite her here and she would fill the room...

As I blow smoke onto bare floorboards I catch his small picture on the wall. The mess of curls, the wide eyes and cherub lips of Mr Thomas. Could I tell Agneshka about him, I won-

der? The small Welsh superstar of the heathers of the hills, and a good friend of mine. He is a companion, dead in the grave whose words follow me like footsteps. Will I be able to play the song I've written for her? The tune that's introduced itself to me and won't go until I've finished entirely...maybe one day...

Then I think I can tell her anything—the silver-haired, honey-skinned girl from the East, and who knows why, if someone asked me I wouldn't be able to tell them.

One Year Later

It was one of those things that he would have dreamt up to sing about, she thought afterwards. A coincidence, a twist of fate, something that usually happens in novels or films. When she saw him coming out of Robbie's on Leith Walk her whole body went cold and she thought she was going to throw up. *Not now*, Agneshka thought, *Not today of all days*. For today was her last day in Edinburgh and opposite, on the other side of the road, blinking into the haze of early evening, stood her reason for leaving.

Stuart Moon, the love of her life and nemesis in the battle for their hearts and minds. She looked at him now, so familiar with his face and body, the way he scratched his head through his hair, the way his face fell vacant when concentrating on a book or playing his guitar. She would ask him something when he was in the middle of a song and he would completely ignore the question but look at her, or *through* her as he sang out his new lyrics.

Agneshka felt a huge wave of sadness engulf her, the street swam in and out of focus, the traffic roaring and hushing to a whisper in her ears. She couldn't move, but just stood and stared at him across the road. He had been engrossed in rolling a cigarette, but at that moment a truck shook itself past and he looked up and saw her, staring at him. He smiled instantly, that broad grin that came naturally to his face and conveyed only happiness. Agneshka's heart broke all over again as she could see that he felt no awkwardness on seeing her, that for him all those feelings, bad and good had just melted away into a sense of fondness. There was no longing or thrill for him, as far as he was concerned she was a firm friend with whom he had shared some nice times.

If there was one word in the English language she detested it was *nice*.

Stuart looked back at Aggie, his wee Aggie that was. '*What a sweetheart,*' he thought, her hair was now a deep shade of fuchsia, glowing on top of her head, making her skin look even paler. She looked thinner, he thought, if that was possible, as her bird-like figure never seemed to gain any weight, no matter how many pastries she bought from the Polish deli or pints of lager she chugged. Stuart used to worry at the amount of alcohol she would put away sometimes, he'd wonder how her pixie-like figure could hold that much.

A river of time swam in front of them as they stood on opposite sides of a busy road and looked at each other. Two humans who had known and loved each other deeply. But now they stand apart and alone again, watching each other's well-known faces and mannerisms.

He made a move as if to cross the road, and she mimed looking at her watch and shrugging as if to say, *I haven't got time to talk,* but she knew she had, and was only heading back home to her flat on Easter Road. Inside her bare flat sat two fat rucksacks, packed to bursting with her belongings, ready to be strapped to her back tomorrow afternoon and taken on a plane, a train and then perhaps a taxi to a small town just outside of Lodz. Then they would sit with her in her parents' spare room which had once been her room, and she would look out of the window at the views that made up her childhood. The clothes in the rucksacks would soon smell of cabbage and fried potatoes as they always did when she stayed with her parents, as well as wood smoke and her father's tobacco.

Stuart ignored her hasty gestures and was already looking from one side of the road to the other, trying to spot a free space in which to cross. Agneshka wanted to run, to just flee this whole encounter, as she knew what would happen when they spoke; all the yearnings and sorrow would return, and she didn't know whether she would be able to keep from crying. Many times she had been bewildered by this rush of emotion that she felt for this man, this had never happened to her before, this heartbreak—for that's exactly what it was—the books and the songs and the films weren't lying, heartbreak was exactly what happened, the sudden weight in your chest, the *pain* which dwelt there was indescribable, the whole body grieving. Agneshka braced herself and she stood rooted to the spot as Stuart made his way over.

He couldn't remember exactly when it was he last saw Aggie—*Aggie*—when had he stopped calling her Agneshka, as he always swore he would? It must have been a good five or six months, perhaps even longer. But it was good to see her, he could say that to himself truthfully now, the absence had been good for both of them, diluting the strong rages and loves which had battled between them in those last few weeks.

The final words which had exploded between them like a bitter firework had been at yet another party, this time to celebrate someone getting out of prison, someone Stuart didn't even know, and he felt odd being there, welcoming this lad Michael back into this other world where they were all unlocked yes, but just how free were they? His black mood was made even darker when he spotted Aggie hunched over with a five pound note stuck up her nose, her eyes narrowed in concentration as a large bearded man steadied the mirror which held the fragile powdered lines. In Stuart's eyes, someone who needed these man-made drugs to become themselves were further away from their soul than even they knew. When he and Aggie had got together, they had moved out of the orbit of partying, drug-taking and staying up to meet the sun. They hadn't needed it or wanted it, adrift on their own island of each other, not needing to be rescued by anything else. Now, seeing Aggie raise her head up and sniff loudly, he felt rejected, and that he wasn't enough for her.

Early on in their relationship, when the world had consisted of wrinkled sheets, coffee and cigarettes and laughter, Agneshka had tried out her usual speech on

Stuart, one that after a few nights together, she would say to most men after gradually disappearing from their lives, "Stuart, I'm having lots of fun, but really, isn't it better to keep ourselves separate? My soul is my own, and I find it really hard to join up with someone else's… I don't like to be trapped…I don't like to collaborate."

And instead of receiving begs and pleadings from the man next to her, insisting that he wouldn't tie her down and that they could do it her way *just as long as they were still together*, Stuart simply turned his head to her and said, "Shut up, Agneshka, don't talk shite," and they had both smiled at each other.

It was then that she fell in love, sweetly, swiftly and without compromise. Coincidentally it was also the same moment when he took a small step back from her in his head and wondered. The words that she had obviously used on so many others rankled him, couldn't she just keep her 'independence' crap and just go with whatever was happening? He hadn't made a plan for them, he hadn't dreamt of a future with her and her presumption that he had, annoyed him.

But he placed it to the back of his mind and got on with loving her. Weeks passed, months leapt by, she met his mum in Ayr and although there was talk of maybe going to Poland together (she was keen, he less so), it never materialised. Jobs came and went, Agneshka gave up her job at the Balmoral, and began to work in an underground bar that held open mic nights where serious long-haired men sang songs of Iraq and poems about women's thighs. The same men dreamed moonily at Aggie's pale shoulders while Stuart sniggered at their writings and, much to Agneshka's dismay, shrugged off any thoughts of jealousy.

She thought Stuart was in love with the thought of love, he never seemed to inhabit it fully. He was a brief lodger, decorating the walls of the relationship with poetry and songs, but when the landlord came knocking on the door, demanding rent, or in his and Agneshka's case, when she wanted them to move in together, he couldn't agree, his pockets were empty.

Love was pulled this way and that, Agneshka would tug at her side of the rope, trying to tie Stuart closer to her, Stuart, in return would relinquish his frayed end, holding up his hands to let her do as she pleased. He stopped going to parties with her as he thought she became a different creature, and it was one he didn't feel anything for. Her face, which at one time encapsulated beauty as it appeared in the dictionary in his head, now blurred into familiarity, and with drugs in her eyes it even swayed into ugliness.

"I don't recognise you when you're on that stuff."

"Stuart, you're such a hypocrite! You were completely out of it the night we met."

"I know, but I don't do it every single bloody night! I've got more important things to do."

"What—staying in your room, reading your books? Staring

out of the window?"

"There was a time when you were quite happy with that."

"But I want to go out now, and I like coke—what's the problem? We had a great time when we did it together." Aggie crawled up to the bed where he lay and massaged his thigh. "You used to say such beautiful things to me, what happened to all of that?"

He didn't answer. But he wondered too.

"I used to think that you loved me more than I loved you," she said, the silence speaking for itself. It was one of those blunt statements with a hidden sharpened point that he couldn't stand, you would never find a Scottish girl saying things like this, he thought, so openly. But he felt his heart sway as he swam in the curled consonants of her accent. He turned and held her, sinking his face in her hair.

Eventually, the rope of love disappeared entirely. A new fire was lit, one of passionate arguing, and lost in the flames near the centre, the last kindles of tenderness were lost.

"For fuck's sake, Aggie, what are you doing here? You're completely gone." Three in the morning and Agneshka's wide eyes are looking over him.

"I thought you would be pleased to see me!" Her voice is messed, her hands already finding him under the duvet, "I thought, 'I know, I'll go and find my moon in his bed'" she giggled, "the man in the moon!"

"Yeah well," he got out of bed. "I'd prefer if you called first."

"Stuart, I'm your girlfriend! I shouldn't have to call."

"Well maybe I'd like a night alone once in a while! And I definitely want one where you don't come in fucked out of your skull!" Tears pour out of her black-

58

lined eyes. "*You* fuck with my skull, Stuart Moon, you get in there and you have a good *fiddle*

After that, the fiery embers smouldered with sadness and the two humans broke away.

Now, as Stuart came hurrying over the road, Agneshka felt her insides tugging. How she had loved him, she thought, how she still loved him. She just hadn't known what to do with it and in consequence had ruined it. She suddenly thought of the night they had got together, only a year ago. The calm before the storm that led to the present events now being played out. Agneshka remembered getting ready in her bedroom that night. How she had finished work at the hotel, and walked home in the sunlit evening of a Saturday night. How she had felt the swell of expectation in her chest and the feeling that anything might happen. She had looked at herself in the mirror, sipping at whiskey— and liked what she saw. Stuart slowed to a jog as he approached and started smiling, unable to control it. She smiled at him back, and then looked at her boots.

"Hi," he stopped in front of her, breathing heavily. She blinked up and looked into his face.

"Hello."

There was a pause and a million thoughts and images passed into them both, flooding their minds. Stuart hated this, how they had spoken so much to each other, knew each other's dreams and memories and private thoughts, but now—they couldn't think of a thing to say. Agneshka sighed inwardly, heavily. She wanted him to look at her like he used to do, with an expression of awe. Eventually he spoke.

"How are you?"

"I'm fine, I'm ok," she squinted up at him, wanting him not to believe her.

"Good, that's good, what–"

"I'm leaving, Stuart," she interrupted. "I'm leaving tomorrow." His set face fell, and she felt a rush of gladness. "Oh, Where are you going?"

"Poland, back to my parents." "Why? Has something happened?"

She swallowed, a lump forming in her throat. She looked away, across the street where she saw a couple walking hand in hand, both smiling at the ground. Behind them walked a woman and child, her mother she supposed; the little girl dressed as some kind of princess or fairy, the cheap sparkly wings bent and splaying out behind her, and Aggie momentarily felt a ferocious jealousy of the child in her own fantasy world.

"No, I just wanted to leave," she looked back at him, bang in the eyes, "I've got nothing here now."

He was silent, but looked back squarely at her, then he couldn't stand it anymore. He took a step forward and grabbed her, held her small body tightly. Tears welled in both sets of eyes. She held him back, stroking his broad shoulders, nestling her head in the crook of his neck.

"I'm sorry, Agneshka, I'm sorry."

She said nothing, but pulled away from him, he reached for her hands, stroked her fingers. They both looked at the ground. She frowned as she tried to summon up the courage to speak, to say the words that were rolling through her mind; she tried to look up to his kind face.

"Will you come and see me, Stuart? Would you come over some time?"

He looked into her crumpled face and wondered when he had told himself that he didn't care whether he saw her or not. And then, just three minutes ago, he had felt such a jump in his stomach at the sight of her figure across Leith Walk. Ten minutes ago he had been laughing and drinking with Jimmy, and he hadn't thought of her at all, but then suddenly, here she was, and there they were, crying and holding each other. He was confused and half drunk and tasting salt. He smiled at her, wiping a tear from her cheek.

"I think I'm going to have to."

After holding each other for a few more minutes, they decided, against their better judgement to go together to the Port of Leith Bar and drink three pints of lager each. They talked lightly of the news in their lives; but with a renewed energy that comes like a phoenix rising from the ashes of anger and resentment. They followed the lager with shots of vodka and whiskey, laughing and enjoying the underlying flirtation and rough knowledge that they would end up in bed together, which is exactly what happened.

Entering Agneska's bare skeleton of a flat, Welchie, having moved out two weeks ago, Stuart felt the surge of excitement at the familiar. He knew this place and all the bitterness of the last few months were washed away. He felt a rush of emotion for Agneshka, coupled with the sheer certainty that this time was *not* over yet, that they might still have a chance together.

It was only later, a few weeks later, when sober and quiet and honest with himself, Stuart realised that the night after the meeting on Leith Walk was the last time, that really, it had been the gap of not seeing Aggie, and glimpsing her afresh like that; small fragile and thin, which had aroused him so much.

And so he never visited Poland, and he never saw her again. He had meant to, that was true. There had been emails to each other and at first they were friendly, chatty with hints of love scattered throughout. They were careful not to mention their social lives in depth, of flirtations with others and even, a couple of months later, a bedding on Stuart's part of a girl who was on the same evening course he had just started. It was then that he knew Agneshka would never really return to his life, she was now purged from his heart, wrung and rinsed out.

When Stuart stopped replying to her e-mails, Agneshka knew he had found someone else and she felt as if they had only just broken up again. He didn't have to explain, she finally wrote, she knew that he no longer loved her, and now, she supposed, this really was good-bye.

He never found the strength to reply to her and was ashamed at himself. But it was easy when there was technology involved, if asked he could always say that he never received her e-mails. He could say he was out of Edinburgh, away from a computer.

Agneshka didn't leave Poland again. She moved from Lodz to Warsaw with two of the old friends (those who she thought knew her well, better than anyone in Edinburgh could have) but as it turned out they didn't really know her at all. They wondered at her constant tears for this 'Stu-art'. Agneshka was no longer the party girl she used to be, she could have once been depended on to be the first one up to dance, or to know where the next party was, but in the months after she returned to Poland, she could only be found in the corner, chain-smoking, with a bottle of Vodka, which she wouldn't share. She stopped doing cocaine when she couldn't take the familiarity of the sensation. She could only associate it with the early days, and the later ones with Stuart. The buzz felt all wrong, she preferred the heavy, cumbersome weight of alcohol to the light quick sparkle of white powder.

Stuart never consumed any more drugs in his life, except when entering middle age and his eldest son began to smoke pot. Stuart, in an attempt to strike up a bond (and unbeknown to his wife, a yearning for his youth) joined him. He found he enjoyed the feeling and discovered a new aspect of the drug, one that he had ignored when he was young and had obliterated with alcohol.

In the years after Agneshka left Edinburgh, Stuart himself moved out of the city and over to the west coast, feeling a need to be nearer his childhood home of Ayrshire and to cleanse himself of the city, and all that it had brought to his life. He didn't forget Agneshka but since he moved from the streets they had walked down and didn't talk to the friends they knew any more, she was now folded into the pages of his past.

He met his wife three years after saying goodbye to Agneshka. Annie was Scottish and they shared a love of walking in the hills, of Jura whiskey and nights by their open fire discussing Dylan Thomas. Stuart would play his guitar and Annie would sing. Years later, one day by accident, the tune he had written for Agneshka popped through from his memory, through his fingers and onto the guitar strings.

He had been gazing out of the rain pelted window and looked down to find his fingers picking out the tune he had written for her, the one which he had played over and over and apparently annoyed his neighbour so much that they had taken his guitar away. He smiled at this memory, shaking his head at the bizarreness of it all, though at the time he had been very upset, it was just before he moved out of the flat too; what with mad neighbours and a sky-high rent, it was more than he could afford at the time.

Aggie's face snapped into his mind, he remembered its pale elfin look, the smallness of her arm. It saddened him as he remembered that year with her, he had never seemed to reach the point in his life where he could think of the women who had shared time with him, and smile. The memories were always tinged with either sadness or a bitter taste; the loss of love always having left a small but violent gash.

Stuart would have loved to look through his rain spattered window and glimpse into her life, to watch her face change expression, even for just a second.

Thousands of miles away in a small stuffy flat in the east end of Warsaw, Agneshka looked at the tip of her newly lit cigarette, but there was no stranger sat opposite her from whom she needed protection. The smoke wafted, dipped and rose throughout the still flat, as if in time with Billie Holiday's voice.

4

Clarence blindly put out his hand to the cut-glass bowl of dolly mixtures and fumbled a few into his palm. He held up a soft neon green cube of sugar up to his eye and absently popped it into his mouth; wincing as it touched an ulcer growing on his tongue. Still, he thought, chewing solidly, an ulcer was better than cancer; something which might have easily developed had he kept up his thirty-a-day smoking habit. A sore tongue was certainly better than the hacking cough that shook his lungs awake each morning, better than the ache in his chest and a mouthful of ash. But he couldn't help thinking that popping kids' sweets didn't suit him half as well as the wreaths of cigarette smoke. He used it to enhance his image, that of an enigmatic and mysterious writer of horror and crime.

His bookshelves were lined with the prolific work of C Blackwood (a slight deviance from his own name Clarence Wood, the 'Black' being obvious but it did lend itself to the genre). The black and silver spines sat in chronological order, all of them there from '*Sticks and Stones*' to Clarence's latest, '*A Fool's Game*'. His portrait on the shiny dust jackets depicted every inch the mind that created the macabre stories within. C Blackwood's slight smile and half-raised eyebrow in the photograph could be translated as one who plays cruel games with his characters, and in turn, the reader. Clarence was happy

66

with that image and so were his fans, and consequently, he had not changed it in ten years. If you looked closely you could even detect the faint wisp of smoke wafting into the frame, evidently from a cigarette in the ashtray or sitting snugly between his yellowed fingers. With that thought in mind, Clarence now held up his hands in front of him and saw—yes, it was still there, a small indent on the right of his index finger and left of its neighbour, the hollow bed where his cigarettes had lain for twenty-five years. He sighed. *A mouth ulcer was better than cancer.* Wasn't it?

"Are you sure you want to do this now, Clarence?" his agent Jules had said.

"What? Give up smoking or start a new book?" he had replied. "Well…" Jules had paused, unsure of how to go on. "Both I suppose, it's a big thing you know, giving up fags." He fell silent again and then offered, "Are you sure you don't want to leave the book until you feel more…more…"

"Grounded?" finished Clarence. "I've got to give up Jules, the doctor said it in no uncertain terms—I don't really have a choice in the matter. I think starting a new book is just the right thing at the moment, you know, keep my mind off it. Besides, you need me to start it, don't you?"

"Well, yes," conceded Jules, "but I don't want to see you get strung out either, have you got a clear plan of how you're going to go about it?"

"I'm not going to have a cigarette Jules, that's my plan." Clarence had rolled his eyes down the phone, snorting mentally at his agent's over-emotional response to everything.

That conversation was four days ago, and Clarence had to admit to himself that he had been blind to Jules' misgivings. Nicotine had a vicious little bite on his tail and it hung on like a feisty terrier. Clarence had never thought so much about cigarettes before in his life. They were a stalker, an obsessive fan who never let him be. When he had smoked, cigarettes had been quiet and docile; they were happy to let him go about his business, but as soon as he had thrown what remained of his packet of Marlboro out with the rubbish late on Sunday night, the cigarettes had raged; they had risen up as a whole and attacked him. A revolution of smoke.

He couldn't think properly, couldn't settle on anything. And write? Reluctantly, Clarence had to admit that Jules had a point, as his routine of writing used to include a big pot of coffee and a fresh box of cigarettes. If a sentence wasn't coming, or he simply wanted a break he would reach out for the pack, light up and reread his words through the wisps of smoke. Cigarettes allowed him to break, to think (and ironically) to breathe. Without them the ideas had just stopped coming, a thought would just about be wriggling its way into his mind when it would suddenly hit the brick wall of craving, keel over and die.

On the sixth day of biting his nails to the quick, shouting at Annie (his longhaired grey pensioner of a cat) and chronic head-aches, Clarence succumbed and went to buy cigarettes at half-past eight in the morning. A few puffs, a sigh, and when the nicotine rush had died down, he coughed violently and he remembered why it was he was supposed to give up in the first place. He threw them away.

That same afternoon, Clarence had returned to the flat with a large paper bag, stapled at the top. He unlocked the door, walked in and opened his bag of loot. Annie slunk round his legs, curious to see what would appear from the crackling paper. Clarence took out the small box and looked briefly at the instructions to the nicotine patches, he scrambled the box open. He pulled what looked like a circular plaster out, peeled the back off, and unleashed a smell of pure chemical, Annie caught it and hurried off fearfully. Clarence rolled up his shirtsleeve and unceremoniously slapped it on at the top of his forearm. He pulled his sleeve down and waited a few seconds. Nothing extraordinary happened so he went into his small kitchen and filled the kettle.

Ten minutes later the skin under the patch started itching, but he remembered the chemist warned him this might happen so he tried to ignore it. Sitting down at his computer he knew he was trying to ignore a good many things, and wondered what it was he was *allowed* to think about. Definitely not cigarettes.

And not about the fact that he had an itching arm.

Which was brought on by the fact that he was trying to give up cigarettes.

And not cigarettes and not cigarettes and not–

There was a thud from upstairs and Clarence looked thankfully at the ceiling, grateful for the interruption. Loud voices followed it, and someone whistling. Another two thuds and a bang, a chorus of cheerful swearing. Clarence frowned at the noise. Newcomers surely, and not quiet ones either which was all he needed when trying to write a book and trying to give up- *No*.

"I don't know," he shrugged to Annie, "but how about that for an inspiration, hey? Have we done a villainous neighbour yet?" Clarence's mind whirred back through his previous story-lines; policeman and thieves, vengeful wives, psychotic professors, psychotic doctors, psychotic priests…but no, he couldn't remember a good claustrophobic trapped-in-the-house-with-a-psychotic-new-neighbour yet. The mystery behind closed doors and all that. "That's good, Annie," he nodded to himself, an idea starting to gestate, the cat looked at him, eyes still on the alert. "Yes, that'll do nicely."

By five o'clock and another two packets of dolly mixtures gone, Clarence had managed to squeeze out a page on the laptop; *not* his usual standard, normally he could have written ten pages easily, the words drifting out like smoke…But today he had to literally prise them from his mind, and the sentences were stilted, bitty without his usual flourishes and wit.

Clarence sighed and Annie mewed in reply. He looked at the clock and felt relief that the day was almost done, and his working day was certainly finished. Annie was good time-keeper and he obliged her by opening a cupboard and fishing out an individual tin of cat food, dumping the contents into her bowl, Annie's head was already in there, wolfing down as much meat as she could push in.

Clarence saved his one page of work on his laptop and closed the lid. Enough for today. He went to his 'drinks cabinet', a spare cupboard in his sideboard where he kept a bottle of Famous Grouse in a decanter. He poured himself his usual two fingers into a heavy whiskey tumbler and sipped. The liquid swelled in his throat and he breathed deeply. Something was missing—obviously. His body was held in expectation, everything except his brain was at a loss as to what was happening; where was the cigarette? Where was the smoke to go with the drink? Clarence apologised profusely to all his body parts; his fingers, his lungs, his blood, his lips. *It's for the best everyone, honestly, you'll thank me in the long run.*

Although the craving had hit him with his evening drink, he had to admit that it had lessened during the day, his fingers still twitched for the want of a cigarette between them, but on the whole, the small itchy patch was doing its job.

At seven p.m. Clarence sat down to eat his evening meal of fish and steamed vegetables. His glass of chilled Pinot Grigio went well with the fish and Clarence thanked himself for the small mercies left.

After washing up he settled himself down in the only armchair to sit out the evening engrossed in a book, written by one of his rivals, Martha Exe. Reading his competition reminded him of what was out there and it pleased him when he found a clumsy sentence or a stereotypical character.

At nine-thirty he heard his new neighbour return, Clarence could feel himself twitching at the heavy footfalls of this newcomer and the sudden blare of a stereo breathing into life caused him to shut his book with a slap, but when the volume was hurriedly turned down, Clarence paused in his judgement. Still, he had been re-reading the same sentence for the last five minutes and his eyelids were beginning to droop.

He got into bed and lay listening to the dull roar of traffic from distant Queen's Street but as much as he breathed deeply and slowly, sleep did not even poke its head in the room to visit. Clarence stared at his swirled Artex ceiling and thought about the new book. He couldn't even picture his main character and this was important, if he could at least visualise some aspect of them, it might help...where was the neighbour from for a start? Why had he come there? What was his intent?

Clarence heard the sound of a guitar plucked loudly from upstairs, followed by a fast series of other chords as the instrument was tuned. He shut his eyes in disbelief and thumped a pillow over his head. But the chords echoed through the feather-down and he sat up quickly, switching on the light, illuminating his immac-ulate bedroom. After ten minutes of the music dripping through the ceiling, Clarence's anger dissipated and seemed to melt. He tried to read a little more but the melody from above kept creeping into the story and the macabre theme was lost as the music was uplifting, joy-ous even. And now he was lying back in bed listening to the dreamlike notes dance around his ears it painted a smile on his face. The music washed over the room and soothed him into sleep.

He is a solider, running across a fog-drenched no-man's land alone. The enemy is behind him firing, he looks back and doesn't see anyone, but he knows they're still there, in the trees, behind the smoke screen. In the distance he can see a forest and he knows that it's there he needs to go. There's a bright rosy glow coming up behind the trees and now he can hear a voice. It's singing but he can't discern the words. He has to get to the singer. He runs and runs, stumbling over rocks and blocks of wood that litter the ground. He has trouble breathing and begins to choke, he stops to catch his breath and feels that his mouth is full of something, he coughs and spits out a lump of fur—he can feel the spiked threads catching in his throat—he's got to have water, something to wash out the hair which is absorbing all the saliva in his mouth…

The scene changes and he is back in the house he grew up in. Everything is as it was, he can even sense the smell of the house; damp mingled with the polish his mother used on the table and a faint whiff of morning toast and tea. Sun is streaming through the threadbare curtains and as he goes through to the kitchen his mother is there, wiping potatoes and chopping violets. She smiles at him and explains that his father is dead but Gwen is here to see him, look there she is behind you. And there Gwen is, looking younger than he remembers her, and she picks up the violets and places one behind his ear and smiles, then tips back her head and laughs. The sun catches her hair and her teeth…

Clarence was woken by Annie sniffing his face. She seemed to be puzzled as to why he wasn't in his usual place of soft blankets and warm air. Clarence blinked and for a moment he was just as confused as his cat. Why was he at his desk? He hardly moved when he was asleep, let alone *walked out* of his bed. His bleary eyes took in the blank computer screen in front of him, he slapped the keyboard and the computer whirred awake. On the screen was a message stating that he had successfully sent an email to JWhite@whiteandbrownassociates. com. He'd sent a message to Jules? Clarence twitched in confusion. When and why had he done that? Nervously he pressed the previous page button and saw an email which he had no recollection of writing;

Dear Jules,
Here's something I've been working on for the next manu-script, let me know what you think.
Yours, Clarence.

There was a document attached to it and Clarence, with a small dread fluttering in his chest clicked buttons to find out what it was. What he saw next, made him want a cigarette more fiercely than he'd ever wanted one before.

It was *poetry*, that's all he could think of. The flowery words dropped onto the screen, with no discernable structure or story. The sentences didn't even seem to make that much *sense*. Clarence sat, mouth agape, trying desperately to think why and *how* he had written them. The phone on his desk broke the silence. Still staring at the screen, Clarence reached over, knocking over the bowl of sweets and picked up the receiver.

"Hello?" he croaked, his mouth parched. "Hi Clarence."

"Jules, I–" he started and then stopped, what the hell would he say?

"How are you feeling?" Jules asked, though he did not really sound that concerned, but it took Clarence by surprise.

"I'm fine, I think."

"Really? Because I assumed you had a bit of a heavy night of it last night."

"No, I...I don't think so." Clarence's head whirled, had he drunk a lot? Had the dreams been due to too much whiskey? But no, looking across at the decanter of Grouse, still on the sideboard, the level had not changed from last night and besides, Clarence never drank to excess.

"Right, well in that case," he could hear Jules's voice tighten, "could you please explain exactly what you sent me at 3.30 this morning? I mean Clarence, I'm all for practical jokes but you know we're both on a deadline–"

"I can't remember writing it though," Clarence interrupted hurriedly, "honestly Jules, I don't know what happened last night, I wasn't even drinking, but then this neighbour upstairs started playing music, and I don't know, it did something to me," he paused, breathless. There was silence on the other end, Clarence wondered what Jules was thinking.

"Are you sure you're feeling alright?" said Jules finally.

"I'm fine," Clarence lied, "I've just had a funny night," his eyes searched around the flat, "it was probably something I ate."

Clarence didn't feel like his usual breakfast of muesli and fruit so he settled for a tea with no milk, but it tasted rancid in his mouth so he added an uncharacteristic spoonful of sugar. He sat at the tiny kitchen table, the troubled night slowly ebbing away with the morning light settling in through the window. He thought again of his dream, the sight of Gwen laughing so heartily still pierced his heart, but the edges were beginning to fade and the tea helped restore some warmth to his bones.

His brain popped up with the thought of a cigarette and although Clarence knew he *should* want one, his body was repulsed at the thought. Instead he went through to bathroom and turned on the shower. Inside, the hot water pummelled his muscles and helped smooth out the knots. He peeled off the nicotine patch and rolled it into a sticky tube. He got out, dried himself and chose a fresh shirt from his neat rows of similar dark shirts in the wardrobe.

Feeling refreshed and optimistic he took out a new patch from the box, murmuring a short entreaty to it. *A new day.*

He had spent two hours scribbling down notes for the new book, when he heard stirrings from the flat above. Clarence tried to ignore the misgivings that were beginning to clutch his heart. He heard a faint toilet flush and tried to concentrate on his train of thought.

Cheap flat—run down—damp, paint peeling, dark, etc. audible noises from other flats.

Other neighbours? Odd characters-'fallen through the cracks' types-prostitutes, elderly lady with dark past, etc. alcoholics.

It was only when the first strum of the guitar sounded did Clarence sink his head into his hands. The force of the dream hit him again and to his immense surprise Clarence felt his eyes water.

This would not do. The tune that had swung him to sleep the previous night echoed down from above and Clarence shuddered, it placed memories behind his eyes that he had long since buried and had tried to forget. He tried to concentrate on describing the sinister feeling to the block of flats that his protagonist feels on first encountering the tenement;

Building looms up over him—stone smoked black by years of city pollution—which part of town is it? Blank windows like eyes...is there a face at the window? Yes, a woman's face, pale and lovely, ethereal looking with long dark hair, she gazes down at him wistfully and–

No. Clarence physically shook his head as if shaking out a fly. What was he thinking? *This is not a love story* There was never any 'wistfulness' in his books—lust yes, if combined with psychological menace, but never lonely faces at the window, and never pretty faces with hair like Gwen's.

Clarence grabbed a book of fluorescent pink post-its. On the top one he wrote in capital letters;

I WORK AT HOME, COULD YOU R EFRAIN FROM PLAYING YOUR MUSIC BETWEEN THE HOURS OF 10 AM AND 5 PMC. WOOD-No. 6

Without pausing he stood up and marched out of his flat up the stairs to No. 9. Purposefully he slapped the post-it on the door, unwilling to actually knock and confront the musician himself.

Nodding satisfactorily he turned away in time to hear his own door slam, and lock. His heart jumped as he realised he had no key with him and Clarence felt himself break out in a blush, his whole body reddening, even though there was no one to witness his embarrassment. It was something he hadn't been able to control since he was a child and he cursed himself doubly. This was so unlike himself, he thought, he would *never* have stepped outside without a key before. Clarence sank down on the cold stone step, feeling utterly weak. The patch on his arm itched and he longed for a cigarette and a strong cup of coffee in the comfort of his small sitting room, instead of being marooned in the no-man's land of the tenement stair, the freezing concrete seeping into his skin and the music which made him both jump for joy and cower with fear, now even louder in his ears and heart.

Three hours later Clarence was back in his flat. After having to wait for the neighbour in No. 1 to return (the landlord's daughter, Meredith, who held spare keys for all the flats in the tenement. She had stared at Clarence and silently handed the key over).

He was exhausted and didn't feel that he could go back to his desk. His head still hummed with the tune he had heard in the stairwell, following him about like a personal soundtrack. Dazed, he plodded into his bedroom, drew the curtains and lay down, fully clothed on the bed.

"Look what I've done," she says and held out her closed hand to him. On opening her fingers he sees a tiny child sat on her palm. It has blonde hair, similar to his when he was a child, white blonde. She wraps the child in purple tissue paper and pops it into a leather handbag as if it's a bag of sweets. Then she is gone, around a corner and when he follows her she has disappeared out of sight.

Clarence woke with a start, a sheet of paper stuck to his face. He blinked and it fluttered down to the desk where he found himself sitting. The computer screen glowed eerily in the darkened living room and Clarence's heart sank as he realised what had happened. He could hardly bring himself to read what was written on the screen's stark font. His whole body felt empty whereas his brain fizzed with an overtired energy like a stretched muscle.

He wondered what time it was and found that he didn't care if it was after five or not, he needed a drink. He poured double his usual amount into the heavy tumbler and downed it in one. He shakily poured another as upstairs he could hear the music start up again. Dully he wondered if the guitar player knew anything else as he tried to block out the tune, but already it was there, the chord changes that made hairs stand up on the back of his neck and wrap itself around his lungs, making them heavy with emotion. Clarence swallowed the whiskey and gritted his teeth as he started to read what was written.

The moment he opened the door, something leapt within him. For a moment he didn't even take in her face and body, for the whole of the doorway was bathed in light. It blinded him, it touched his skin like the sun on a summer's day, filling his being with warmth. Had he known love until now? Could he ever compare another soul to this one opposite inside a long slim body with its mussed up dark curls...

Clarence could not read on. This...this *romance* was not him, in all his days as a writer he had never written anything like this. He shut the lid quickly, wanting to distance himself from this other author. Where had *his* writing gone? Tales of the darkness within human nature? He felt stripped and exposed in these descriptions of light and bodies and love–

Gwen. Even her name conjured up a sense of fragility, an eggshell, perfect but bitterly delicate. She was the only woman Clarence had ever loved, and there it was, the simple truth of it smiling smugly back at him. Not that he had admitted it to her at the time. They had been young, they had been naïve. They were together for two years, and with the tragedy of hindsight Clarence could now see that it was the happiest time of his life—he was fully himself, from the top of his head to the tips of his fingers and toes; through another person, he had come into being. He finally knew what people meant about finding the missing piece of the jigsaw—the completed 'o'.

And then something unexpected and unplanned had happened. Gwen announced she was expecting a baby, and Clarence had run away, screaming inside his head. He had never wanted anyone else to join their seamless unit, not even a baby born of both of them.

They separated.

She got rid of the baby, so he heard.

She was ill for a long time, a mutual friend said, not physically, but mentally.

And Clarence felt so guilty that he didn't think of her for seven years.

Until now. Until this...this stranger moved in up above him and started playing his music which unravelled him like a rope, dredging up the carefully pressed down memories and scattering them to the winds. There was something in the notes that floated down which caused Clarence to see Gwen's face so clearly behind his eyes that he feared to shut them.

He sat at the desk trembling, too scared and sad to move.

"This feels so wrong, Clarence, doesn't it feel wrong to you?" she had pleaded, her face pale and thin, her hands grabbing at her wrists, scratching the soft skin with her bitten fingernails. He didn't meet her eyes and said nothing, it was only when she had turned away from him and began to slowly pull her coat on that he managed to mutter, "Don't go, Gwen—please."

But she didn't hear him and was already moving towards the door. Inside he was bellowing, but outside his throat couldn't manage a whisper.

Upstairs the guitar reached a crescendo and Clarence remembered simultaneously, the clouds in her eyes as she walked out the door that last time, and a look she gave him when they had woken up together that first morning. He collapsed at his desk in sobs, not knowing how to go on.

Something had to be done.

Come the dawn, Clarence is sat upright at his desk. His eyes are dry. In one hand is a lit cigarette, its smoke winding round his head like a grey snake. In the other hand he holds a small cup of fresh percolated coffee, its scent dreamily powdering the smoky air. Clarence feels calmer than he has done in two weeks. The air is still and he is silently watching the small gold clock on the mantelpiece, steadily counting the seconds and the minutes and the hours until a certain hour comes and he can say goodbye to this awful, awful night.

"Good Morning, Force control centre, Noise service, Tricia speaking."

Clarence could hear a voice inside him, high pitched, almost feminine, was it even Gwen's? He took another strong pull on his cigarette and inwardly stamped on it.

"Yes, I'd like to make a complaint about one of my neighbours…"

Clarence heard footsteps on the stairs that very afternoon. He went to his door at the sound of No. 9 opening, and listened through the crack.

"What are you talking about? What complaint?" came a male voice, evidently his new neighbour, Clarence realised he didn't even know what he looked like.

"You were warned Mr Moon, unofficially."

"No I wasn't."

Clarence frowned at this, how could he have missed the neon pink post-it? He should have put something through the letterbox, something dated and formal. The young neighbour's voice came again.

"I didn't receive anything."

"Well, there's been a complaint now, and we're asking you to keep your playing to minimum or else there will be official action taken."

"Come on, it's not as if I'm playing loud drum and bass at one in the morning!"

The other man did not answer but started to walk away from the door, Clarence's neighbour ran after him, still yelling, "Come on man! Don't you have a soul? Who is it? Who's doing this complaining?"

The Force Control officer ignored him as he walked past Clarence's door and through the crack Clarence saw his neighbour appear. He looked carefully at his face; he had dark hair that flopped over his eyes, broad-chested, with strong tanned arms under a thin faded green t-shirt. He was young—beautiful even, and a spiteful part of Clarence, (related to his younger self who was prematurely bald, nervous and blushing) rose up, *well this might bring him down a peg or two.*

The neighbour from No. 9 sighed heavily and ran his fingers through his hair. He looked about him at the seemingly empty blank doors and wearily plodded back to his own.

Clarence's afternoon passed in contented silence and if there were any uncomfortable feelings in his mind, he obliterated them with another cigarette. His writing came thick and fast, his fingers almost couldn't keep up with his thoughts and he smiled broadly as his characters came alive on the screen.

At five o' clock he wrote a short email to Jules explaining that he now had his storyline set out in his head and was confident it would work. He didn't mention anything about starting smoking again, or his recent behaviour, hoping that Jules would forget it quicker if nothing was said.

He gazed fondly at Annie who snapped awake from her chair the moment he opened the cupboard for her cat food. He settled back in the armchair with his glass of whiskey and lit another cigarette, blowing the smoke up to the silent ceiling. Later, as he lay in bed, Clarence wondered if he had done the right thing—a pang of guilt pricked him as he thought of the young neighbour alone in his flat with his now muted guitar, and Clarence compared it to someone taking his computer away—or Annie…his thoughts faded as he drifted off into a silent sleep.

He was woken by a knocking at the door. Foggily he got out of bed and padded through to the dark living room. The knocking stopped as he neared the door, but as he gripped the handle it started up again, not loud, but a polite, restrained knock. Clarence opened the door a crack and peered into the darkness of the stair…

He was nearly pushed backwards by a hand that held up a bright pink note and before Clarence recognised it as the one he had written, he was barraged by a flurry of notes on a guitar. He opened the door fully to see what was happening and was confronted by his adversary, the resident of No. 9, Mr Stuart Moon who was serenading him very loudly with the one tune that Clarence now feared. His neighbour's face was set in a forced smile and he looked Clarence directly in the eye as he sang some words over his playing, "Oh Mr number six, how sad and old you look, does my playing really interrupt your book?" Clarence opened his eyes wider in surprise at this but his neighbour just nodded and kept on singing.

> *"Yes, I've been reading all about you.*
> *With your cheap trashy books and your prejudices too,*
> *You just can't handle hearing about love,*
> *It's something you obviously know nothing of,*
> *Well I can sing it because I know,*
> *What it is to find love and let the joy flow."*

His tune ended in a flourish and Clarence found himself unable to speak. All he could think of was Gwen, of time lost and un-regainable love. He shut the door in the beautiful boy's face and crawled to the phone.

The next morning, No. 9's guitar was taken away with its owner shouting obscenities at both Clarence and the Force Control officer. By the evening Clarence could hear laughter floating down through the floorboards, his young neighbour and a girl's voice, accented and carrying.

Clarence sat in his flat with Annie on his knee, a burning cigarette in the ashtray, couldn't even feel his own fingertips such was the emptiness inside him.

A Series Of Events

Two days later Stuart Moon opens his door to the sight of his guitar leaning against the wall, like a casual guest come to dinner, with a note reading;

With all my heart I apologise, thank you for reminding me of the love which is out there. Warmest regards, Clarence Wood.

Three months later Julian White of White and Brown Associates received a large rectangular parcel wrapped in brown paper. It contained a completed manuscript from his client, C. Blackwood. The novel was entitled *Writer's Block* and the synopsis told of a claustrophobic thriller in which a writer is terrified in his own tenement by a new psychotic neighbour. It ends (controversially in Julian White's eyes) with the writer being killed. The revelation being that the he has previously been involved with the killer's daughter, getting her pregnant and then fleeing, scared of the commitment. The girl went on to kill herself and her father swears revenge on the flimsy hack who caused his daughter's death. 'So so,' thinks the agent, not exactly original but it'll have to do, especially considering the short handwritten note that accompanied it;

Dear Jules,

Here is the last manuscript I'm going to write as far as crime novels go. I'm sorry to leave White and Brown Associates but I feel this is the end of the line for me. Thank you for all your help and support over the years, I shall miss you.

Your friend, Clarence Wood

Julian White raises his perfectly shaped eyebrows. *I shall miss you*—overly emotional for Clarence. Something had happened recently, midlife crisis probably. It happened a lot, particularly in creative types.

Jules stays up all night reading the four-hundred page novel. It is completely unlike anything else Clarence has written, and although he has doubts as to whether he'll be able to sell it to die-hard fans of C Blackwood, he is enthralled; he recognises the odd romantic writing which Clarence sent to him, but it has been tweaked, the syrupy sweetness removed, a dark threat lurking, enough to keep the reader in suspense. Although the plot was not original, the writing was unique.

At nine a.m. the next morning, Jules phoned Clarence to offer him more money than his usual commission; he was that excited about the new book. But instead of Clarence picking up on the fourth ring as was his habit, the answering machine clicked on. "Hello, this is Clarence, I can't come to the phone right now, or for the foreseeable future in fact, I've gone to seek my destiny," there was a pause, " I might be some time."

Julian White rolled his eyes. Bloody writers. So melodramatic.

5

The knocked door echoed around the concrete stair. "Tam! Tam are you in there?"

Bang bang bang.

"Tam! Come on, open up," Meredith called through the thick mahogany door, bending her ear close so as to hear any discernible sounds from inside. Traffic shouted in from the outside world of bustling Morningside going about its business. She knocked again, louder and longer this time and from behind the door she thought she could hear a slow, laborious shuffle.

"Tam!" she roared moderately, desperately trying to keep her voice to a minimum, lowering the sounds in the top of her mouth so they came out in an oval hiss. "Are you in there?"

There was a hacking cough on the other side of the wall, followed by a snort and a gurgle and a collected pooling of phlegm.

'Oh God, not on the floor,' Meredith thought as she rattled the doorknob.

"Who iss it?" a voice slurred through from the inside. "It's Meredith!" she hissed, "open the bloody door." "Who?"

"Meredith Macefield."

"Mer-dith?"-

"Open the door, Tam."

"Mer-dith the landlord's daughter?" She rolled her eyes and leant her head against the wood.

"Yes, that one, can you please just open the door?"

The gravelled voice suddenly burst into song. *"Much has been said of the strumpets of yore, but I sing of the baggage that we all adore, the land-lord's daugh-ter."*

"Tam?"

The voice came louder, she could imagine his mouth raised to the roof, eyes closed.

"And when her name is men-tioned…"

"Tam–"

"The parts of every man–"

"TAM! Open up now!

"Do stand up to atten-shun!"

Meredith spun the doorknob again, but this time the door had been unlocked and she fell into the Cream of Magnolia painted hallway and onto the reeking coat of Tam Conway. She inhaled a mouthful of cigarette smoke, dull strong whiskey and air that had been circulating around Tam's stagnant lungs for the best part of three months. She coughed involuntarily, gagging on the thickness of the atmosphere that tasted rubbery with alcohol, long since drunk.

After shutting the door hurriedly, Meredith ran to the nearest window, unlocked it and heaved up the sash, sticking her head out, gulping in deep breaths of clean, leafy autumn air.

"For fuck's sake, Tam, could you not open a window once in a while?"

"But I sing of the baggage that we all adore," Tam was still singing and smiling at her, waving a bottle in one hand and enjoying his song, *"The landlord's daugh-TER!"*

"Will you shut up?" Meredith shouted at him.

Tam mumbled something into the collar of his great coat, shuffling from the hall to the kitchen in his socks.

"And I told you not to bloody smoke!" she called through after him, pacing over the slate flagstones that led into the stark white and steel kitchen, complete with breakfast bar, dishwasher and microwave. The gleaming glass and chrome gadgets sat on the spotless surfaces and hung from bars suspended from the ceiling. It had the air of a morgue or butcher's shop and Meredith could see no evidence that Tam had used any of the kitchen equipment at all. In contrast to the smell and Tam's appearance, the condition of the flat looked remarkably good. Tam was now shambling into the spacious dining-cum-living room, the main focus of which was a huge semi-circular window on one side, through which the bright old light of the year was streaming.

She could now see that Tam had made himself a nest in the corner of the room, the biggest leather armchair was lined with an old mouldy army sleeping bag, bursting with stuffing. Next to it lay his faded green duffle bag, the bottom smeared with something very old and unrecognisable. In the crook of the broad arm of the chair nestled an overflowing ashtray and around the feet were mounds of empty wine bottles, growing in clumps like glass flowers.

Meredith sighed, Tam blinked up at her through his half- closed eyes, his gums gnawing and smacking.

"Why didn't you use the kitchen?" she asked, hands on hips. "Pf!" he snorted, "Ah cannae cook!"

"You could've just made beans on toast or something."

"Aye well, ah didnae want tae mess anythin' up like," he mumbled. Meredith sighed again.

"Tam! It wouldn't have mattered! I could've come in and cleaned up," she looked at him, hands gesturing all around her, "this was what all this was for! That's why I offered you this place, so you could sort yourself out."

Tam's eyebrows danced by themselves and he grinned toothlessly and self-consciously at Meredith.

"Ah ken," he said quietly, "Ah'm sorry, Meredith."

"Well this is your last day, Tam, I'm really sorry but there's gonna be people moving in next week, I heard from Norma." Tam didn't seem to react. He looked away and shuffled towards his dying clothes and heaps of bottles. Meredith watched his threadbare back.

"I'm sorry, Tam."

"S'alright Mer-dith, ah ken ah cannae stay here forever." "Will you try and sort yourself out at least?"

He turned and grinned at her. "You're a fine lass, Mer-dith." She dropped Tam off at Babylon café on Nicholson Street where he knew the owner and they would give him a free breakfast. Meredith slipped him twenty notes as he got out of her Lexus and called after him, "Don't just spend it on drink, Tam."

He didn't turn round but simply enacted a royal wave as he staggered towards the bright green door of the café. Meredith watched his retreating figure in the wing mirror, knowing he would never change, never get off the drink. His life as it was now was far too engrained, like the dirt and smog from the Edinburgh streets that his clothes had inhaled over the years. In five months' time Meredith would read in the *Evening News* that Tam had been found dead next to a dumpster behind the Central Bar. She would feel anger mostly; a frustration at his sheer laziness and bloody-mindedness, but there would also be a deep knot in the pit of her stomach, because although she knew that she had given Tam a couple of months under a roof with central heating (albeit unused) and a good few bottles of cheap whiskey, she could have really tried harder. She could have gotten him off the booze, found out if he had family and—No. Meredith had sworn that when she had started her small crusade she would only offer what was there already, i.e. empty houses. She wasn't a saint, she wasn't a worker for Shelter or the Samaritans and it would be too much to try and sort out people's lives as well as their housing situations. But then, wasn't it just that she couldn't be bothered?

It had all started as revenge. A pure act of vengeance on her father for...well, Meredith hadn't quite decided specifically what for, but various multiple choice boxes could have been ticked. The affairs for instance; such was Hugo Macefield's attitude towards women that Meredith's mother, Audrey, had lived her life as Mrs H Macefield on a strictly need-to-know basis. She had rarely known where her husband was at any given time; he was either 'at the office', 'abroad on business' or 'working late'. Meredith had seen him even less. When Meredith was sixteen she had told her mother that she was at a friend's sleepover, when in fact she was drinking vodka and lying to a doorman about her age at The Dome nightclub. That was when she had spotted her father, fast-tracking the queue, his arm casually fondling the bottom of an unknown blonde, may- be only a year or two older than Meredith herself.

Other good reasons for a few hits on Hugo Macefield, could be that he had not been robustly present during Meredith's child-hood. He had typically missed birthdays, school award ceremonies or performances of *Twelfth Night* and *Les Miserables* (in which Meredith had a lead role at Watsons). As well as his own business, Hugo had the pressing commitments of Freemasons' meetings or lunch and dinners with vague yet important acquaintances. He was strong supporter of the Scottish National Party, albeit on a more right-wing level, and to the consternation of his friends (and the police) Hugo had a habit of writing to the local MSP with none too subtle suggestions of 'ethnic cleansing'. He had no dealings whatsoever with anyone from over the border, refusing even to stop down in London when travelling abroad. He had slapped Meredith smartly round the head when she had suggested that she might like to move down to Manchester.

"No family of mine will pay taxes to English bastards." Vengeance might be too strong a word, and it wasn't so much a cold dish that Meredith was serving up to her absent yet domineering *pater familias*, but a lukewarm two fingers; a prolonged practical joke. Every time she thought of who was staying in the spacious and luxuriant flats Hugo owned, dotted around the desirable leafy parts of Edinburgh, it made her feel as though ends were tied up, the snake had eaten its own tail and her father was getting his just desserts. He never gave money to charities and the sight of the homeless 'cluttering up the streets' made him splutter up on his old soapbox of 'what's wrong with Scotland today...'

As well as doing a bad turn towards Hugo, Meredith had long since thought that she needed something to do with her time. Not having to worry about earning a living, she spent her time entertaining a mildly amusing cocaine habit and visiting friends either abroad or in and around Edinburgh. She had friends who worked in spite of not needing to, finding within in it a sense of fulfillment and satisfaction. Meredith had vaguely tried her hand at this, setting up a shop in Newington (courtesy of an investment from Hugo) where she had sold clothes and ornaments shipped over from Thailand, retailing them at twenty times the price she bought them for. The business had largely consisted of Meredith trolleying to and fro between Edinburgh and Bangkok, smoking copious numbers of Thai sticks and bartering with the local dress- makers—all of which she had greatly preferred to sitting in the empty shop—*Thai Times*, staring at the grey drizzle of an Edinburgh spring.

She resented the fact that her father thought she should work for a living, or that she should go to university come to that.

"For fuck's sake, Meredith—you've got to do something with your life; make it mean something, girl! Do something that you're proud of, or at least get off your arse and get an education, I never had the chance when I was your age…"

…Yeah yeah, he left school at fourteen and had to support his poor mother when his dad upped and left, blah blah blah, she'd heard it all before.

As far as university went, Meredith had never seen anything she particularly liked the look of, she already had the student lifestyle without even having to do a course and it was so hard to think of a career when at the back of her mind she knew that really, she didn't actually have to have one.

Meredith didn't feel any guilt because of this and she hated the way that some of her friends tried to disguise their wealth, as if it were an embarrassing disease. Her friend Chloë had actually chosen to live in Broughton Street because in her words 'it was more *real*'. Well, Meredith could do reality; look at the people she encountered nowadays—Tam for example, you couldn't get closer to the streets than Tam as he still reeked of them (it also made her smile to think of that same smell lingering in the Morningside flat when the new people moved in). Maybe she'd introduce Chloë with her grotty dreadlocks, torn trousers and fifty grand a year trust fund to Tam Conway one day…

Yes, Meredith could do gritty thank you very much, but when her work was done, (when she knew where people were staying, and the dates she had to get them out on) she liked to return to her desirable residence on Dublin Street, (with its generously sized rooms and real oak panelling with original gilded cornices) and forget. She would forget that there were people like Tam or Maggie who was on the game, or the obviously disturbed girl she had just put in No. 6, Canaan Lane.

At night Meredith would close the tall shutters on the dark, cold and unforgiving city, and turn inwards, into the womb-like living room that was painted deep crimson, light up a joint and watch *River City*. It was true she had the nicest flat in the tenement, having investigated them all with Hugo before he bought it. Meredith's only duty was to be a key-holder for the rest of the flats above her, and the other tenants hardly bothered her at all.

She would hear of any empty houses through Norma, Hugo Macefield's secretary, who had worked for him for twenty-five years. Norma was the closest thing to a parent that Meredith had, it had been Norma's chest which Meredith had sobbed her heart into when Audrey had died under a privately starched hospital coverlet, and it was she who Meredith trusted with more information than any member of her family, (Norma had answered Meredith's one call from St Leonard's when she had been charged with possession of cocaine and it was due to Norma that Hugo never found out.)

So Norma would tell her which houses were empty and if necessary cut a few keys that she would hand over to Meredith, colour coded with labels. Norma had always despised Hugo herself, but with jobs (and rent-free houses) hard to come by, she could satisfy her rising bile with these sizable acts of fraud and deception. Norma's filing system at Macefield and Co. was a minefield of double turns and dead ends to Hugo, and she was confident of never being discovered.

It was Meredith's prerogative that she chose who to house. As with her father's own business, Meredith had her contacts; friends would mention someone they'd met at a party where they'd been slumming it for an evening, there'd be an odd character in the corner, down on their luck—maybe even a former member of their own set, Phillip Morecombe for example. Phillip was an ex-banker, kicked out by his wife and his company, after he'd been found to be shagging his secretary (such a cliché, Meredith thought) but the man was a miserable wreck.

Phillip had taken full advantage of one of Meredith's 'hotels' (as she liked to call them) and after a few days at the flat in Duddingston village he had stopped drinking, cleaned himself up and got a job at an accountancy firm. Phillip became Meredith's poster boy for what her set-up could do for people. Tam Conway she had helped out as a matter of her own convenience, she would be constantly tripping over his feet on the way into Waitrose as he lounged just outside the doorway, and so for the sake of her ankles she had set him up on Comiston Road for a few months. Meredith had met Maggie in a bar, leaking tears into her Gin and Slim. "My bloody man's gone and died!" she sobbed when Meredith asked what was wrong. "Selfish bastard, who's going to look after me now?" Maggie had two children she said, who social services were threatening to bag so Meredith had offered her a flat that was going in Abbey Hill for Maggie's protection and a decent address for her to give the social. So far she'd managed to persuade her father that a friend of hers was interested and if he could keep it free? Reluctantly Hugo had agreed and then with Norma's help, Meredith had managed to waylay all the concerning papers and not mention the flat again to Hugo…Maggie, Caitlin and Jordan were still there, and Hugo was none the wiser.

The Canaan Lane girl bothered her though. There was something about her that Meredith really didn't like, she left a nasty taste in her mouth and she really should just tell her to go. The idea found her nervous though, and she was annoyed at herself. Meredith didn't get nervous, especially about confrontation.

She had met the girl at a party in Leith when Meredith had consumed enough cocaine and vodka to put her in excellent spirits. The girl had been eyeing her from a corner, Meredith had felt the heavy-lidded eyes fixed upon her face and she had wondered whether she was one of those girls going through a gay phase. Meredith, with her slim tanned forearms and carefully mussed blonde hair was quite used to women sidling up to her and confidently slipping an arm around her waist. After another line Meredith was bored of being stared at and simply called across to her.

"What exactly are you wanting, love?"

It was the signal the girl had been waiting for. Her eyes widened and she swiftly crossed the room with her head down towards Meredith, who stood waiting with a raised eyebrow. The girl was dressed all in black, a paint-spattered hoodie and tight ill-fitting jeans. Her dark ratty hair was pulled back in a ponytail, her pale face free from any make-up and Meredith felt her eyes pulled towards two angry spots on her cheek.

"Well?"

"Are you the one with the houses?" the girl asked.

Meredith narrowed her eyes suspiciously. The girl spoke with an English accent, one that Meredith couldn't quite place.

"What do you mean?"

"Are you the one who can get people into places, you know, if they've got nowhere else?"

Meredith twitched her mouth, this had never happened before, someone asking *her* about having a house, she was worried, word must have gotten about in certain circles.

"I might be, how do you know about it?"

The girl met her stare confidently. "I just heard that's all—can you get me somewhere then?" Her tone was aggressive and demanding and if Meredith hadn't been swimming in a powdery false confidence she would have felt uncomfortable. Instead, she adopted a patronising tone.

"Look love, I don't know who told you all this stuff but it's strictly exclusive, ok? I approach people, not the other way round, ok?"

The girl stared at her; a filthy look on her face and Meredith smiled her half-baked benign smile, which said, *I'm sorry for your situation but not enough to do anything about it*, especially reserved for beggars and charity fundraisers. After a pause, in which Meredith lit another cigarette and aimed her eyes away from the girl's angry wasp-like gaze, the stranger continued.

"So you get to choose who gets a house and who doesn't? You get to play God?"

Meredith rolled her eyes in mock despair. "It's not like I own the whole of Edinburgh! I know of a few spare places which certain people in certain situations can have access to for a limited period only."

"Jesus Mer," Tiffany said next to her. "You sound just like your dad," which made them both explode with laughter. The dark- haired girl continued to stare at Meredith until they both had calmed down and then she gripped Meredith by her silver-chained wrist and hissed urgently into her face.

"Please. Please just give me a place for a few days. I've got to disappear for a while and I've got to get in touch with my boyfriend first but I don't have a phone."

Meredith sighed, gushing smoke through her nostrils. "Can't I just buy you a phone?"

"You just don't get it do you?" the girl hissed, tears near her eyes. "What would you know anyway? It's not like you'd ever be homeless."

"No. You're right, I wouldn't," Meredith snapped back, bored with the girl already. "I won't ever have to worry about not having any money," she paused, pulling hard on the cigarette and exhaling blue trails through her teeth. "Anyway, what is it exactly that you're supposed to have done?"

The girl looked at her suspiciously, "What do you mean?"

"I mean, why do you have to disappear?" Meredith said, waving her arms about melodramatically, she raised an eyebrow again, "boyfriend got you up the duff, did he?"

"No!" the girl snorted, looking almost relieved, her face softened slightly. "Look, I'm sorry for being weird, I'm just a bit desperate," she paused and allowed herself a shy look at her feet, " just if there's anything going at all, I'd be really, really grateful."

"Yeah well," Meredith stubbed her cigarette vigorously into an ashtray. "I'll have a think about it."

It proved that Meredith didn't have to think too long. The next morning she was nursing an enormous hangover when a text from Norma appeared on her mobile.

6 CANAAN LANE FLAT AVAILABLE FOR VIEWING FOR 2 MONTHS +

Well, she supposed she *could* put that girl in. She didn't like it though, didn't like it at all. Her guts churned with doubtful instincts, and the lava of alcohol and drugs that bubbled inside her. Lying back on her pillows and looking at the shadows play on the ceiling, she closed her eyes against the forthcoming day.

The girl wouldn't be hard to find, she'd be hanging around Daisy's flat; waiting for her presumably. Meredith thought it probably would be a good idea to keep this one sweet, she didn't want any ridiculous counterattacks, dead rabbits pushed through her letterbox for example and she looked that type, the girl; she had fire in her eyes. It angered Meredith that she *did* have to placate this stranger who she'd never met before- and was probably a good ten years younger than her. But to be fair, she had dipped her toe into the murky waters of Edinburgh's Mr Hyde; why should she be kept clean? After all, she concluded, pulling up her Egyptian cot- ton duvet over her head, it would only be for a few weeks at most, then she'd tell her to scarper.

That was nearly two months ago and the girl was still there. Meredith didn't even know her name; the girl had refused to tell her, on account of Meredith maybe passing it on to someone else; "Oh come on," Meredith had scoffed, "what I'm doing isn't exactly kosher—who the hell would I tell?"

But the girl just looked at her with narrowed eyes. She wouldn't even tell her when she'd be going and it was this fact that Meredith really got nervous about. Of all her 'clients' the girl was the only one who Meredith was uneasy with; the rest she could tell what to do. Maggie would go whenever she told her to, she was that grateful, but Meredith was quite happy to let her stay there; knowing that of all the people she had accommodated, if there was anything that was going to bring down her father's reputation, it was going to be a hooker in one of his places—a *lower class* call girl at that. When Maggie finally left, Meredith thought, she might have to dribble a small story to the newspapers…it would make a good headline. And Tam was gone, folk due to move in any day now. There was another flat which she rarely went to as the reformed junkie who lived there hardly ever stayed at the place; his girlfriend living nearby and the flat itself was due to be redecorated so she wasn't bothered about him. But that girl, the girl in Canaan Lane was the thorn in her side—she wanted her out.

Sitting in her car on Hill Place puffing on a newly lit joint and having watched Tam Conway saunter off, Meredith decided she wanted her out *now*.

Meredith drove home and cut herself a couple of lines to boost her up a bit—she'd need some confidence…then she drove jaggedly over to Canaan Lane, making sure her phone had a full battery, just in case.

Walking up to the flat, she had a rotten feeling in the pit of her stomach like a cankered apple, she half wished she hadn't had any coke as it sharpened her paranoia to a knife's edge. Her heart thudded in her chest as she approached; she couldn't see into the flat at all—the blinds were down. She felt for the key in her pocket and was surprised to find her fingers slippery with sweat. Meredith let herself into the stair and her heart sank as she instantly spotted the graffiti'ed sign to the right of the door. It was one of those stencil things, made fashionable by Banksy and bought for thousands by clamoring celebrities. Tiffany, who liked to think of herself as an amateur art critic had one hanging, framed in her large bathroom. Meredith was always slightly alarmed to lift her head up from the lid of the toilet and be confronted by a large picture of two policemen kissing.

But this one, placed next to the solid oak paneled door consisted of words, one line of black and then a block of red capitals that read.

HE'S LY ING YOU'RE LY ING

CAN'T WE BE LYING TOGETHER?

Oh God, Meredith thought, not only was there vandalism it was bloody awful *poetic* vandalism—and what the hell did that all mean anyway? But for all her bluster, she still had the uneasy sharp feeling in her guts. Taking a deep breath, Meredith banged on the door. The stair was exceptionally silent and all of a sudden she couldn't hear a sound from the outside world. There was no noise from inside the flat either, not that Meredith was surprised. She put her ear to the door, trying to snatch at anything that signified a human presence. Her eyes flickered too quickly, and Meredith nervously cleared her throat, feeling queasy as she did so.

"It's Meredith, ok? If you don't let me in I'm coming in, ok? I've got a key here."

She paused, hoping to hear footsteps. When she heard nothing, she breathed hard again and reached for the key in her pocket. It slid into the Yale easily and there was a smooth click as the catch was turned back.

The smell hit her instantly and her empty stomach heaved, it was a blend of the metallic odour of warm blood and an underlying richer smell of something long dead. Having never encountered these smells before, Meredith was at a loss as to what was the source of them, all she could think was that something had been left in the fridge and had *seriously* past its sell-by date. It was stiflingly warm in the flat, and Meredith, with one hand over her mouth and nose, gingerly placed a hand on the radiator in the darkened hall, it was red hot to the touch, and she rolled her eyes at the thought of the forthcoming gas bill, as long as Hugo *never* knew she had been involved, it was another sting in the tail she supposed, mentally shrugging. It was with this dismissive, casual gesture in mind that Meredith turned the corner into the open plan lounge/dining room/kitchen (a converted bedsit if ever there was one, she thought grimly) and was confronted by a scene which changed her mood dramatically.

Although it was dark in the room, the corpse and it's small buzzing inhabitants were thrown into relief by the light of an Art Noveau Lamp. Meredith could make out the slender bronze body of a nude nymph, arms outstretched under the stained glass shade of a multi—coloured flower. She concentrated her gaze on the small imperfection on the statue's left hand, a break in the fingers where it had been dropped and an attempt at mending had been made. If she kept looking at the lamp, the girl's beatific smile, then she wouldn't have to look at the sight of a rotting cadaver, decomposing peaceably, on the fake Moroccan rug.

Inevitably she *had* to look at it though, with the same dull- eyed wonderment as she might stare at a car crash, or someone throwing up, she was compelled to snatch mental photographs of the body in close up lurid technicolour. Flies flew in and out of the holes in the flesh, the skin already green and where the blood had flooded out, it had now dried to a deep sienna crust. Meredith breathed deeper through her mouth, her hand on her chest. She vainly tried to visualise her 'good place' which she had discovered several years ago, but she couldn't quite remember where it was; desperately she tried to think of a cave, or a hilltop, or a field, anywhere except this red-hot oven of a flat where a dead body was stinking at her.

Who was he? Because it was a he, it had *been* a male, she could definitely make that out with a glance at the trousers and the shoes confirming this. But what was he doing here? And where the hell was the girl? Had she done this? Was that what Meredith couldn't trust about her? The fact that she could kill a man and leave the body here in one of Meredith's places...*is that why she wanted the flat?* Maybe that's what she thought Meredith did, maybe she thought the whole flat lending business was really a cover for unspeakable crimes, that Meredith herself hid murderers in her father's flats...how long ago had this happened? Meredith was no expert, but she guessed the body had been here a long time, time enough for the face to shrink-wrap itself onto the bones like wet tissue paper.

There had actually been a killer, someone's life had been ended—here in this flat. Someone had brought this man here with the sole intention of ending his life. How did someone (any-one) get to that kind of place, Meredith thought, emotionally *or* physically? How do you go about it? Her spinning brain was slowly unravelling itself, the coke wearing off and her thoughts slowing down, and now she felt brittle, spiky and slow. *We're talking Taggart and Rebus,* she thought dazedly, and remembered that there was a new series of Rebus on that evening which she'd promised herself a seat on the sofa for...

Fucking TV?

There was a dead man here, in front of her eyes, and she was thinking about sitting on her comfy couch, a glass of Baileys and a single skinner in her hand? That life seemed very far away, as if she were looking down the wrong end of a telescope...*Burke and Hare—we're talking the underground crime world of Auld Reekie here...* again the surreal voice of normality hit her—*Hah! This is reality, Chloë! How do you like them rotting apples?*

Suddenly the door behind her clicked shut and Meredith whipped around. The girl, her tenant, was standing behind her, her eyes wide and bright. She had a peculiar expression on her face, her smile only half finished.

"Well?" she asked Meredith.

"Well what? What the fuck have you done, you mental cow?" The girl rolled her eyes, as if attempting to explain something for the umpteenth time to a particularly slow person.

"It's really none of your business."

Meredith nearly exploded, forgetting momentarily that she was in the presence of a corpse and a potential killer.

"What do you mean it's none of my fucking business! In case you've forgotten missy—this is not your flat—you have not paid money for it and I lent it to you out of the goodness of my heart–" The girl snorted. "Don't make me laugh," she said sourly, "it's all a publicity stunt isn't it, this Good Samaritan act—you're not doing it out of kindness."

Meredith narrowed her eyes. She glanced again at the dead body, the flies sounded louder in her ears.

She fumbled about in her bag and drew out a crumpled packet of cigarettes. She was alarmed to see how hard her hand shook as she withdrew one and lit it. The girl noticed too and smiled.

"Do I make you nervous?"

"What do you think?" Meredith glared at her, inhaling hard on the cigarette. "What are you going to do then? About–" her eyes flicked to the body. The girl shrugged.

"Dunno," she looked at it doubtfully. "I'm leaving now so…" her voice trailed off. Meredith's mouth dropped.

"What do you mean, leaving?" she could hear herself shrieking, a volume she rarely hit. "What am I supposed to…where are you…" Meredith spluttered questions, not finishing them, eventually she settled on, "Why now?"

"Well, you're here now," the girl said simply. "I don't have to keep him company anymore."

"You've been *living* here?" Meredith asked quietly, incredulously, "With that?"

But the girl just nodded and smiled, her eyes innocent. She moved towards the door,

"You did kill him?" Meredith called after her, "didn't you?"

The girl rolled her eyes, *"Duh!"* she said, and went out of the door. Meredith blinked slowly and automatically followed the girl's exit a moment or two later.

Once outside the flat, the cool air hit her and her knees buckled. She staggered to her Lexus and fell in behind the wheel, breathing heavily, her head rushing.

What the fuck just happened there? Who was that girl?
Why had she killed that man—*killed*. A newspaper story, a news report waiting to happen, back there, somewhere she had just been...Where was the girl now? Why
had she waited—*waited* in the stench of a flat, like she
was waiting in a bus station for Meredith to come and
somehow relieve her of her position? What time was it?
What *day* was it? Was it time for *Rebus* yet? All Meredith
could think of was to get home and somehow drove in a
wrought-iron dream back to her flat, where once inside,
she collapsed onto her couch- and sobbed

The next day, Meredith closed down her hotels.
Apologetically she helped Maggie and her children
move out (with a slight- of-hand favour to a removal
man who Hugo sometimes employed) and paid three
months rent in advance on a flat in Oxgangs for the
three of them, promising to keep in touch with Maggie,
who swore once again to get off the game.

Eventually one winter morning, Meredith opened
the *Evening News* to read of the gruesome discovery in
a Morningside flat of a decomposed body, as yet un-
identifiable. It was the smell, a neighbour said, as most
folk had their heating on this time of year, it wasn't long
before a very strange and unpleasant odour crept down
the stair to the neighbouring flats.

It was rented accommodation, said the same neighbour, and there hadn't been anyone in it for months,
the previous tenant having left a year ago. She had
thought she'd heard voices though, a few weeks ago
now, but with what had just happened she dreaded to

think who it had been. No, she couldn't think how they had got in, she'd only supposed it was a temporary let, someone who knew Mr Macefield, the landlord. No, he hadn't been in touch; she thought he might be on one of his holidays. Meredith checked the journalist's name at the bottom of the report and smiled to herself. Hugo wasn't on holiday, she knew that much, but she could let the journalist, Stacey Kirnan know where he was—for a favour of course.

6

The Wall was the only view from Gerald's kitchen window. It was not just his wall, but stretched the length of the row of houses, divided by clipped hedges and fences. There was also a narrow footpath that ran between the houses and the wall, sharing it with the general public.

In recent years the wall had not seen much action, but occasionally things were written on it—

'DEBORAH LOVES NIGEL FOREVER IDST'
'JAMBOS RULE'
These had been in harmless biro or felt tip and easily got rid of. Every year, around springtime, one of his neighbours would rally together the other residents to dab paint over the scribbled entreaties and declarations of a stumbling walk home, making the wall and the neighbourhood respectable again. And then somebody had bought a spray can.

Numbers 38-42, Ashcroft Row looked out of their kitchen windows one morning to see their first tag, pink and gleaming in the April sunshine. Someone had unskillfully combined the letters R, E, G into a single-symbol squiggle.

"Oh! It's shocking behaviour—what are we going to do?" Peggy had asked, (number 38, blue rinse, yellow housecoat, fake pearls, duster).

"Disgusting! How are we going to get it off?" Brenda had said, (number 40, beige cardigan, pink-rimmed glasses, white hair).

"Shall we call the police?" Peggy had trilled, wringing her hands fearfully.

"At once!" agreed Glenys (number 56, small, wiry, blue house- coat, tufty hair). "I'm not going to say goodbye to my neighbourhood."

A second tag appeared the next night, this time in front of numbers 44 to 48, then all along from 26 to 32. And then from 48 to 52. Three months on from the beginning of it all, Glenys had pushed a sheet of photocopied paper through every letterbox on the road.

Tackling The Graffiti Problem

*As most of you must be aware by now, the wall behind our houses is rapidly becoming a target for vandals. The police claim there is nothing they can do without evidence, but we can make a concerted effort to be on the look out **at all times**, and help put a stop to this growing problem.*

I hope everyone takes this matter seriously.

Gerald had done his bit. He now sat in the kitchen to drink his morning tea, had pulled his chair to face the window directly, so he could watch the wall without appearing unnatural. Through thick-rimmed spectacles and recovering cataracts, the eyes of Ashcroft Row constantly scanned the wall.

In the circles of the youth there came talk of this newly-found bare stretch of canvas; it was out of the way, freshly painted and perfect for works—the area was safe too—no cameras and virtually no lighting either.

More signatures, graphics, cartoons, and mottos, arrived. Gerald found himself noticing two distinctive styles on his section that shone out, they held more weight compared to the rest and he felt oddly privileged to have, what he considered, the best part of wall. Gerald didn't even feel it was vandalism, there were no insults or threats, not even swearing and the pictures were some of the best he'd seen in the whole city. He found himself looking with interest at other pieces around Edinburgh, compared with a lot of graffiti, which in his eyes looked tatty and not thought through. It would have been a strange sight; an elderly man in his shabby green coat, squinting at a fresh piece of graffiti which consisted of swearing, brash boasting and topless girls.

One of Gerald's pictures was indeed a woman, but it was just her head. The stencil block of her hair gave the impression of being demure, conservative. She was not looking directly at the viewer, but had her eyes downcast, the lashes brushing her cheeks. To Gerald she looked sorrowful, but he liked looking at it; he liked the peaceful face.

The other artist on his section dealt mainly in words, but again he seemed to really think about his marks. His writing was strange, *poetic* even, what it all meant was Gerald's guess but it didn't matter.

I WHISPER INSIDE UNTIL I FLY

Gerald liked that. Gone were the days of Deborah loving Nigel. These kids thought about it, and meant it. They actually went out at night and sprayed their writings on a wall for the world to see. Notebooks and diaries were not enough.

It would never have happened in his day, Gerald thought, emotions and feelings were good and repressed. As they said, sex wasn't even invented until the sixties—especially in Presbertarian Edinburgh. And artwork? Unless you were in the throws of a marijuana trip, or whatever it was, down at the university, paintings were a nice vase that went with the colour of your lounge—it was nothing like this.

But sure, he had been born a lifetime ago in these kids' eyes, he'd never forgot his daughter Sandra's withering look when he'd laughed at her teenage outfit of miniskirt, pink and black striped tights and boots that a navvie had probably died in.

"God Dad, you don't know a thing about fashion," she had snapped at him.

Not that she dressed like that now, it was all smart suits that went with her job at the insurance company— and something inside him, although happy to see her in a successful career, wished she still wore the stripy tights and bomber boots.

The following spring, the row decided to take action. Another piece of photocopied paper was pushed thorough letterboxes requiring a whole weekend being dedicated to the Clean Up Of The Wall. If the police couldn't do anything, they would have to take the matter into their own hands.

"Think of what it could lead to,"said Shirley, (number 58, arms folded across her bolstered red cardigan, pince-nez on chain). "A wall of graffiti can send out all kinds of messages, even that we encourage this sort of thing. It'll attract all the wrong kind of people...and think of number 42 who are trying to sell."

Sandra and her boyfriend Derek came to visit Gerald one Sunday afternoon. He brought them out to see the graffiti, saying proudly, "It's the best of the lot."

Derek had agreed with him. "I don't see what the problem is, it's not like the usual crap at stations or tunnels."

"Aye, but you can't keep it there," said Sandra, "I mean I'm all for art but it's not to everyone's taste, is it?"

"Times were you'd love it, Sandra," replied Gerald, knowing it would wind her up, "you know, when you went about with that lad from the art school."

Sandra rolled her eyes. "Dad! That was bloody fifteen years ago! And just because it's good doesn't make it legal—it's still vandalism you know."

"Ach, you're just like the rest of the ol' wifies around here," Gerald snorted, "whose side are you on?" he folded his arms. "In the deeds to the house it says that my land goes right down to the wall, so really it's mine to do what I want with."

"Blimey Gerald," smiled Derek. "Have you put an electric fence up too?"

"No but I'm thinking about it," Gerald said, laughing.

"But you're going to get rid of it, aren't you Dad?" Sandra looked at him pointedly, putting him in mind of Alice when she was telling him (not asking) to do something. He sighed.

"Aye, well I s'pose I'll have to."

The Clean Up weekend came and Gerald approached his wall with a sense of reluctance. Although the rest of the wall deserved a scrubbing over, his own paintings seemed too good to cover up. He paused in front of them, scourer and bucket in hand, studying the woman's downcast eyes.

"Come on, Gerald!" shrilled out Brenda, "We'll show them who's boss!"

But for a while, it seemed like the graffiti artists were silently winning, this paint was not going to come off simply with a scourer and bleach. In the end Bernard went to Hermiston to buy five tins of Magnolia paint and by Sunday afternoon, the wall had been restored to its former blankness; Gerald thought it looked oddly bare, like a house with its Christmas decorations taken down.

Two nights after the great Clean Up, Ashcroft Row caught themselves a vandal. Spray-can in hand he had been jumped upon by Glenys in curlers. She had rushed outside armed with a hairbrush, her husband Bernard; an ex-security guard had lumbered out after her and had him under his knee in minutes.

In certain circles word got around that a tagger had been arrested, had blurted certain names to the police. With the help of security cameras a lot of Edinburgh's graffiti artists were caught and pictures were left unfinished around the city—signatures without their signers. It was shame, said some, sadly shaking their heads, now the amateurs were wiped off the new wall, it was now ripe for serious pieces, quality works.

Ahh, thought some wistfully, that huge blank space haunted their dreams.

Ashcroft Row wall received no unsolicited writing for the next two months. The inhabitants looked out of their kitchen windows at the plain magnolia bricks with satisfaction. Gerald still had his morning tea in the kitchen, gazing at the spot where the woman's face had been, remembering her delicate eyelashes.

It was on one of these mornings that he noticed a line of paint on the very bottom of his piece of wall. He squinted out of his window and saw that it was writing, but from this far away, indecipherably small.

Gerald crossed the lawn in front of his house, glancing over his shoulder to see if Brenda was watching from her living room post, but all was clear. He squatted down to peer at the small neat writing—undoubtedly sprayed on and Gerald wondered how they kept the letters readable and at the same time have a distinctive style to them.

HELLO, IT'S ME, IS THAT YOU?

That was all it said. He stood up, considering the sentence. He was sure it wasn't meant for him, but it was for definitely meant for someone. He patted the grass to cover the words up and walked away.

Three days later, the message had been answered. Gerald spotted it at once, on his way into town. It was at the same level as the first, but a few feet away from the first.

118

Y ES, ARE YOU READING?

Gerald turned his head quickly away, and smiled to himself. There was no way he was going to cover this up. Something was happening, a play of sorts and he was excited to see how it would unfold.

A few days later the first writer appeared, the same colour,
> the same style of writing.
> *AND WRITING...TO YOU*

The next messages came in consecutive days;
FOR ME?

A NOTE JUST TO SAY....I'VE MISSED YOU

MISSED YOU
A conversation was taking place between two people who were strangers to Gerald, but he felt honored that they had specifically chosen *his* piece of wall to write on, maybe they knew he'd like it, maybe he actually knew them? But no, that seemed impossible, he didn't know any young people. And they must be young—who else would spray their longing onto a wall? Sandra, now in her early thirties, didn't count as young anymore he supposed, and it's not as though there were any young people living in the row. It seemed like an affair of some sort, as if the words couldn't be spoken aloud, but had to be written, silently, and in secret, if you could call his wall 'secret'.

Gerald was pondering this when the doorbell rang. On his doorstep stood Glenys, Brenda and Peggy, wearing three identical forced smiles. He knew why they were there the moment he saw them.

"Gerald," began Glenys with saccharine sweetness, "we were all quite concerned as to whether you'd be at home or not."

"Why's that?" asked Gerald innocently.

"Well…we were all sure you'd been away for the past few days." "No,' shrugged Gerald, "I've been here all the time."

"I see…well in that case why have you not done anything about the vandalism on your wall?"

"What vandalism?"

"Now Gerald," smiled Glenys, as she would with a child, "surely you must have seen the new stuff that's appeared there—I do hope you intend to take responsibility for your section."

"But it's only on my piece," answered Gerald defiantly. He had not even considered painting over it, he had been too eager to see what was going to be written next.

"Yes, but it only takes one to start it off again. Now–" she smiled icily, "are you going to take it off?"

"Have you read what's on there?" he asked suddenly, apparently taking the three women off-guard.

"No, I haven't, Gerald, " snapped Glenys impatiently, "does it matter? It's making a mess on our wall—now, are you going to take it off?"

Gerald made a quick decision on the spot.

"No, I'm not," he said bluntly. "I like the writing, it's poetic and lovely—something you lot wouldn't know about." Glenys, Brenda and Peggy looked aghast, Brenda's glasses actually slipped off her nose and swayed on their chain. Gerald ploughed on, "It's not a mess. It's a message board, and it's got to stay there for them. "For WHO, Gerald?" squawked Glenys. "Exactly whose wall is it?"

"It's more mine than yours," replied Gerald simply, "and the writing stays."

And with that he shut the door swiftly. That afternoon he painted over the words with thick clear varnish-ensuring a water- tight seal which was impenetrable to any dabs of magnolia.

I WAS WRITING TO ASK...

Came the blue writer a few days later,

I THINK I LEFT
A PART OF MYSELF WITH YOU, COULD I STOP
BY AND PICK IT UP?

The recipient was silent for a few days and then suddenly surfaced, sounding, Gerald thought, urgent and somehow despairing.

THERE ARE TIMES WHEN I CANNOT BEAR TO WRITE YOUR NAME,
BUT NOW YOUR IMAGE IS EVERY WHERE, IN THE WALLS AND PAVEMENT

"Blimey," Derek had said again on his and Sandra's fortnightly visit. "You've got a real life love story going on outside your house." "I know," Gerald had grinned, "Isn't it nice?" He was pleased to see that even Sandra had moist eyes whilst reading it. He was proud that Derek and especially Sandra understood the messages; saw how beautiful the words were, and that somewhere—not too far from his house—a love was blossoming. It gave him a little faith, he thought, that not all romance was dead.

CITIES, HOUSES, PEOPLE, GET STUCK IN YOUR TEETH,
LIKE FUDGE, LIKE SUGAR, WEDGED IN, SHATTERING THE ENAMEL
—SOMETIMES I CANNOT EVEN THINK OF YOU

Gerald's lip trembled when he read that, one grey day. The writing had seemed so sad recently, it sucked Gerald back to a similar day, when he had said Goodbye to Alice as she lay trembling and dying under an angular white sheet at the Infirmary. He would never have dared to speak, or even write these words, but looking at them now, they described what he had been feeling perfectly.

The next night, one small word seemed to glow, set apart from the rest of the messages, it just read,

STOP

Stop? thought Gerald in a panic, *No, please, don't stop.*

No writing appeared for the next two weeks. He worried for these two strangers who had unknowingly drawn him into their secret. Had they been found out? Who or what was stopping them from being together? Maybe it wasn't even a man and a woman, Gerald suddenly thought, what was it they said about it 'the love that dare not speak its name'? This was the twenty-first century after all...

He tried to put the two writers out of his head, tried not to think of when they would be back, or what had happened to them. Maybe they had walked off happily into the sunset together after all, able to spend the rest of their lives together, maybe this was all an elaborate hoax and any minute now that bloody beardy man would leap out and the joke would all be on Gerald. But deep down in his gut, Gerald knew that it wasn't all finished yet.

Then just as he was adjusting back into his usual routine of having his morning tea in the living room, he was filling the kettle and noticed a line of blue paint, new yet familiar, that had not been there before.

WE CAN'T DO SUCH VIOLENT ACTS
TO OUR HEARTS AND MINDS—NOT YET.
MEET ME NOW.
P.M.

Gerald's heart gave a jolt, he knew what the writer was implying, it wasn't finished, something was about to happen.

He watched the wall on and off all day and by half past three he had fallen into a light doze and awoke half an hour later, his neck jerked towards the window, another line had been added.

THIS LINE TELLS OF M Y PROMISE

He cursed himself for falling asleep. Whoever the red spray can belonged to, had come that very afternoon, and taken a huge risk by writing in daylight, but it was a response, and a dedicated one at that.

That evening Gerald took up his post at the window, eyes constantly glued to the darkened Wall. For five hours he waited, sat in the darkened kitchen. He could just make out the dim outlines of his small garden, silhouetted by a far off streetlight.

Keeping himself awake with countless cups of tea, the street outside was so quiet that he could make out Bernard and Glenys's television blaring next door. At around 2 a.m. Gerald was startled by footsteps on the path and he peered into the darkness. A small figure appeared, dressed in black. It was a girl. When she glanced behind her, Gerald caught sight of her face and was astonished at how young she looked, fifteen maybe sixteen, she had black tatty hair pulled back into a rough ponytail, and dark flashing eyes.

Surely that can't be her, thought Gerald. The mature words did not seem to fit with this young girl who looked slightly awkward and gangly. There was a coarse rattle and the thin hiss of a spray can, and then came Gerald's second shock of the early morning,

WHATEVER YOU DO, DON'T WALK AWAY

The girl was writing in *blue*. Gerald had always supposed the blue message to be from a man, he never imagined them to be female. He thought again of Alice, did she ever think or feel so passionately?

The girl had finished her message, edgily looking quickly up and down the row, Gerald watched her with a growing sadness, now knowing who she was waiting for, standing there and risking more by each second.

Minutes passed. The girl took one last long look in both directions and then turned to face the wall, her shoulders heaved a reluctant sigh, as she lowered her head.

And walked away.

Gerald leant back sadly in his chair, feeling a finality in what he had just witnessed. This was to be the last test of them both, and the other writer had just failed the girl. A new sound shook him, there was another set of footsteps on the tarmac. Another small figure, though taller than the girl, and dressed identically, carrying a rucksack. A boy. Gerald watched him with pity, as he read the new message.

Whatever you do don't walk away.

But *she* had walked away.

The boy stood for a long moment. Deciding. Then he reached in his bag. Gerald thought quickly, and took action. Slipping from his seat he hurried to quietly unlock his back door. He tiptoed towards the boy, the vandal, the other author. He touched his arm gently and as the boy whipped around Gerald immediately put a finger to his lips, his shush urging the boy to trust him. Gerald looked down to see that the lad was holding a stencil.

IF YOU HAVE TO READ THIS, REMEMBER ME IN SMILES

Still in silence, Gerald frantically pointed to the last message written by the girl. The boy saw that this old man knew all about their story, that it was probably him who had allowed their writing to continue. The boy shrugged, gesturing around him to indicate that she was not there, his face was set in anger and dejection as he raised the regretful sentence to the wall, and set his spray can ready. Gerald grabbed it; he and the boy silently struggled, Gerald made a final thrust for the can and aimed it at the wall. As he sprayed, the writing came out straggled and uneven, but readable;

sHE HaS Not GONe—WAIT

Gerald did not know this for sure. He had put his neck on the line by writing this, but he felt certain that the girl had not left entirely. The boy looked to the sentence, and then back to Gerald who nodded.

"GERALD!" came a shout. "What on earth are you doing?" A flashlight shone in their faces and behind it

Gerald could make out the shape of Glenys (curlers and dressing gown) standing on her lawn, open-mouthed. The boy bolted, leaving Gerald rooted to the spot, spray-can in hand, unable to speak. He suddenly felt a rough arm around his neck, and a knee dug in to make his own legs buckle.

"It's alright, Glenys! I've got him!" came Bernard's rough breath in Gerald's face. As he fell to the path Gerald's eyes followed the boy's retreating figure; as he reached the end of the row another shape stepped out of the shadows, revealing itself to him in the yellow pool of street light. Gerald could just make out the two shapes moulding into one, separating again and quickly fading into the enveloping night.

He smiled.

7

Inside the white walls of his flat, Derek sat perched on the edge of his leather sofa, as if ready to spring. He could hear his phone ringing but there was no way he was moving from his spot to answer it, and there was no way he could relax back into the cushions either. He sat, poised on the cusp of movement, but unable to move. The phone clicked onto the answer machine as it had been doing for the last two days, and Derek wondered nervously who it could be, *please God not the office,* he thought to himself, and please God not his mother either. He couldn't deal with strangers or family or friends or anyone. He couldn't deal with anything. "Hi…er… Derek, it's Michael," came a voice from the machine, Derek stood up—Michael.

Now there was someone he really wasn't expecting.

Maybe he should pick up the phone, he started to cross the floor and stopped—but if Michael was calling from the prison it would be from a payphone—someone else might be listening; someone who could easily get Derek's number, from a redial or something, he didn't know—Michael's voice continued breezily. "Yep, well, I'm out and well…" There was a pause and Derek could hear his brother breathing, "it would be great to see you, I'll er…I'll give you a call later."

There was a click and the line went dead. Derek stared blankly at the silent telephone that now flashed a red light signaling a message.

So, Michael was out of prison, his only brother was free to roam the streets once more. Derek didn't know how to feel.

Two years ago, Michael had been put away for violent assault- over a dog of all things, and it wasn't even Michael's dog; he had seen a man kicking a terrier and had gone over and kicked the man. Hard. He had punctured a lung, ruptured a kidney and broken his nose. Derek shuddered at the thought, he was all for animal rights but he was of the charity donating kind rather than Michael's hands-on approach.

His own brother, nearly killing a man.

This event served to confirm Derek's theory that everyone potentially had a violent streak and this idea had grown inside him, like a dark pulsating seed. It had kept him from visiting Michael in prison, kept him from all contact with his brother, lest this horrific trait was somehow passed on. When Michael had gone into Saughton, it had made Derek think more and more about his family and about how he and Michael had turned out, where had this side of Michael come from—their parents? Derek could maybe see a glimpse of it in his father Derek 'Deek' Senior (in his younger days or after a drink or two), but his mother? Try as he might, Derek couldn't imagine the little immaculate woman who had a place for everything and everything in its place even harming a fly.

The small kernel of brittle paranoia had squirmed inside Derek for months after Michael went down, its roots curling around his memories of childhood; where exactly had this side of Michael been nurtured? Had there been a trigger? Had something happened to Michael that Derek had ignored or missed?

He had gone round to see his mother as soon as he'd heard that Michael had been arrested, and she blamed herself entirely.

"What did I do, Derek?" she had sobbed, eyes puffed with tears. "Didn't I bring you boys up to know right from wrong?"

"It wasn't you, Mum," he said reassuringly. "You know how

Michael felt about animals, remember that baby bird he found?"

Valarie Lambert smiled through her snuffles. "Aye, he nursed that thing for days and then it only died—I told him it would," she sniffed, "its mess got everywhere."

"But that's what I mean. Michael's a good person, Mum, he was only doing what he thought was right."

"What? Beating someone up?" his mother had shrieked incredulously. "Aye, that's a fine way of doing something right."

Derek had fallen silent at this, but the conversation had stayed with him—what if it was his parents who were to blame?

He thought of all the times he and Michael had been told off for not saying 'please' and 'thank you', all the times they had been shushed for speaking too loudly, the groundings, the curfews, the disapproving expression on his mother's face—the blankness on his father's, at some of his and Michael's friends when they'd appeared in the house;

"Does his mother know he's going out looking like a homeless person?"

Or girlfriends.

"I mean I like the girl, but, well isn't she a bit on the wild side for you?"

Derek began to feel more and more claustrophobic at the thought of his parents, how everything and everyone had been boxed up neatly, pressed down on and sewn up. There were things you did and things you didn't, and stepping outside the bounds of acceptable behaviour was one of them—obviously Michael's actions were out of anyone's limits, thought Derek, or were they? Wasn't Michael's reaction perfectly reasonable? Not so much the violence but the fundamental thoughts behind it, wasn't it simply that he cared?

And there he was trying to do what he thought was right but all society had done was suppress it, the phrase ' *freedom of expression*' kept running through Derek's head.

That was what was wrong with his family he thought, his parents had turned out the same as their parents and so on, no one moved with the times, branched out or thought for themselves and this had gone on for generations. Any behaviour that was not in keeping with what had gone before was shushed down, stamped out and this was the result; Michael nearly killing a man and

Derek was so messed up that he couldn't see straight. So much for survival of the fittest.

"You can't blame your parents for everything," Sandra had argued with him. "You've been an adult for a long time now Derek, stop acting like a teenager."

But he couldn't stop thinking about it. There must be reasons why he didn't feel like he could talk to anyone properly—about anything; all these new feelings and thoughts were popping up and there was no one he could tell. Everyone had earplugs in or just their 'minds on other things'.

Work had become a sea of faces he hardly knew and bobbing alongside them, he felt he was drowning. In the past when he and his colleagues had all gone for drinks on a Friday night after work, Derek could be relied upon to be the life and soul of the group; having something to say to everyone and the first in line with a joke. But lately he had felt like a puppet who began to dance, chameleon-like, to whatever tune the crowd of the duke box was playing. There was no-one there who *really* knew him, who he could sit down with and tell all this to. Who could he tell that he was having nightmares nearly every time his head hit the pillow, that headaches came and went as frequently as buses, and life now seemed like it had cling film wrapped around it; edges seemed blurred and air bubbles rippled throughout it, rupturing reality.

He started forgetting things, or thinking he had forgotten things. Had he locked the door properly? At first he would only go back once or twice to double check the handle, worried for the amount of expensive equipment he and Sandra owned in the flat. Both of them had computers for their work, as well as the hi-fi, digital camera, mp3 players and some expensive prints that they had bought in Prague. He cursed himself several times for their choice of living in Leith, albeit in one of the new builds on the Shore, but near enough to some of the rougher pubs and estates for Derek to worry about burglary. His visits back to the door began to get more frequent; he would arrive late for work having spent an extra ten minutes checking that the front and back door were definitely locked. He took to constantly patting his pockets to check whether his wallet and phone were still there. His imagination went into overdrive; if Sandra was late home from work he would be pacing the floor, nails bitten to the quick, envisaging all sorts of horrendous situations—Sandra lying in a gutter, bleeding, unconscious, or kidnapped, raped.

Nothing seemed real and it was this feeling that had kept him inside this past week and was now so strong that he was petrified to go out. He became afraid that he no longer knew what he was doing. Derek found he would go to bed at the end of a day and not remember what had happened, and this shook him. If he couldn't remember what he had been doing then he could have been doing anything. Anything. He had read, with horror, stories of people who had no recollection of making illicit phone calls, committing crimes or even in one horrendous case, beating their lover to death in their sleep whilst having a nightmare. He could no longer trust himself, what if all this childhood suppression (if that's what it was—if that's what Michael had inside him) was inside Derek and was slowly oozing out of him like jam out of a doughnut, bright red liquid spilling out of a tiny hole within him.

Again and again the thought came to him;

If my brother has this streak, won't I have it as well?

If he went out, he might see something, or someone he didn't like.

Something might flip in him, just like that, as quick as a light switch being turned on—or off. Maybe it had already. Maybe he had killed someone and *never known*. Maybe he'd seen red and blacked out.

In Derek's mind he had become *watchful* of people, mindful of everyone. He looked for the wrong kind of eyes, studied faces for a twitch of the mouth; anything that might signify a glimmer of violence, the hope of a fight. Not that he wanted a fight, in fact the very thought of one would bring saliva rushing into his mouth and sweat break out on the back of his neck. He would do everything in his power to stop a fight, but then, by contrast he was attracted to the thick wave of violence, half curious to know if the bloom of brutality really lived within him, as it did with Michael.

It was a cough, he decided, a cough that would do it. A cough could be interpreted as a comment, or an insult. A word might well be hidden within the cough and to the ears of the Angry Man who Derek would be inevitably standing next to, the cough/words would lead to a fist and blood and pain. So Derek would not cough, could not cough, certainly not in public and even at home could be hazardous as their wall were so thin (he never know who was listening) Sandra was forced to cook with windows wide open, and be careful not to burn anything. She couldn't spray deodorant in front of him. Derek, himself stopped wearing it. Sometimes at his work, when Derek could feel a cough rising in his chest, he would hurry to the toilet, make sure all cubicles were empty and then hack his guts up.

He took to constantly drinking water to keep his throat moist, as long as he couldn't feel the tickle, that awful tickle which would lead to The Cough. He now flinched when Sandra cleared her throat, something she did now, after her second glass of Pinot Grigio as she handed him a scrap of paper.

"Derek darlin', I think you should talk to someone." He eyed the note suspiciously. "What's that?"

"It's the number of a therapist my friend Julie goes to." "A therapist?"

Sandra nodded and there was a loud silence. Derek looked at her. "You really think I need to talk to someone?"

"I don't think you're yourself at the moment love, that's all." "You think it's that bad?"

Sandra reached forward and rubbed his knee. "I just know that you're not the same Derek...and I think it might help you to talk to someone."

"I talk to you, don't I?"

"But I don't know what you're going through, really Derek, I don't know what's triggered all this stuff off," Sandra frowned and looked away from him, "and I don't know if I can cope."

Derek looked up sharply, "What do you mean?"

"I mean that I'm finding this hard as well Derek, you've been like this for months now."

"Like what? Exactly what am I like?" Derek's voice rose.

"Well, you're not right for one thing," Sandra's voice matched his for volume. "I don't know what sort of state I'm going to find you in when I get home these days—you haven't been to work for a week, you're not eating—you jump if I even cough, you sometimes seem to be nearly gagging on something in the back of your throat- you look like you're about to puke sometimes"

Derek breathed "Ok"

"And I'm afraid to say it Del, but you really stink- there'd be a time when it wouldn't have bothered me- but we're not exactly going through our honeymoon period anymore" She took another sip of wine. Derek stood up and ran his fingers over his hair head. "I'll be alright, it's just a phase, a...a midlife crisis or something." He could hear himself gabbling. "My aunt Isla was like this once, I remember Mum telling me, the doctor put her on something and she was fine–"

"No Del!" Sandra interrupted quickly and firmly. "No pills, they're really not a good idea."

"Why not?" Derek looked at her in surprise.

"They're just not the answer, I've seen people on them and they change—not immediately, but they're never the same, the pills flat-line you, I don't want to see you like that."

"Well what then?"

"This!" Sandra held up the slip of paper with the number written on it. "Honestly love, Julie says she's really nice and a really good listener." She put the paper on the coffee table.

"Will you just give her a ring?" she asked. "For me?"

Derek sighed, knowing when he was backed into a corner, Sandra looked at him, her green grey eyes wide.

"Alright I'll ring her, but I'm not promising anything."

Sandra flicked a wink over the top of her wine glass. "Thanks Del."

Derek had grunted.

The piece of paper sat next to the telephone and Derek looked at it from his position on the sofa. He got up and went over to the small table where both objects loomed, the sleek black wireless telephone with its flashing red L.E.D looked menacingly up at him. The piece of torn paper with Sandra's scrappy writing looked innocuous enough, but to Derek it signified the lid of a whole other can of slimy worms. It was times like this that Derek wished he still smoked, if there were a pack of cigarettes in the flat this would be a perfect opportunity for one, he would light it up, puff calmly, breathing in his thoughts with the smoke and make a decision. Maybe he could go out and—no. He couldn't do it- what was he thinking? He hadn't smoked for a while, surely the first thing he would do is light up and…cough.

And there was the rub, he couldn't go out to get cigarettes because he was too afraid—if that was the right word, he knew even stepping onto the street would do him in; the noise, the traffic, the people—everything moving so fast. And then having to actually go into a shop and ask a stranger for something, if it was milk or something that he could grab from the shelf then it might, *might* be a different matter, the whole exchange could pass in silence, the shop assistant only murmuring the price and Derek wouldn't have had to speak at all. He baulked at the thought of actually having to ask for something like cigarettes which were behind the counter, and then if they didn't get the right ones he'd have to correct them and—God. It would all be too much, they'd think something was wrong with him if he freaked out and—No. He couldn't do it.

He looked down at the piece of paper again, and now he noticed the name above the number, *Maura Hadley*. An unusual name, but not that unusual, a middle class name he was sure of it, and besides, who had ever heard of a working class therapist? This thought hit another nub in his mind, as there had been a time when one of his favourite soapbox rants was about the middle class's 'urges to talk'—why couldn't they just get on with things like everybody else? Why was everything picked apart and mulled over? Just because you didn't get a piano for your birthday like everyone else in the private poncy school you went to, apparently meant you were headed for serious depression in your thirties whereupon you had to seek out a therapist for forty quid an hour to properly understand why your head was stuck halfway up your silver spooned backside…There weren't any therapists in Leith, that was for sure, or Pilton, or Muirhouse or–

"But you don't live there," Sandra had said soothingly as he paced about the floor, ranting.

"I live in Leith, don't I?"

Sandra rolled her eyes. "Aye, in the expensive end!" she threw her head back laughing. "It's not exactly the Banana flats is it?" Derek scowled at her, she gulped at her wine and relented. "But that's not you Del, you're not working class."

"My Da is."

"Aye, but he's not you, is he? You might have been brought up on an estate but you're not on one now, are you?" Derek absently stroked his hand up the beige floral curtains of the living room window, saying nothing. "Besides," said Sandra, reaching for the bottle for a refill, "class is a state of mind, wouldn't you say?"

Well, thought Derek, here he was terrified to go out and genuinely considering calling in the services of one of these 'middle- class ponces' for help. Yes, Help is what he needed, because he couldn't see another way out, (had he now inadvertently become middle class? Maybe this is what a high salary and studio flat did to you, you suddenly stopped worrying about having to make ends meet, and started having panic attacks). But he didn't know what else to do, and Sandra was right, pills wouldn't be a good idea, he'd be too scared to take them anyway.

Derek took a deep breath, his palms were sweating and his heart thudded in his chest, it was the first time he'd picked up the receiver in weeks, the dial tone buzzed loudly in his ear like an angry wasp and he slammed the receiver down. The phone seemed to grin smugly up at him, Derek frowned at it and picked the receiver up again, he grabbed Maura Hadley's number and jabbed at the buttons, his fingers slipped stickily over the plastic moulds, and before he knew it there was a ring tone at his ear. Derek's heart jumped up to his throat. He had no idea of what he was going to say and wondered if this Maura Hadley was accustomed to strangers phoning her up to either say nothing at all or simply screaming,

'Help'. Derek was trying to gather his thoughts and translate them into coherent sentences when there was a voice on the other end.

"Hello?"

It was a male voice, with a thick Scottish accent. Derek supposed he must be a receptionist. He cleared his throat;

"Hello, er…" he faltered, what should he say? "I… er was given your number from a friend of mine and wondered if you could help me."

"What is it you're wanting, pal?"

"Well, I er…" Derek stuttered, he didn't know how to say to a complete stranger that he felt he was going absolutely insane and couldn't actually leave the house for fear of killing someone…or something. Derek could hear the man on the other end getting impatient.

"Is it painting or papering you're wanting, pal?"

"What?" Derek was surprised at this sudden leap into the abstract, especially as the voice didn't sound like it regularly delved into the human psyche and made metaphors out of it.

"Erm, well," Derek searched his brain to try and understand what was being alluded to. "I suppose I've got a few cracks."

"Is it inside or out?" asked the man.

Derek felt on firmer ground here, "Oh inside, definitely in side."

"An' what room is it, pal?"

"Er…" Derek paused again, this allegory was really being stretched but it felt a bit easier than saying things outright. "I suppose it's the whole house?" He tried experimentally.

"The whole hoose? You've got cracks in the whole hoose?"

"Definitely," said Derek with confidence.

"An' are ye wantin' the cracks filled in or just papered over 'cause it would cost ye more to fill them in, but if ah were you pal ah'd git it done 'cause it'll only give ye trouble in the long-term, know what ah mean?"

"Yes, I do, you've got a point there," agreed Derek, doing a slight double take on the subject of money, obviously the therapist would charge, but he was under the impression that money was always a sore point in this field of work, a subject to be handled tactfully and carefully, almost like it was an afterthought—a courtesy which it only seemed right to adhere to. He certainly hadn't expected the cost to be brought up so obviously.

"So when dae you want me to come round?" asked the man, and Derek blinked in shock and surprise—someone coming *to him?* Surely that wasn't right, and anyway, he couldn't have a stranger in the house, he couldn't even entertain the thought. Derek's palms sprang out another batch of sweat and his heart thudded.

"You…you want to come here?" he croaked.

"Aye, ah've got tae come round tae give you an estimate, when's a good time?"

"Don't I have to come to you?" Derek was beginning to panic, this wasn't anything like he imagined it would be, maybe Maura Hadley did things differently, maybe she was an experimental therapist or something. The man on the end of the line sounded irritated.

"Look pal, how can ah come and do work on your hoose if ah dinnae see it? Ah've got tae see the state of the place haven't ah?" "But it's a mess!" Derek cried. "The whole house is a complete mess, that what I'm telling you!"

"What dae ah care?" the man shouted back. "It's your walls ah'm gonna be looking at, not your bloody carpets."

Derek's brain ached, he couldn't think what the man meant now and could only suppose that it all came from a specific philosophy of someone he'd never heard of. He fell silent and breathed heavily.

"Hello?" asked the man. "You still there pal?"

"Sorry," Derek spoke softly, wearily, "I'm just a bit lost." He paused. "All I want to do is make an appointment with Maura Had- ley, is that possible?"

"Who?" the man snorted.

"Maura Hadley," Derek repeated, "I want to make an appointment as a new patient."

"Sorry pal, ah've never heard of her," the man replied. "Well..." said Derek slowly, "who are you?"

"Ah'm Joe McKenzie pal, ah do painting and decorating." "Painting and decorating?"

"Aye."

Derek ran his hands over his face dumbly and coughed. "Sorry, sorry," he mumbled, "I've got the wrong number." "S'alright pal," Joe McKenzie said shortly, Derek could almost hear his eyes rolling down the phone line. "You take care now," and Derek knew when he was being mocked.

Two days later when Derek looked through the spy hole set in the ash wood door, he caught sight of who was there and his heart thudded louder in his chest than it did when the doorbell first rang. *Well* he thought *it had to happen sometime.* Derek held his left hand by the wrist to stop the shaking as he pulled back the double locks, the chain, the mortis lock and finally the Yale and yanked open the heavy door.

Michael had his back to him, and Derek could already see how much broader it had become, how his brother's shoulders had squared in the two years he had been away. Michael turned around at the sound of the door being opened and Derek looked into the eyes of someone he wasn't sure he knew.

"Alright Derek, how's it going?" Michael's voice seemed deep- er, quieter but Derek just wondered if it was because he hadn't heard it in a while. There was a pause as Derek blinked at him nervously. He could feel blood rushing around his body, his hands, forehead and neck sweated. He swallowed, his throat was sandpaper and he thought he might gag.

"Hi Mikey," Derek breathed out loudly, hoping he sounded as casual as possible. "What a surprise like!" he was talking too loudly, he knew it. "How long have you been out?"

Michaels' eyes narrowed as he took in the sight of his older brother who was usually so jovial, so full of *bon homie* (so superficial, Michael thought darkly), sweating in the doorway of his über- modern flat. Something had happened. Michael felt smug at the thought of having the upper hand over Derek, who in the past had never missed an opportunity to patronise or tease. Now Derek looked nervous and uneasy at the sight of his *wee* brother—or was it simply that he was an ex-con? That he now represented a side of life that Derek knew nothing about, and consequently feared.

Derek had the wide forehead and stocky frame of Deek Lambert whereas Michael had inherited the dark curls and wide hazel eyes of Valarie Lambert. Michael always felt they each had the same parent's personality as well; Michael shared the emotional demure- ness of his mother whereas the two Dereks both were gruff, quiet and about as emotional as a wooden spoon. Until now seemingly.

Instead of answering his question, Michael shouldered his way past Derek into the flat. It still looked pretty much the same as he remembered. Stark, minimal and completely devoid of personality; a bit like Derek, Michael had often thought. The rented rooms dotted around the city which Michael had passed through like a series of carriages, had always been stuffed full of sentimental bits and pieces which Michael trailed around behind him; stuff he couldn't bear to throw away—photographs, books, letters, bits of writing he had started and never finished, keepsakes from abroad which he'd forgotten why he'd kept them. In contrast, Derek had never been one for memories, or objects with memories and with Sandra's influence of keeping rooms clear of clutter, Derek had settled happily into the bare white walls and sanded floorboards of minimalist living.

Michael didn't trust Derek's flat, he always wondered where the rest of Derek's possessions were, he knew he owned more—all his Hearts stuff for a start, he wouldn't have got rid of that and he was pretty sure their mother didn't have it, she didn't have the space in her tiny flat. Anytime now Michael expected a cupboard in Derek's flat to burst open, and for the whole of Derek's childhood and teenage years to spring out in a mountain of toys with chewed ears or smelling of perfume from ex-girlfriends—Lauren McKee for example. The thought of him running into Lauren recently made him smile, but Michael decided to leave bringing that one up till later on. He'd keep it hidden up his sleeve, a miniature grenade.

Derek was still hovering in the doorway, his feet almost dancing, Michael noticed and turned around again, Derek's feet shuffled and hopped around, not knowing what to do with themselves. Michael quickly decided on tactics, could he be bothered with this? He felt distinctly intolerant towards his brother, and although he could see something was wrong, he decided to ignore it for now.

After Michael had gone in, Derek quickly ducked his head out into the hallway to glance at anyone who might be waiting there. The hallway was echoingly empty.

"This place is still the same I see," he could hear Michael say and Derek hurriedly shut the door and locked it again, just in case anyone should suddenly appear.

He almost ran through after Michael's retreating figure, but then held back and stood in the doorway of the living room, scratching the back of his neck. Michael sat back comfortably into one of Derek and Sandra's wheat-coloured linen armchairs. There was an excruciating silence.

Derek blinked nervously. He frowned and licked his lips, trying to find the right words. He inhaled as if about to say something but then changed his tack and looked Michael directly in the eye.

"Do you want a cup of tea, Mikey?"

"Aye, go one then," Michael grinned, he stayed where he sat, thinking it best not to follow Derek into the kitchen. It was weird to be back here, this first taste of familiarity after the no man's land of pubs, friend's gaffs and one night in a stranger's bed. Michael smiled to himself, *quick work you cheeky bugger.*

Ironically, Derek and Sandra's flat was the one of the most uncomfortable places he knew, and yet he had ended up here because he couldn't find, or get hold of the rest of his family.

After a couple of minutes in which only dead air could be heard coming from the stainless steel kitchen, Michael got up and went through to investigate. He saw Derek standing, kettle in hand staring at the gleaming tap, as if wondering what he should do next.

What the fuck was he up to?

Michael walked slowly towards him, head cocked on one side as if approaching an animal whose movements he was unsure of.

"Derek?"

Derek appeared not to have heard him. His eyes were flickering from the kettle to the tap and back again. "Del? You ok?" Michael tried again. When he got no response he went over and slowly levered the kettle out of his brother's hands, the thought rippling through his head that it should be him who was staring, shell-shocked, at the wall; him, the ex-con re-adjusting back to reality- but instead its his bloody wanker of a brother who seemed to have gone loop the loop.

On gaining control of the kettle, Michael took it over to the sink and whooshed the water in, banged it down on its stand and flicked on the switch, the actions feeling novel and slightly disjointed after two years of not being allowed to make his own tea. Derek was breathing hard, swallowing audibly.

Like an overbearing relative, Michael led his brother of thirty years to a more comfortable chair in his own home.

" Del, are you going tell me what the fuck's going on?"

Derek didn't say anything for a long time. And when he finally turned his head to look at his younger brother, Michael saw that the skin around his eyes was criss-crossed with more lines than he remembered, there were dark shadows too. Derek ran his fingers over his shaven head, the tips pressing down on the gentle slopes that shaped his skull.

A deep inhalation.

"Have you got a fag, Mikey?"

"Shit Del, are things really that bad?" Michael said smiling, trying to keep things light, patted his pocket and took out a flattened packet of Richmonds. He shook out two cigarettes and handed one to Derek. Fag in mouth he said, "Sandra won't like this you know," and lit them both with a black clipper, Derek watching his every move in silence, suddenly got up again.

"Don't move, I've got an ashtray somewhere," his voice squeaked through from the kitchen. "Don't spill any ash for fuck's sake."

Michael carefully held his cigarette up so the ash wouldn't fall. Derek came back with a shiny aluminium orb with a small dip cut in the side.

"God it's smoky in here," Derek muttered angrily. "For fuck's sake Derek, you wanted the bloody fag!" "Well I'd forgotten how much smoke they make."

Michael looked at his brother incredulously. Derek pulled hard on the cigarette and exhaled quickly afterwards, the smoke hardly having a chance to reach his lungs. He wouldn't meet Michael's glance but looked carefully at the burning tip of his cigarette, as if expecting to see something truly amazing. Then without warning and without looking he told Michael.

"I'm not right, Mike. I'm not doing well at all."

"How do you mean? Are you ill?" Michael snapped, "you don't look ill."

"In a way."

"In what way, Del?"

"I've been to see someone." "Who? What a doctor?"

"Sort of. I s'pose she's a doctor."

"What—she's not a proper one then?"

"No, she's kosher like, she's got letters after her name and all that."

"Well who is she then?"

"She's a shrink Mikey, I s'pose." Derek was silent for a time. "She's a therapist."

"Fucking hell!" Michael nearly laughed, nearly snorted on his fag and with his eyebrows still in his hairline he asked, "Has something happened? Are you and Sandra ok?" Then Michael's brain raced, "Are Mum and Dad ok?"

"Aye, they're fine," Derek answered leisurely.

"So what's going on?"

"Nothing amazing, Mikey," Derek breathed out smoke slowly, "I'm just going round the fucking bend, that's all."

"What does that mean?"

Derek inhaled noisily again, his eyes screwed against the rising smoke.

"I've been told I've got high anxiety."

Michael did snort now, he couldn't help it this time. "That's a bit fucking obvious, you and five million other Scotsmen."

"And OCD." "Come again?"

"Obsessive Compulsive Disorder."

It was Michael's turn to inhale aggressively. "Isn't that what the kiddies get?"

"That's ADHD." "What's that then?"

"Attention Deficit Hyperactive Disorder." "Oh," Michael sniffed, "not what you've got." "No."

"How do you know about this...this thing?"

"I've been looking it up, Maura—the therapist told me about it, she's given me books on it," he paused and looked at him. "Charles Dickens had it you know."

"Ri-ght," said Michael slowly, rolling his eyes. "Well, at least it's respectable then."

Derek noticed the sarcasm in his voice but before he could answer a mobile phone rang, shattering the solid air. A grating digitalised version of *Scotland the Brave* emitted from a mobile phone in Michael's pocket. Michael was still getting used to the fact that he now owned one, having been without a phone in prison. He was now in possession of a smooth black oblong which buzzed and vibrated (in a few days time, the jarring sound of *Scotland the Brave* would fill him with a wary dread as to who might be on the other end).

"Oh shit, yeah that's me," he said after a few rounds of the tune, whipping the phone out from his pocket and scanning the keypad frantically for the right button.

"Hello?" he shouted and Derek winced. He studied the floor beneath his feet, the pale biscuit shade of the carpet. Michael's nonchalance flooded his head, why was his brother so calm? Did everyone go through this madness? How the hell did people cope- surely not everyone kept sane? In the last few weeks Derek's imagination had won creative awards for grotesqueness, scenes that flashed before his eyes sometimes brought saliva into his mouth, churning his stomach. Did everyone have to deal with this? Or did folk simply become skilled at ignoring these fears? Sailing blithely through life with blinkers on, smiling gaily and obliviously–

"Who is it? Joe? Joe who? I don't know a Joe," Michael was saying, then a pause and, "Oh…oh yeah, ok—the other night, yeah…yeah man, it was good shit," suddenly aware of his older brother intently listening, Michael turned his back and lowered his voice. Derek's eyes widened, what was he talking about? It must be drugs, he was talking about drugs in Derek's flat—his flat, what if someone heard? How thick were these walls? Where did he get that phone? Was it bugged? Were the police listening? Maybe it was a trap. Maybe he was being set up. Michael's being set up and he'd be found in his flat—Derek jumped out of his chair and came round to face Michael, who batted him away with a flick of his hand, Derek mouthed a silent shouting.

"Who is it? What are you doing?"

Michael broke off from his conversation and hissed.

"Do you mind? I'm on the fucking phone." He spoke back to the caller, "Nah, its ok, look are you in Leith? I could meet you somewhere?…aye, yeah—nah, I'm just at my brother's like, yeah…down at the Shore."

"Shut up! What are you doing?" Derek screamed at him, making a grab for the mobile. What the hell did Michael think he was doing? Was he telling a *drug dealer* where he *lived?* This was it, this is *exactly* what he'd feared would happen—he was sweating, liquid pouring down his back, but his mouth dry, scorched from the cigarette and angst. He knew it! He bloody knew it! Seeing Michael again, Michael coming *here* was just such a bad idea—he'd just increased Derek's anxiety a hundred-fold, and now a drug dealer, a gangster even, who knew? A murderer who'd come back and burgle the house when he and Sandra were out—or not even that—they could be sitting here, watching TV, eating a meal with a glass of wine and these guys probably wouldn't even wait until they were *asleep,* they'd just knock down the door, armed to the teeth; his heart leapt to his throat and he could feel the bile rising as he heard Michael say, "Look, just come up and meet me, man. I'm at 22 Tower Street, yeah that's right, near the Shore pub, yeah I'm there now, just come up like, ok, yep…right…bye."

Derek sat, hardly able to move, he could not believe what Michael had just done.

"Who was that?" he asked faintly as Michael jabbed the off button.

"That was Joe" replied Michael calmly, lighting another cigarette

"Who's Joe?" Derek croaked, "and why the fuck have you just told him to come to my house?"

Michael sighed. "Will you chill out? He sells a bit of dope, I got some from him the other night, it's no big deal." He exhaled smoke. "Don't come all high and mighty Derek, you used to smoke the stuff too."

"Michael–" Derek got up out of his chair, forcing himself to stay calm, "you just don't get it, I'm really not right, in myself like, it's not like some phase or something—I've been going mad here…I can't go to work, I can't even go out, I've been climbing the walls, and now, after fucking months of thinking I'm going bonkers, someone's actually put a name to it—it's a thing, it exists like, it's not just me cracking up." Before Michael could answer, Derek swept on, his voice rising to a screech, "and have you any idea what it's doing to me? The thought of this Joe coming here and you buying drugs off him—I mean, who is he? Is he ok? Do you even know him?"

Michael stood, eyeing his brother through the smoke, "Not really, Del," he said slowly, enjoying seeing his brother getting so wound up, "but he seemed to be harmless, just your average nutter from Leith—we got talking 'cause of the football like, he's a Hibbee, and a right mad one at that," Michael grinned.

"He's a Hibbee?"

"Aye, pure mad on it, used to be one of the CCS crew."

Derek sank his head into his hands, he felt like he was going to cry, he looked up through his fingers. "Let me get this straight, you've invited a nutter who you hardly know, up to my flat, and to top it all, he's a fuckin' mad Hibbee who probably indulges in a fair bit of casual violence on the weekends! I mean, Michael, you support Hearts for Christ's sake and besides that, haven't I just told you I'm not well? Didn't I just tell you that I had OCD—"

"Ah Del, isn't this just some middle class posh name for something?" Michael said, dismissing his brother's speech with a wave of his fag, "Isn't this just you in a rut? Having a mid-life crisis or something?"

"Michael!" Derek screamed, "I am ill, can you not just see that? I need help—not some dodgy stranger turning up...oh God...God," he was now breathing heavily, his chest heaving. "I can't do this, Michael—ring him back now, tell him he can't come here, I can't deal with it."

Michael reached over and stubbed out his cigarette into the shiny aluminium globe.

"Any chance of that brew?" Michael asked nonchalantly. "Mikey! I need help! I'm going to be sick–"

"No, Del, this is just shite—will you get a fucking grip? I've been inside for fucking two years—you never came to see me, even though I asked you to, why the hell was that? Then when I do get out, you don't try and find me, I have to fucking ring you, and then I'm expected to listen to all this crap? How no one understands and you're going loopers...well welcome to the fucking club mate...no one I know is sane...you try doing two years...you wouldn't believe some the guys in there, man...you think you're going mad? Try looking the wrong way at a lifer and see what happens, just look around the city...I got off the bus...just out of Saughton like, and there's all these fucking nutters protesting about something or other...there's an Indian family looking at it all wondering what the fuck is going on...there's a guy off his head just blowing a whistle...and he doesn't even know what he's doing there–"

"Alright!" shouted Derek, chopping the air with the palm of his hand. "I get it, I'm not special, I've got fuck all to worry about—I get it!"

"Too right matey, there's a lot more insanity about than you've ever noticed anyway. If you'd only taken your head out of your yuppie poncy arse for a second you'd have thought how fucking loopy our family is for a start—just look at Mum and Dad."

"What about them?" Derek looked at him sharply. He had sat down now, head bowed as if taking penance.

"Well they're not exactly what you'd call model parents, are they? Chances are most of this shite you're going through stems down to one of them; Dad's mad as a hatter, he just doesn't show it...doesn't show anything, and Mum's slowly winding herself round the bend now she's retired...get this—she used to write to me in- side about the bloody stain in the sofa cushions that she couldn't get out! Other guys were getting letters from their Ma's telling them deep family secrets, or professing real love for them—stuff which the old wifie's couldn't say out loud, mostly because they've all been brought up on dour Presbyterian shite which doesn't allow any time for emotion or love or feeling for that matter—but no, I get the pros and cons of Scotmid's brand of stain re- moval to that of Vanish—where the hell does that leave me?" Michael paused to catch his breath. "All I can say is that I'm not really surprised, call it what you like, OCD, anxiety, depression—whatever, at the end of the day it's the messed up human condition which twists out of us all in different ways. But don't go thinking you're fuck- ing special, Derek, or that it gives you an excuse to treat people like shite—like not visiting your own brother in prison."

Michael was on his feet now, chest pumping, Derek stared back at him caught between anger and helpless- ness. There was an almighty pause, which exploded with a banging at the door.

"Awright Michael! It's Joe, are you in there?" Thud thud thud. The two brothers looked at each other. "Michael! It's Joe McKenzie—let me in would ya?"

Derek had now entered a nightmare, this could not be happening, this could not be happening—not Joe McKenzie—*not the Joe McKenzie* and hearing the voice now, it was the same; *Ah'm Joe McKenzie pal, ah do painting and decorating.*

"Hang on mate!" Michael called out as Derek fell from the wheat-coloured armchair to the biscuit coloured carpet in a heavy faint.

Intermission

He had been alarmed at the speed at which she'd said 'yes'. He hadn't even got up from his kneeling position when, daring himself to look up into her eyes, he saw the eager expression on her face and she was nodding vigorously.

"Yes definitely," she'd said, obviously pleased but not overcome with the emotional rapture he'd secretly hoped for. He'd heard men's tales of their proposals to girlfriends and how they'd been met with coy indecision, the girls didn't know, they'd have to have 'time' and 'space'. They weren't sure if they were ready for that kind of commitment, etcetera, etcetera. The men had planned their proposals immaculately, with a preparation more suited to taking an exam or executing a battle than asking the one Big Question. They'd organised engagement rings in champagne glasses, violin players to serenade, expensive restaurants and dim lighting.

John made an effort in his own way, but as soon as Lily had readily accepted, he saw that his attempt at romance (a picnic rug overlooking the public park, where they had shared their first hesitant kiss) might have gone overlooked. If she did appreciate the gesture she never told him outright. At the time John was simply relieved that she'd said yes, than if she'd noticed he had chosen the very spot where they had stood trembling, their lips shakily meeting, on which to spread the red and blue tartan rug.

The reason he had been attracted to her in the first place was not that she was unlike other girls but the fact that she was. There was nothing outwardly unusual about Lily Peters. She was pretty but not uncommonly so, although John would later see photographs of Lily as a child and be astounded at how beautiful she was. She told him that she had grown out of it, as if it was a childhood game that she now saw as immature and silly. As the years went by, Lily's features seemed to grow a little plainer, a little more ordinary. But at seventeen Lily had clear skin, a distinctive laugh and bright curly black hair that she took trouble to comb carefully and separate into ringlets each morning. She drank vodka and coke and didn't object to the odd cigarette.

At the small business college where they had met, Lily had blended in well with the rest of the girls, she wore modest feminine clothes that although showed off her slim figure, said nothing in particular about her personality; only that she knew which colours suited her (dark reds and earthy greens) and which length skirt was the most apt. Lily would never have made so bold a statement such as to advertise which music she enjoyed or that she belonged to any social group; she wasn't a pale-faced Goth, she wasn't a dreadlocked hippy, she wasn't a short-skirted playgirl. She didn't like to wear labels as she liked to think that she was happy enough with herself that she didn't need to shout about it through her skin and fingernails. John always thought that she didn't feel the need to stand out and scream that she was an individual.

Lily was quieter than her friend Angela but not as demure as Beth, and once she and John had been out a few times to the cinema or the pub on the corner of her road he found that she talked just as freely with him as with the friends she socialised with. She liked cats and small children and walking in the rain, all in all being a picture of normality and to John's thinking, she posed no risk of bizarre behaviour. He compared Lily with his sister who had embraced the loud thudding club music and pierced herself with safety pins. Kate was now involved with an older man who owned a dog on a chain, had two children by different women and managed to supply an entire high rise with a full menu of illegal drugs. Irregular behaviour scared John. Being naturally shy and timid as a boy, he had disliked anything loud, unprompted or spontaneous. He re-read books, or watched the same film three or four times over, comfortable in the knowledge that he already knew the end. John saw Lily's non-descript cardigans and subtle make-up as a distinct bonus, as he found his sister's erratic life positively exhausting.

Being attracted initially to the feeling of security and or-dinariness that she gave, Lily's attitude to sex was a great sur-prise to John. He had seen her as modesty itself; the only bare skin that peeped out during the summer months belonged to her forearms, lower knees and legs. Her toes, always daintily paint-ed in a neutral shade of pink, sat shyly inside sensible white sandals. She never drank to excess. Whilst at the fag-end of a Friday night in the student bar, other girls could be seen loll-ing slushily across tables or straddling the legs of an unknown boy who they may or may not recognise in the morning on the pillow, Lily (if she had even stayed until closing time) might be giggling tipsily while getting into a taxi, but would always wake in the morning, bright-eyed and full of clear conscience.

Having been out with similarly quiet girls, John had experienced the looming battlefield of physical intimacy and guessed Lily would be the same slog of trying to convince her of the beauty of sex rather than any stigma attached to it.

But it was Lily who startled John by allowing him to kiss her passionately on the first night, unhook her bra by the end of the fourth evening out together and agreed to stay with him in a cheap hotel on the outskirts of Manchester after a week of officially being a couple.

"You're full of surprises, that's for sure," John lay on the starched and slightly rough duvet cover, a small puddle of sweat lying on his chest.

"Well," Lily said lightly, inhaling shallowly on the ciga-rette that they passed between them, "I'm grateful to you to be honest with you, it's some- thing I've been wanting to get out of the way for ages," she said quite nonchalantly, though she knew something was lost to her now. John pushed himself up on his elbow.

"That was your first time?" he breathed incredulously "you're kidding me?"

"No," she said, turning to look at him, "it's fine…I want-ed to do it…but I'm glad the first time's over now…it's a relief… that's my childhood finished with now completely, thank god."

John lay down heavily again, taking the cigarette from her, he blew out heavy smoke and said, "God—don't put it like that, it makes me feel awful."

"You shouldn't do, honestly," she turned over and rubbed his shoulder. "I'm so glad it was with you," she lay on her back again, conversing to the ceiling, eyes looking into the swirling artex, "but bloody hell, its taken long enough, I mean I'm sev-enteen, that's virtually an old woman in some girls' books, I should've lost it ages ago," she sighed, "but I'm so glad to not be a kid anymore, that's what I feel like, I feel like a proper adult now, it's a real relief."

All of this small speech didn't make John feel less uneasy; up until now Lily had played the part of the confident, yet slightly naïve, happy-go- lucky girl who knew her place in the hierarchy of her group of girlfriends—and that was not at the bottom with bespectacled boyfriend-less Justine, yet not at the top with the ever-popular, wide-smiled, sashaying Angela.

But John had meant it when he told her she was surprising; he hadn't imagined it would be so easy a path to her near-naked body, or that she would be quite so thankful to him for relieving her of her heavy burden of virginity.

That evening they never got dressed. The grey dying light of an autumn afternoon dimmed in the warm stuffy room while they heard the distant rattle of the railway pass by, filled with commuters on their way home. They opened another bottle of wine and ate the sandwiches and crisps that Lily had packed, knowing they wouldn't be able to afford room service, or even a hotel with room service.

Stretched out on the coarse beige duvet, Lily told him snapshots of her childhood; drew thumbnail sketches of what her parents were like, what she and Barbara got up to at Christmases and the school holidays, family pets long since dead and buried in the back garden. And then there was the time when Lily was—

"…Well, it wasn't what you'd call kidnapped, or abducted, but that's what the police called it anyway…well they would, wouldn't they? And the few papers who got hold of it hyped it up like anything…but I didn't see it like that…it's not like I was away for days…she just took me away for a day that's all… we went for a walk round Edinburgh. She bought me an ice cream." Lily shrugged, "It was nothing really."

"I bet your parents didn't see it like that."

"No way! They went ballistic—we went straight home again. Barb never forgave me I think, she'd been looking forward to going to the castle for weeks, we'd never been to Scotland before, we were really excited." Lily paused, gazing at the small

panes of glass that made up the lampshade, rimmed with gold plated plastic. "I know she always thought that I'd done it on purpose—for attention," Lily winced very slightly. "I was that kind of child I suppose, I always liked being the centre of attention," she looked at John's raised eyebrows, "I'm not now," she smiled, "obviously."

The pause filled the room, until John asked, "Who was she? The woman who took you?" Lily frowned.

"The woman who took me," she repeated, "it's odd, hearing you say that, but she did, didn't she? Take me, I mean." she paused, eyes abroad somewhere, "I don't know—I remember her looking at me when we were waiting at a bus stop, Mum and Dad were arguing over the bus times and Barbara had her head stuck in a book—Barb was always like that, she was always reading something...Malory bloody Towers most of the time, it used to really annoy my Mum...anyway, I was only six and I had on my pink fairy wings...I'd got them for my birthday... Mum told me this...and I loved them so much I'd never take them off, she could only unhook them once I was in bed...but thinking of it, it's probably what she, the woman that is, noticed first about me—I read later that her name was Deborah Bennett, but she told me just to call me Debbie."

"And was she—" John stopped, not knowing quite how to continue, "you know, was she right in the head like? Did she do anything?"

"No, not at all," Lily shrugged "she seemed perfectly normal to me, but afterwards it turned out that she thought she'd won the lottery—really believed it—but she said that she couldn't tell anyone...I think she was just confused...I remember that she did seem really excited about something, and we rushed around, she didn't let us hang about anywhere...I re-

member being so tired at the end of the day, I just wanted to go to bed, but the police kept asking me question after question...and Mum and Dad were really frantic. It might have been different if it had happened in Manchester, but neither of them knew Edinburgh, they didn't know where to start looking, and there was this mist, this really thick fog which had closed in round the city—the Haar they call it up there—it happens sometimes, the cool air off the sea meeting the warm air inland, it creates this fog and you can see hardly a thing...they were so scared, Mum and Dad...they hardly noticed Barbara who had to traipse after them everywhere."

"What happened to Debbie?"

"Oh, she was arrested," said Lily airily, "I don't think she was charged with much; they couldn't really pin anything on her, and Mum and Dad didn't want anything else to happen once they saw that I was ok, they probably felt a bit sorry for her...and there was no way they'd have wanted a huge court case or anything."

"And you weren't scared at all?"

"Not really...I thought it was a bit of a game, I remember being a bit nervous when we went to find my parents, I wondered what they would say, if they would be angry. But I was so trusting at that age, I'd never met an adult who didn't like me or who frightened me...adults were always so nice to me," Lily sighed. "I suppose I was an attractive child."

"Ahh, I can imagine," John pulled her close, fondly imagining Lily darting around, aged six, fairy wings wiggling, feet tapping. She went on. "I can't really remember what she said to me...but I do remember that as the day went on, I began to talk less and less...I began to wonder where my parents were, why this woman was just dragging me around this weird city, she *didn't seem right, she was talking really quickly, and she seemed to go off me as I got tired and didn't want to do as much…and then…and then—"*

Lily tailed off, frowning as she tried to recall something— something important about the day but she just couldn't place her finger on it. When she couldn't catch hold of the elusive memory she shook her head to scatter the thoughts.

"What did happen though…when I'd got back to Mum and Dad, when we'd got home…I stopped showing off, I didn't go in for dancing in front of the family or school plays or any- thing…I suppose I was just worried that I'd be taken away again…so I didn't do anything to draw attention to myself… just in case."

That conversation was one of the last times John and Lily spoke about the incident. That day wasn't spoken of dur- ing their four-year courtship, when each of them met the other's parents, nor come the engagement on the blue and red tartan rug, or when there were children running all around them in the shining grass. It wasn't an anecdote told at Lily and John's wed- ding, when all their friends and relatives rose their glasses in the back room of The Rose and Crown to toast the young couple's future.

That day in Edinburgh was stowed in Lily's mind, hid- den until her children, David and Megan, had grown old enough to start running about and Lily would constantly be rushing and grabbing at them around shops. She thought back to that day, when she had trailed after a stranger in amongst the toy-town buildings in her pink silky shoes.

Now she was a mother herself, she could understand what her parents must have felt; the sickening rise of panic in the chest which flooded into her throat when once she'd turned round to hand Megan a banana, only to find that an empty space now occupied the place where Megan had been standing seconds ago. She had not gone far, and David had found her two minutes later looking at a row of teddy bear slippers thirty yards away, but Lily had remembered well the leaden dread which had occupied her stomach in the intervening moments between Megan disappearing and appearing again.

The episode in Edinburgh was never mentioned by either John and Lily; not out of awkwardness or that Lily found it hard to discuss, but on the understanding that it didn't need talking about. As far as John was concerned, Lily had told him everything there was to know, and for Lily it wasn't a subject she felt the need to discuss any more.

Their lives together passed quietly, with only some storms to weather. Lily's father succumbed to Alzheimer's disease, and saddled with her mother's and her own guilt, he was finally donated to a care home, albeit not The Beeches Retirement Home where Lily was assistant manager. She regretted that she couldn't pull enough strings to allow to him to stay in one of the refined yet modest apartments which the affluent occupants of the retirement house called home, but their policy was not to take anyone with medical needs; and these rules were not for bending.

Once, Lily had relieved her mother of her father's confusion for a day and taken him on a shopping trip. They had been looking for woollen socks in Marks and Spencers when Lily suddenly looked around and in a lop-sided repeat of Megan's three-year-old wanderings, she found her head whipping around frantically in search of the full sized frame of her eighty-six year old father. Again she felt the sickness in the pit of her stomach, and the blood pump furiously around her body at the recognition of loss, the realisation of disappearance. He was found at the bottom of an escalator, two floors away, pacing up and down, trying to find a way out.

Lily saw that her mother was also terrified of losing him on days out; they stayed knotted, hand in hand down the streets, in and out of shops and all the way home on the bus until they had reached the safety of their own house. Strangers to the elderly couple would see the sight as sweet and endearing, secretly wishing that when they reached that age, they would still be holding someone's hand. Only Lily and Barbara knew the real reason why their parents journeyed around with their fingers folded around the other; and it was because they were both scared stiff of losing each other, of their fingers loosening their grip and brushing away, the companion hand gone forever. In the same way that parents forget how their children are as babies, Lily forgot how her parents used to act when she was young. She'd missed the point when she had overtaken them and become like a parent herself to the couple who'd created herself and Barbara. She empathised with them when her own children had arrived, but now she felt their dependence on her and it seemed they'd always been the fragile people in the cardigans which were buttoned up wrongly and with liver spots on their knuckles. Lily didn't recall the vitality in which Alan and Susan had led their children around strange cities or over beaches on holiday. She knew that her mother used to have black hair, but she couldn't really remember what it looked like, and it now sounded like an urban myth, like the fact that her father had once ran in the father's race on Sports day.

Lily and John Maxwell's son David grew up. He met a girl named Gillian and they got married. Their daughter Me-

gan met Patrick, had his baby and didn't get married. Lily now found herself with her own family spread all around her like a blanket, and on her forty-forth birthday (a meal out with John, David, Megan, Gillian and her mother) she finally felt settled; as if everything had been working up to this moment when she felt contented and safe. John looked across the table at his wife of twenty years and could see that she was happy, and he himself was pleased with the fact that he had played a part in making it happen.

So when a year later, Lily announced she was planning on going to the Survivors of Childhood Abuse group, John suddenly wondered if he'd got this reckoning wrong, if he had in fact been hopelessly ignorant of Lily's experience, had he never seen how haunted she was by it all? Had it been lying dormant within her, ignored by him and slowly eating her away from the inside? John wondered if he'd ever really known his quiet wife who, when she was seventeen, used to walk with such a bounce that her hair never sat still on her shoulders for a second.

8

Joe threw the phone down. For fuck's sake, what the hell was that twat on? Didn't even sound like it could be justified by drugs. Mind you, that guy was just a nutter through and through , didn't need any Columbian Marching Powder to get him going…some folk—he just didn't get it.

Joe picked up the polystyrene cup and slurped at the stinging hot coffee. Good coffee too, he wouldn't call himself a coffee snob but that Polish place did do blinding stuff…What did the fucker *think* he was talking about if it wasn't bollocking painting? He lit another cigarette and narrowed his eyes against the rising smoke. Joe peered through the van's rapidly steaming window, at the busy criss-crossing of legs on Leith Walk.

'…*Steamy Windows, coming from the bod-y heat…*' The dated song wormed out of the tinny radio. Fucking great song, getting on now was Tina but a great old doll, the legs on her–

Anyway. Anyhoos. Joe checked his watch, three 'o two p.m. The day was nearly over but there was still a lot to do. He took a deep breath. Phone Davie, that was the first thing, make sure he had tickets for the game for a start, he could just imagine what it would be like if they turned up at Easter Road, the old ER, without tickets, the whole crew there; everyone there; like old times, he couldn't believe it was really happening; he felt like a lad again, ever since that message from Davie had appeared on his phone, wondering if this was still his number? If so, did he feel like meeting up?

And they had done, him and Davie, they'd gone for a pint in Shakespeare's on Lothian Road, there'd been a game on, but it was fuckin' English teams and neither him nor Davie could be arsed with it; they'd both ignored the big screen until they'd finished their pints and decided to move on to somewhere else

They'd talked about old times mostly, once they'd got all the formalities out of the way—Joe said yeah, he'd married Mona in the end and that they'd had a son. He now had his own business; decorating jobs all over town, but Leith mostly—business wasn't booming, but folk will always move and buy houses and not many of them want to do their own decorating so there was always a slow trickle of work flowing through. Nah, he didn't get to games much, Saturdays were usually taken up with jobs, but he tried to catch the Hibee's games on telly...

'I ken it's not the same...'

Joe missed the old days, course he did...and that was when Davie had gazed at him across the head on his pint of Tenants and asked him what he would think about getting the old gang together, whoever was left in town that was; those who weren't in Saughton, or had left for Weedgie land or south of the border, those who hadn't gone yellow-belly on their asses, how about getting together after a match like? Depending on who the opposition were, there was surely going to be another firm there, or at least *someone* up for a spot of aggro...too much time had gone by without the CCS showing their faces...folk had forgotten who was top around here...

'The time has come,' Davie added quietly, and it was the most powerful thing Joe had heard in a long time, he felt his heart start thudding in his chest, this was important.

"The time has come," Davie added again, not looking directly at him, but into the middle distance, "we've got to reclaim our title like. You know Joe, I was on a train the other day—had to go over to Dundee for a spot of business, and there's these bastards on the seats in front of me—must have been about six of them, maybe eight- and they're younger than us, boys really, when we were around they were still in fucking nappies...but they're acting like they own the fuckin' place...they were part of Dundee Utility as far as I could tell, probably just out of the baby crew—all in that clobber—I hardly recognise it to be fair. Stone Island—heard of that? Or fucking Ralph Lauren—new stuff, it looks ok I s'pose, but not really like our stuff; not a Burberry cap in sight man, or any Lacoste...anyway, there's these young twats, lording it over, and I'm thinking, if there was just one other guy with me, I'd show them who's who...we aren't known enough any more Joe, there's been no-one like the CCS, but we've fizzled oot man—what happened? Even the baby crew seems to have gone to ground."

Joe shrugged in sympathy,

"Ah dunno Davie, ah'm the same as you like, ah've never stopped being part of the firm like."

"Ah c'mon Joe! When was the last time you went to a game? You said it yourself like, you don't manage to get oot any more…tell you what…" he added, waving a newly lit cigarette in Joe's face, "that's what birds do tae you, ken? Soon as you settle down with one and have a bairn, that's it, they've got their claws in and they dinnae let go, an' your life stops…you can't go oot, you can't see your mates…it's birds man, they fuckin' ruin your life," Davie smoked angrily. Joe didn't really know what to say, he had a point like, but then Davie had been royally shat on by the mother of his children quite a while ago, when she'd run off to New Zealand with the brickie who had done their extension; she'd taken the two boys and Davie hadn't seen them since, he had every right to hate her of course, and the rest of womankind, but for Joe, it wasn't really like that.

Mona had never really stopped him from doing anything, and since they'd had Mark, he'd not really wanted to go out anyway…mind you that was years ago now, and with working a forty- five hour week, Joe hadn't the energy to do anything except eat a meal and then fall asleep in front of the telly.

"Aye, but it wasn't just the fitbaw, Davie," Joe swigged at his pint, confident that Davie would see his point, "it was everything—the claithes, it was buzz—it was fuckin' chasing the scouse soap- dodgers down Shandwick Place, man!"

Davie laughed with him, shaking his head at the memory. "Aye…you've got a point."

It was a coincidence like, seeing Davie, thought Joe. Lately he had been feeling something was missing, Mark was in his teens now and didn't need looking after, or so Joe was led to believe…Mona had started going to her evening classes at the Uni (good on her like) but it left Joe to start wistfully thinking more and more of the years just before he and Mona had got married; it had been the most *awesome* time, the Capital City Service was in its hey-day—they were even talked about in *parliament* like (Mona had never believed him about that, he'd had to show her the *Daily Record* clipping, proudly pinned to his wall) and him and Mona were loving each other.

He'd known when he'd met her that she was going to be the one he'd spend his life with—he couldn't explain it, but he'd known…ever since they'd seen each other down the west-end Wimpy…they'd smiled at each other, and then one Saturday afternoon they'd found themselves running away from the pigs together, up round Toll Cross and she'd looked down at his feet and said breathlessly, "Nice trainers like."

And she was right, they were; fuckin' Adidas Gazelles 2X600, he'd only just bought them too and they were shining (he was terrified that they'd be taxed by another crew and for a few weeks he didn't move out of Edinburgh on the weekends, even though he'd missed out on some fuckin' stunning Away victories for the CCS).

But for him and Mona, that was it. They were inseparable from that moment.

She was tough Mona, she'd shout and kick and punch as much as the guys when it came to fending off the Huns or the Dons, and Joe loved her for it. She had been lovely looking too, it being the late 80s, it was all tight stonewash skirts and peroxide hair, not that Mona looked like that now, but she still had a good figure like, Joe had to admit that.

"An' the truth is, Davie," back in the bar, several pints down "we just ran oot of folk tae fight like, we were at the top of our game and no one could beat us."

"But that didn't mean we had to stop!" Davie thudded his fist down on the table, making the glasses shudder, "we had to defend our title like, keep pounding them again and again, until there was no one who was even willing to have a go." Davie breathed hard, Joe stared at the table, nodding alongside him, but hardly daring to look at the other man, he felt ashamed.

"You're right, Davie, of course you're dead right man." Joe took another swig of lager, and swallowed, shaking his head. "I should've been there man, on that Saturday—you ken, when we fucked the Dons down at Waverley." It was his turn now to thump the table, and people at the bar glanced over. "I always regretted not being there, not chasing that scum out of our town forever."

"Mmmm," Davie grunted, teeth bared open at the mouth of his pint glass as he poured the remainder of his pint down, he smacked his lips, and looked away from Joe. *'He's ashamed of me too,'* Joe thought.

"Aye, that was a good one," agreed Davie darkly, "where were you anyway?"

Joe sighed, he knew exactly where he'd been; fucking bored at Mona's parent's house while Mona and her mother looked through wedding magazines, cooing at table arrangements and cakes. When he'd heard later about the CCS battering the Aberdeen firm he'd cursed himself for even proposing to Mona in the first place. She hadn't been hanging around him and the guys so much since she'd started college; she'd got new friends there, had calmed down, much to her parents' relief, and now that Joe and her were getting hitched, she'd decided she needed to just call it a day with the crew— and so *he* had stopped meeting the guys in pubs on a Saturday afternoon.

She'd never told him as such, never *made* him do anything, but she'd give him this look whenever he'd start talking about the firm, or fights or a new Lacoste shirt that was doing the rounds. Mona would look at him in a kind of pitying way, like he was a child who was describing their favourite toy, or what they got for Christmas, Joe would feel like a twat, knowing that she had moved on from all this, why couldn't he? It was clever

"Ah was sick like," said Joe, now lying to Davie, "chronic diaorhea, I remember seeing the footage on the news though, and laughing so much at the looks on the Don cunts' faces, ah nearly shat myself again!" Davie chuckled into his glass, draining the dregs, Joe felt relieved, getting up from his chair and nodded to- wards Davie's empty.

"Same again?"

"Aye, cheers mate," Joe smiled at Davie, smiling at him.

Joe didn't have to think twice about getting together with the crew; or at least whoever Davie could track down, course he would, he'd never been more up for it in his life.

"Cannae wait, Davie," he'd said at the end of their night, "it's time we got back to what Saturday afternoons are all about."

And now, here he was in his van on Leith Walk, and it was all organised for tomorrow. It had been years—*decades* on, but he had the same tingling in his fingertips that he used to get twenty years ago...he thought of the clothes he'd dug out; he hardly wore the shirts anymore—he couldn't at work, the amount those shirts cost there was no way he could afford to get paint on them but he'd found his old favourite Tachinni shirt, the white one with the navy stripe across the chest. A mesh of memories netted him; Saturday afternoons—weren't all the memories from a Saturday? That was the day he lived for back then; working week finished with (or at least college where he was doing his apprenticeship) tea with the olds done with, and then shower and gear on; the shirt, the trousers, the trainers, the cap and jacket. A single line of gold round his neck.

He could actually remember the feeling of the Kappa kagool against his wrists, the dry rustle of the one he'd once had, and the snug fit of the cap round his head. He was a casual, he was a Hibbee, he was part of the amazing Capital City Service and as identities go, he wouldn't have had it any other fuckin' way. The buzz of meeting the guys, the knowledge that there were invaders in their city who were going to be shown exactly whose town this was—it all that...the pure shot of adrenaline which ran round his body faster than any snort of Charlie would, something again which he used to go in for, but had given up when he had embraced the life of the three-piece suite and the footie on the telly, instead of the aggro on the stands.

And tomorrow would take him back there, a step back in time, he felt younger just thinking about it, he couldn't stop his knuckles flexing, involuntarily. He wondered if the other guys were like this, as nervous and as psyched up as him? Three coach loads of fans in from Aberdeen—so Davie said anyway, for the three 'o' clock match at ER.

"A good time," Davie had said, "I always liked the later matches—time to get tanked up"

"Aye," Joe had agreed and although he was excited, he still felt quite nervous; he hadn't done anything like this for years, it would be weird like, getting back in the saddle—but the thought of a few pints before seemed liked a good idea, take the edge off things…

Let's face it, he thought. It wasn't the fuckin' football he was excited about, it had never been the footie—oh he loved the Hibs—always would, but in the past it hadn't been the thought of seeing John Collins put one past the opposition that would spread a grin on Joe's face come Saturday morning; it would be of standing side by side with the rest of the boys all decked out in their finest, ready to take on anything that was thrown at them. It would be the smack of his knuckle on a stranger's cheekbone.

As luck would have it, Mona had decided to have a weekend away at her mother's; she'd had a phone call the other night, Edna had not heard from Mona's sister, Maggie, for a month. Ever since her bloke, the no-good bastard, had gone and died, Maggie was notorious for going on benders and Edna was worried for the kids; Caitlin and Jordan. Mona was going over to comfort her mother, and would try to contact Maggie. Joe had silently thanked Maggie for her unstable ways as he was now left to his own devices for the whole weekend. Mona would have disapproved, that was for sure. She couldn't have stopped him, but she would have made it quite clear that she thought the whole idea was a bag of shite. She wouldn't have understood, that was at the root of it. She wasn't a bloke—hadn't been a lad when the whole scene was kicking off...

Joe sat at the bar in the Four in Hand, trying not to look nervous, trying not to look like he didn't know what he was doing there. The first pint had gone down well, but the second was sloshing around his stomach, fizzing the sides and making him feel queasy. Joe looked at his watch the eighth time in five minutes, wondering where Davie was; *quarter to two—where the fuck was he?* The Haar had been drifting in for some while now, lending a weird feeling to the streets, he wondered how thick it would get, whether he'd be able to see steps in front of him, or others for that matter; folk drifting in and out of the sea fog like ghosts. It wouldn't be good for the fight that was for sure—you wouldn't be able to see the other lads if it got any worse...

He thought of the rest of the guys who Davie had said he'd managed to round up, names he recognised, but none who he'd really cross the street for. He wondered if they were in a bar some- where as well, drinking their pints too quickly, licking their lips, their pockets weighed down with double actions OTFs or if Jase and Ferg were there, rubber batons. Joe could feel his heart racing at the thought of the game, or rather the hours afterwards, destination TBA. *Could he really do this again?* The fog drifted by, his legs shook.

Doubt tweaked at him as he thought of his family; Mona had phoned him this morning and his palm had sweated as he'd casually lied to her about his plans for the day.

"No much. I've got a job to finish, but that'll just take an hour or two, then I'll probably meet Mikey down the Foot." "Who's Mikey?"

"You ken, I was talking about him the other day, lad's just got out of Saughton, he knew Kenny."

"Oh."

He could tell by the tone of Mona's voice that she wasn't impressed by this, but it was better than the truth, and if anything *did* happen that the press got hold of, Joe could just swear that he'd got caught up in the mayhem like...

And he knew what his son thought of him, the wee fucker, thought his dad was twenty-five years out of date for all of this but he didn't know what he was talking about. Mark had never liked football either, never shown any interest from day one...Joe had pretended to Mona that he didn't care, it didn't bother him that his only son didn't give a flying toss about what was his dad's life.

Outside the bar a woman and a small girl walked by, Joe's uneasy eyes followed them, bonny wee thing she was, reeking of happiness. She had some of those pink fairy wings the little girls loved, all feathers and glitter wavering through the foggy air, chattering nineteen to the dozen to the woman who she was with; Joe imagined that if fairies did exist, they'd look like this wee one, with the mist swirling around her she could've stepped out of Peter Pan. Girls though. Things would have been a hell of a lot easier if he and Mona had had a girl, they looked up to their daddies, respected them. But Mark had come along and then no more.

His phone rang, it was Davie, Joe's heart stepped up a beat. "Alright mate, how's it going?" Joe tried to keep the shake out of his voice.

"Not bad Joe, my man," Davie sounded chipper, Joe could feel the excitement in his words, he imagined Davie's large ruddy face beaming.

"Are...are we all set?" Joe stuttered, at the same time quivering a cigarette out of its pack, giving his trembling fingers some- thing to do, distracting his fluttering mind.

"Aye," Davie took his time with his words, in contrast to Joe's jumping script, "you in the Four?"

"Aye," Joe coughed loudly as he lit the fag one handed, "when are you coming, mate?"

"I'll be there soon enough."

"And er...is, you know, are the others definitely on their way like?"

"All present and correct Joe, don't you worry about them." "I wasn't–" Joe began but Davie had already hung up.

Shit. It really was going to happen then. He couldn't even think about the football at this point; in truth he couldn't give a toss about the game, it didn't matter who was playing or what the score was, he'd have to stand there with the knowledge that it was all going to kick off afterwards, that all around the stadium there'd be lads from the old firms itching, just *scratching* for blood, and that he'd have to hit someone, actually *hurt* someone... He almost couldn't take the pressure—if he cocked up or chickened out, Davie would never forgive him. But he felt like chickening out, that's exactly what he felt like doing now, with too much fizzing lager wallowing in his stomach and a light head, and Mona didn't even know where he was–

A clout on the back nearly sent him flying off his bar stool. He turned around to see Davie's broad grinning cheeks and newly shaven head. He was wearing a shining sky-blue Lacoste jacket, newly bought, Joe suspected. He looked down to see a glowing white pair of Adidas trainers with gold stripes on Davie's feet and the sight of them gave Joe a sinking feeling in his stomach—there really was no going back. His mind flicked to the thought of the coaches winding their way down to the city outskirts from Aberdeen, on board thousands of faceless men, dressed identically to him and Davie, new clothes, but the bodies getting past it now, guts spilling over trousers, hair thinning, hearts not quite as healthy and pumping as they used to be...

"You alright, Joe?" Davie was looking at him, eyes narrowed, "look a bit pale like."

"Nah, I'm fine," Joe tossed off the comment, "had a bit of a late night that's all."

Davie tipped a wink at him, at the same time gesturing for Joe to follow him around the bar to the toilets.

"Got just the thing to pep you up then, mate, get your ticker going."

Joe traipsed warily after him, already half-guessing what Davie was up to. If it was drugs would that really be a good idea?

He suddenly felt ancient, old and world-weary, he hadn't done any Charlie for years, another thing that Mona had silently weaned him off...

The urinals were empty but Davie ushered him into a cubicle. Reaching into his slippery pocket he pulled out a small polythene bag, in which sat eight pale green plastic capsules. Joe looked at them in confusion.

"What the fuck's that?" he was expecting some white powder at least.

"Plant food," Davie answered shortly. "Come again?"

"Mephedrone," Davie said, as if it were obvious, "it's a new thing, got it on the internet."

Joe looked at the gleaming capsules doubtfully. "Have you no just got any coke? I know where I am with coke like."

"It's just like coke, man!" Davie cried incredulously, he slipped a podgy finger into the plastic seal and fumbled about until he'd caught hold of a green capsule, he drew it out and held in front of Joe, "gives you just the same sort of buzz but not as expensive, come on, it'll buck you up like, get you in the mood."

"For what?"

"For fightin' man!" Davie put up his fists and playfully punched Joe on the shoulder "for showing the sheep shaggers comin' all the way on their fuckin' coaches who the fuckin' CCS are again!" Joe looked at Davie, he could see now that his pupils were wide and there was a faint sheen of sweat beading on his pink forehead.

"Have you had some already then?"

"Aye man!" Davie opened his eyes wide, "fuckin' buzzing and lookin' for blood, now get one down your throat you fuckin' poof!" and before he knew what was happening, Davie had grabbed a capsule and rammed it to the back of Joe's throat, his reflex being to gag but Davie was already there, his grip strong as he made sure the pill went back far enough to swallow.

The minute it was gone Joe wrenched his head out of Davie's grip. "For fuck's sake man!"

Davie was giggling at his reaction, he spread his hands wide in mock innocence.

"Ah come on, Joe—what's the worst that could happen?"

What's the worst that could happen? *What's the worst that could happen?* well…here's the worst man… here's the *fuckin' worst of it*; his head, sky high, as high as the—*let's go fly a kite…*

And he didn't know where his head was, but it was good for fightin' man, good for fuckin' fightin'.

Shiftin', stompin', wheelin', kickin', bitin', throwin' man let's have it LET'S BRING IT ON THEN. Where *were* these cunts anyway? What had Davie said? Ah Davie man, top bloke, top fuckin' bloke, couldn't wrong him like, couldn't find a thing, they hadn't made it to Easter Road, don't really know why now—nah he wasn't bothered about the match—who gives a fuck about the Hibs–

Hibbeeeee's Hibeeeee's best team in the world like man, but much as he loved them, as he'd *always* love them, god knows no one would love the boys in green as much as he did—this *fog* man, you couldn't fuckin' *see*...see? You could wave a hand in front of you like and it could've been anyone's! This hand—*this* hand could belong to anyone, Davie's it could be–

"Davieeee! Davie Man! Where the fuck are you?"

No answer, what's he gonna do? Where was he? What time was it? Time you got a watch man...where was he now? What was he doing, this *mist* man, couldn't see a fuckin' thing...

The Haar, the thick fog which conjugates in the nooks and crannies of the city. Like spectres emerging from the pavement, the opaque air winds its way in and out of Edinburgh streets, enveloping all its inhabitants young and old, man and woman, Aberdonians and Hibernians alike...And where were these two tribes? These two teams of fighters who are destined never to meet in this pea soup mix.

Joe McKenzie stumbles about Leith, looking for someone to sink his fists into but at the same time, desperate to find his way home. He does not recognise the roads he knows so well, the fog misdirects him, the drugs spell the wrong words on the signposts...*Fuck me, it's no even dark yet, how can that be?* Maybe it would never get dark, maybe this day would just go on forever. People emerged out of the fog like survivors from a war—though undamaged they had an ethereal quality to them, the Haar bleached their faces, clouded their hair, made them step out of historical novels...

"You alright love? Having a nice night?"

Joe heard a voice thread its way out of the dense air, a woman's voice, but he couldn't see a face, just a pair of white legs, hard calves, patent crimson heels...

"It's not night!" Joe screamed, laughing.

"Alright, so I've started early," came the cheerful reply, "so have you by the look of it."

Joe blinked, still not properly seeing the woman, though there was something about her, something about the voice, his brain stretched itself to try and think...

"How about it then sweetheart?" she called, "How does sixty quid strike you?" A hand came out of nowhere and roughly stroked his thigh, he moved back involuntarily.

"Oi hen, what you doing?"

"Oh c'mon, sure I can't persuade you?"

A face was suddenly opposite his—powdered skin, strong cheap perfume—"Maggie?"

"Joe?"

But before he could say anything back to his sister-in-law, she was gone in a swirl of fog, no sign of her except the clipped hooves of her heels on the pavement…

Fuck me…Maggie on the game, what was the world coming to? His riddled brain could not even begin to process this statement, all he could think of—and reassure himself with, was the fact that she would never tell Mona about the state he was in and he would never tell her sister that Maggie was selling her arse in the wrong end of Leith…

He walked through the impenetrable fog, through the darkened mid-afternoon, on and on through streets which he thought were familiar and then turned out to be somewhere else entirely. He'd stopped looking for the fight, that much he knew, the fight had died in him, if there had been any in the first place. Let's face it, those days, the CCS days were long gone, leave it to someone else like—leave it to the next generation if they could be fucked to do something about it…dare say they couldn't if they were anything like Mark…

Joe's brain flicked on and off with moving images, a broken Magic Lantern…the wee fairy girl danced on and off of the lamp- posts…Mona in red high heels and a painted smear of lips…Davie, his face like a slab of raw meat laughing and punching him at the same time… Joe's head ached, spun and was in danger of falling off. He was on his own—all alone, if he'd kept with Davie he wouldn't be in this spot—if he'd kept with the crew like…he was a casual…a Hibbee; these colours don't run the man had said…these colours don't–

He stepped into a space between two benches and a cloud of pigeons flew up in front of him.

"Fuck me!"

Joe clanged into something hard and cold, a metal tower? He put his hands out and felt bands of cold steel spiraling up and up. A skyscraper? In Leith?

"What's that? What are ya? Where did you come from?"

"Are you talking to me?" came a voice, he was going mental like—big metal things talking to him...he was as nutty as that lad on the phone...he got as close as he could to the metal structure and looked up to the top, the fog wrapped itself around the rusted ribbons, Joe's lips came so close to the metal that he could feel the stinging cold of the bar. "Who are you?" he croaked.

"I'm a fuckin' statue you twat," came a reply but it sure as hell didn't come from the metal tower, Joe turned around clumsily, he couldn't see a thing.

"Who's that?"

"None of your business." "Where am I?"

A sigh, a giggle and then he heard the distinctive gurgle of a small child.

"For fuck's sake...you're at the foot o' the Walk you numpty now will you keep it down, my wee one's trying to sleep."

It was a girl's voice, no doubt about it, not the disembodied one of the talking corkscrew, which stood in front of him. The huge metal spiral that stood at the bottom of Leith Walk, though he couldn't see it properly because of the mist. He'd hardly got anywhere, he must have gone in one mad loop.

"Ah man, I just wanna go home like." He felt desperate, the drugs winding down like a broken clock.

"Well go home then," came the girl's voice again, annoyed. "Ah cannae!" Joe whined, "ah don't know ah live!" and he really didn't, his brain just couldn't function, it felt like soft cheese, he knew buses were involved but he didn't know where he could go to get one.

"Where are you trying to get to?"

"Granton."

"Well look," a hand out of nowhere jerked him in a definite direction. "Now just go straight, try not to wander off till you get to the pavement, then cross the road and get on the bus stop on your right."

Joe sighed in sheer exaltation "Ta love, you're an absolute doll—what's your name like, what's your name?"

"Leanne. Now go on, go home mate, and sleep it off."

"Ah will, ah will, listen ah'm so grateful to you hen, you wouldn't believe–"

But the hand had disappeared, as had the girl. Joe staggered in the direction she turned him to, then his worm-holed brain suddenly remembered something else.

"Listen," he called into the fog, shouted into the depths of the Haar, "Do you know who won like? Who won the Hibs match?" "Aberdeen," came the reply, "fair play to them as well, there was a bunch of dozy Hibs bastards trying to stir it afterwards, I heard it on the news

"Aye, dunno what they're thinkin'," Joe mumbled back, head swirling in the ever increasing fog.

9

No one tells you exactly what it's going be like. Well, in a way they do, they tell you all the bad bits. They say, "You won't know what's hit you." They say, "You never get any time to yourself anymore." And then they say, "You wouldn't be without them though." But there's no hint of a smile and they say it with a mouth like lemons. And that's what I was prepared for; my life—watered down for somebody else.

My social worker said I should do this.

"Write it all down," Caroline said, "Keep things ticking over, because it's all too easy to just let your mind fester, to let your thoughts get you down," and she looked at me in a *Know What I Mean* way.

Well, I do know. And apparently if I write stuff down I'll forget all about the fact that I'm stuck on my own in a flat with a fatherless wee one, no money to speak of except what the good City of Edinburgh Council sees fit to provide me with. If I put pen to paper I'll forget that I've got no achievement in the world except popping this baby out.

"You never know," Caroline goes on, getting more excited with her own idea, "you could even make a few bob, you know, if you finish anything, you could send it off to a publisher" (then she gets these pink spots on her cheeks like she does when she's getting worked up

188

and her hands go mental), "you could be the next JK Rowling."

"JK who?" I ask.

"You know," she says, "Harry Potter. She was a single mum just like you, and on benefits," she adds like it's a medal in itself. "She used to go to the Elephant House with her wee one and just write, then she sent it off and now she's a millionaire."

"Right," I said warily, "what's the Elephant House

"On George the Fourth Bridge," she says, "they do the most heavenly cheesecake." Caroline closes her eyes in memory of this apparent ecstasy and then puts on her favourite social worker smile (i.e. 'when you see I'm right you'll remember this moment and thank me'). "You never know, just give it a go, Edinburgh's all the rage in the literary scene, just look at that Irvine Welsh."

"Aye," I said, looking at the cot. "A friend of mine used to serve him in a bar, she said he was a prat."

"Or Ian Rankin?"

"Aye," I say again, and look to the clock. She sees me doing this and sighs.

"At least it'll get you out of the house, Leanne—get yourself a notebook, it'll give you something to do." She pauses to see if I'm looking at her, then she nods at me slowly and I slowly nod along with her, like she wants me to.

Yes Caroline.

"You need to get yourself into a routine," says Caroline on her next visit. "Soon as you get the wee one into a proper routine you can get some time to yourself and you can just think about something else for a while. Is she sleeping through the night yet? Have you got yourself a notebook?"

Notebook—no Caroline, I haven't purchased a notebook, my fountain pen has temporarily run out of ink and I seem to have no blotting paper in the house. Sleeping through the night? Is the woman mad?

"My two were sleeping right through from three weeks, Leanne," Caroline assures me. "Routine—it's all about routine, have you got her baths at a set time yet?"

"She hates baths," I say, "she screams for about half an hour either side of getting in."

"Are you holding her head correctly? Have you got the temperature right?"

I don't answer but get up to go to the kitchen window and light up a fag.

Blowing out smoke down onto Great Junction Street I can feel her eyes on the back of my neck, and she shuffles in the chair making the leather squeak. Routine I'm not worried about, what I want to know is when does this Mothering Instinct kick in? I can appreciate the sweetness of the baby, the tiny fingers and toes, the silkiness of her skin, but I don't know if I *feel* it. It's like eating chocolate with a cold.

When do the good times begin? (If they're ever going to.) When does the harsh reality stop; that being me, watching the minutes tick by in the daytime, waiting for her to go to sleep again. Or me, staring at the wall for the forth time in the night, a sucking foreigner on my chest, the shadows on the wall slightly clearer than the last time I was awake; the dawn creeping in. Me, waiting for this bone crunching exhaustion to go. Wanting to feel something—anything, for this creature I'm keeping alive.

My mind flicks back to This Time Last Year, I was a thousand years younger (recently, I can't stop finding my mother in the mirror) I could go to the pub with friends every night after work (temporary workmates, but 'friends' nonetheless). I wore short skirts, too thin a coat and drank like my life depended on it. I have witnesses to the fact that I was occasionally chatted up. In short, I was an individual.

And now—now I don't feel original, I'm diluted. A statistic—I'm everything to someone (the baby I suppose) and nothing to everyone else. I'm a mother, but really, just a mum.

I've trained my eyes to look away from the sight of new families or even worse, expectant couples. He, with his arm protectively round her, while She absently strokes the neat mound of her belly, the foetus itself obediently curled up asleep inside, still and peaceful, unlike the tornado of a child who had inhabited my council flat of a womb. I did picture it like that, other mothers' uteruses would be tastefully decorated, wall-to-wall shag pile with scatter cushions and scented candles. Central heating. Coasters on the coffee table. Whereas my shelter of hollow muscle was probably dark and dingy, the curtains not matching, crumbs on the floor and a funny smell. My pregnancy was a long and heavy one and throughout the nine months all I could think was that booze and opportunity had a lot to answer for. When else would I decide that an ex-con would be the perfect bed-mate except after seven double vodkas?

There was a dream I had (I had loads of weird dreams when I was pregnant; quite common apparently but they were so real and *mad*. I'd wake up from it and I'd been crying, the pillow wet. Or I'd be angry, a black rage which stayed with me all the following day), But there was one dream that stayed with me and I can still remember it now.

In the dream I'm shopping, it must have been Christmas, loads of folk walking about, in and out of the shops on Rose Street, chatting, smiling, blowing, stressing. Dark cold cobbles.

Still very heavily pregnant, belly swinging about in front of me; even in dreams I'm clumsy, weighted. Staggering about as I've got all these bags to carry as well, I keep bumping into people.

It's dark on the street, I can't see anyone's faces clearly, they're all shadows. I'm so tired, really pissed off, don't know how I'm going to carry on. Everything getting darker, it's raining now—hard, my hair sticking to my cheek. I'm walking heavily down the dark street, folk passing me like ghosts.

Suddenly there's a shop in front of me, all lit up from the inside, glowing like a bairn's night light. I blink through my lashes as the rain pisses down and the light is so welcoming. No-one else can see the shop; it's hiding from everyone except me.

I feel a pull towards it, I have to go in there, and I don't even think, don't even hesitate. And I collapse through the door.

A bell jangles as I walk in. A shining golden bell. Inside there are lights everywhere, gleaming off brass bits. It's quiet and it's calm.

The candles inside waver with the air I bring in, there's heat. There's overwhelming relief and comfort. I'm off the cold wet street.

The owner appears, a small man. He's a dark man, and he's a young and he's an old man. A charming man, a lovely man. Out from behind a purple velvet curtain like a magician, he held out his arms to me.

Thick black-rimmed glasses, huge eyes. A great big grin. He is unthreatening. He knows me, I am a stranger. I'm special, he wants me there. He's pleased I came. He thinks I'm beautiful. He wants to take care of me.

He pulls out a red cushioned chair for me. And I melt into it, like I'm lying down, like I'm under the sea, the weight is off and I can forget how heavy I am. Everything's alright. I'm light as a feather.

I'm almost asleep (asleep in a dream? That's never happened before) and it's the sleep of the light bodied, the unburdened.

The little man doesn't speak. He scuttles around making sure I've got everything I want. He puts a footstool under my feet, a soft blue blanket over me.

A mug of steaming hot chocolate, rich and creamy, it's the best thing I've ever tasted.

A bowl of oranges, the only thing I've really craved in the last nine months.

I now look around the shop. On the packed shelves there's bits and bobs, odds and sods, nick-nacks—stuff I used to own, I couldn't tell you where it is now;

A loo roll doll. Knitted pink wool with plastic arms above her head and it used to sit on top of the loo roll in our house when I was a kid.

A china clock shaped like a dog, which used to tick round Granny's house.

A pair of shiny leather black shoes, size 2.

A wooden red boat with a white sail that sat on a window-sill in our house, but no-one knew who it belonged to or where it came from.

Lip gloss flavoured of strawberry.

Relaxed and happy. The little old young man sits and watches me.

Smiles at me. He asks me if I'm happy. Asks me if I'd like to go to the moon.

Pulls out a teddy bear with eyes made of drawing pins, warns me to be careful but I won't touch it.

'Would you like me to take the baby?' he asks, it's in another language, and I understand perfectly.

And I give birth there and then, easily and quickly. Without screams or fuss. The baby appears in my hands. Tiny but very heavy. A lead figure. I pass it to the little man.

He takes the package and puts his hands together. A prayer to me. He puts the baby on a high shelf, out of reach of anyone.

He tells me I have to go now and I do.

I woke up not knowing where I was or what was happening, the sheets wet with a cold sweat.

'Baby' was never still. 'Restless,' the midwife said, but I silently thought, 'uneasy'.

I don't know what I'm doing.

I don't think I feel anything for this soft whining thing who doesn't even seem like a human at the moment…she's just another animal to me. She doesn't even look like me…she's dark like him—the thief in the night who stole my life.

I haven't named her yet.

Caroline does not think this is a good thing.

"It's not a good thing, Leanne, it doesn't help with bonding." But we don't know each other, 'Baby' and me. We're strangers to each other, thrown together by forces out of our control. She doesn't want to be here, she lets me know this about six times a day, and if I'm honest at the darkest hour before dawn, neither do I.

"Happy Christmas," Caroline hands me a shiny blue package together with a small red one, she pats it and whispers, "Some- thing for the wee one."

"I thought you weren't allowed to give me any-thing," I say dully, but inside I'm secretly envious of the fact that she's got the time and money to even think about Christmas. I can picture her, strolling round Princes Street with a friend, both wearing thick black coats and hats against the wet slush that is city snow. They'd do their shopping then go and have tea and cake in Jenners, returning home to a warm cosy house—the Christmas tree glowing in the corner.

"It's only small," Caroline winks at me. "I'm sure we can keep it between ourselves."

The bairn lets out a wail and I feel a leaden ache in my chest. I manage to mumble a "Thanks" to Caroline and go over to the cot. The baby looks at me her face puckered and red; the crying goes up a notch in the scale.

"Oh dear dear dear," sighs Caroline and she sits down on the unbroken part of the sofa. I go to the only other chair and sit down to feed the baby. Caroline looks at me like she's peering into a dark room.

"How are things, Leanne?" She makes it sound like she's never asked me this question before, but on every visit she leans towards The Way Things Are. The wee one snuffles and grunts on me and I suddenly feel jealous of her, of how the world spins around her tiny oblivious head, the pain and the cold and the loss and the worry, and all there is inside that bald egg is a need for milk, warmth and sleep, it sounds like a nice place to be.

"In regards to what, Caroline?" I ask, not looking at her. "Well…" she starts, and pauses. Honestly, for a social worker she's sometimes as awkward as a teenager. I interrupt her before she *umms* and *ahhs* anymore.

"Do you mean am I still depressed?" "Well–"

"Am I still wanting to do away with myself?" "I wasn't–"

"Am I a…how did your lot put it…'a danger to myself and the child'?"

I look straight at her and she looks away. Then, as if she resolved something with herself she meets my eyes.

"Yes Leanne, are you still depressed? Are you still having suicidal thoughts?"

It's my turn to look away.

"No, I'm not." In the corner of my eye I see her visibly relax, her shoulders shrink. "I haven't got the energy," I mutter.

When she's gone I unwrap the shiny blue package. It's a notebook and I shake my head in wonder at the woman. It's a nice one though, the cover is smooth brown leather and the pages are thick paper—creamy stuff that you know is going to be nice to write on. I put the wee red package under my one Christmas decoration; a glowing Santa with a chipped hat where the paint has cracked.

Hogmanay night. This Time Last Year I was sat on top of Calton Hill, drunk as a skunk on as much Tennants as I could force down my neck before the bells. I was with people who I thought were solid, steadfast. On hearing of my 'condition' they more or less scattered to the winds.

I couldn't really remember how I'd met these folk; they were friends who weren't particularly old but I'd been in their group long enough to feel devoted to them. Fiona, Aggie, Micky, Welchie and the rest; we had such laughs, such good times—Mad Nights In seemed to be the whole point of us hanging around with each other.

But it all started to go wrong when Fi found out I'd been with Michael after he got out of Saughton. For fuck's sake I hadn't meant to—it was one of those things, I didn't know Fi still had a thing for him, she'd never said anything—I hadn't even *known* Michael before he'd gone in.

It was one of those mental nights that had started out as 'a couple of pints'—those nights are the worst for getting steamin' and I should've known it. Me, Fi and Pete had gone to the Blind Poet off South Clerk Street for a Sunday afternoon drink.

My God, It was a Sunday, I don't even have the excuse of a Saturday night...Sundays are for coffees and lounging around with the EastEnders Omnibus, not making babies which change your life forever...

Michael was already drunk and sat in the corner, telling bad jokes to a table of freshers from the Uni. I knew his game, all the lads played it around the time the Uni's go back. They'd go out drinking round George square, put on their best Scautish accent and tell stories of Auld Reekie. The posh Ya girls would lap it up. Fair play to the lads though, it worked every time.

Me and Michael hadn't known each other long when the baby was conceived. We hadn't 'dated' as such. We hadn't gazed at each other over candlelit dinners with the promise of what was to follow, lingering in the air. We hadn't met each other's parents in awkward living rooms, hadn't been embarrassed when the box of our baby photos came out. We hadn't discussed our futures at three a.m. in a stranger's living room, bottles strewn around us. We hadn't told the other what we hoped for, what we'd always dreamt of;

'I know it sounds silly but I've always thought I'd like...'

We hadn't gone through the phase of not being able to keep our hands off each other, when someone *consumes* you, an itch that can never be satisfied no matter how hard its scratched.

We hadn't grown bored of each other, or annoyed, when sometimes you can't even bear to hear the other breathe. In truth, we hardly knew each other. That same night we made a map of each other's bodies and then said goodbye. We didn't even know each other's surnames.

I knew it was going to happen, I could tell by the way he looked at me, and I liked it at the time; although I saw from the outset he wasn't boyfriend material I still wasn't going to pass up a pair of arms to press round me in the darkest light before dawn.

A baby made in the shaking sheets of a drunken night. Conception of a life under the fusty shadowy cover of a Good Fuck.

After the pub kicked us all out, Michael gave me a lift home on the back of his bike. We whizzed round the Edinburgh streets, the city lights blurring my eyes and I suddenly felt wistful for the life I was already living... that doesn't happen very often either...

When he told me he was just out of prison, I just thought it added to his charm. And the fact that he was protecting an animal showed he had a sensitive side; I conveniently looked over the fact that he nearly beat someone to death.

I've often thought about that, the fact that he was two days out of prison and he makes a baby. Didn't hang around did Michael Lambert.

Anyway, last Hogmanay, when we were all friends and it was still only me, (there were no *other dependents* yet) we had been doing rounds with a whiskey bottle and kisses—passing each other to and fro like a poker game. We all declared undying love for Scotland, Edinburgh and everyone in it, even the tourists up for their Hogmanay Experience, packed like sardines into Princes Street, drenched and shivering and stuck there until three in the morning.

I remember running down that hill in my bare feet once the bells had been rung in, Edinburgh swirling around me in fairy lights as I landed in a heap, laughing my arse off—it was a caught moment of happiness.

All that stuff now seems like weed on a pond, floating on the murky surface of deep water. I never thought that the next New Year I would be sat on an itchy chair, a baby feeding off me–

A baby…

A glass of warm Lambrusco and a packet of peanuts.

Tonight in the dim light of my broken flat, the red glow of the gas fire makes it seem almost cosy. I can hear the chaos of voices, whistles and drums in the street below, and it must have been a parade because the music faded and I could then hear the telly again, some band or other.

I used to care about music…

Then I must have nodded off because the bells have been rung and on the screen there's people cheering, that white confetti pouring down on them.

A new year.

I look down at the bairn and she's stopped feeding, she's not doing anything but looking at me with big serious eyes. My heart beats and it feels like we're both waiting for something.

Her eyes crease and the corners of her mouth turn up—not a lot, but enough to recognise as a familiar human gesture; a smile.

It could be wind saying that, it could be anything, but it signifies good, and its good directed at *me*. The moment holds us with strong arms; outside the world's still turning with the other millions of people crawling on it, but inside this tiny place, time has stood still—and I think I've fallen in love.

I name her Mary, after my mother. Needless to say Caroline wholly approves.

"Oh yes, Leanne, she's definitely a Mary."

"It's not religious," I add quickly before she thinks she's somehow converted me (I know of her Catholic leanings).

"Oh no," Caroline shakes her head, still beaming at Mary and me (*Mary and me*—the thought makes me frown, and smile). "*No,*" says Caroline, "I never even thought that."

And from then on things change, not dramatically but that first slight smile fuels me like a full sleep, or a decent meal. I can carry on, it seems I've tapped into a secret store of energy, an extra battery pack that my body's been carrying around and I've never known about.

I start to think about things when I'm feeding her in the middle of the night, instead of staring blankly at the wall, and sometimes an idea flips in my mind that I think *might* be good enough to write down. But Caroline's leather notebook still lies on the floor by my bed, the thick pages still empty.

In the night, when my eyes can open enough to focus on the print, I pick up the first Harry Potter book—feeling like I quite like this JK woman after what Caroline said. And I find myself getting into it, you want to know what happens next—it brings out the bairn in me; aged ten I was right into my fairy tale stuff, witches and wizards and castles and princesses—I would even write wee stories, my favourite teacher Miss McKay liked them, she said I should keep them up.

Well.

Ten's a good age for magic isn't it?

But then I think if a grown woman like JK could still write about it, then why not me?

I even go to the Elephant House. Outside is a sign; 'the birthplace of Harry Potter'. It's a few days after Hogmanay, and the air is baltic. Needless to say, Mary's alright, cosied up in blankets under her 'Toastie Toes'.

"Have you got a Toastie Toes on your buggy?" Caroline had asked, "I'll tell you, Leanne, Toastie Toes are an absolute godsend in the winter Toastie Toes, Bumbie Chairs, Tommy Tippee, Tots Bots. Grown women discussing these things with straight, sincere faces; ("Ah love mah Bumbie chair, ah donno what ah'd dae wi'out it.")

There's not many folk in the café—mostly because of the weather and the huge hangover that drapes over Edinburgh after Hogmanay. There's still a few straggling tourists about, not knowing quite what to do with themselves now that the city has turned back into a pumpkin, after the palace it was on December 31st.

I plonk myself at a table next to two old wifies, and draw up the buggy with a sleeping Mary in it beside me. It's funny, before I had one of my own, other mums with buggies just blended into the background, I just didn't see them. But now I've got one, they're *everywhere*, you can't move for four-wheeled kids, and they come in so many models, I'd never thought there was as many as cars.

Anyway, I'd only enough money for a coffee, and half of its spilt onto the table already. As I was paying I did a rough calculation in my head, coffee £1.70, which would last about half an hour, then I suppose you'd have to get another one a while after that—how the hell did JK afford it? I'm thinking she must have spent a bit of time here if she had written a few books, and surely they wouldn't have let her sit there with one cup of coffee all afternoon?

With the wee one still sleeping, I grab my chance and get out Caroline's notebook, my heart beating a little faster. I open it carefully on the first page, creasing down the fold. My biro poised, the page inviting me to write something down. I have a flash through my mind of me having written a book, and it getting published. Getting handed a cheque and us never having to worry about money again, there's one of those signings and I'm in the paper—*Another JK?* The headline says–

"Oh isn't she gorgeous?"

It's one of the old wifies, bending over Mary who's now stirring because of the noise and the woman's voice. (I never realised this, but there's an unwritten law that says anyone can push their head into your baby's pram and talk to it, and it's always followed by the question...)

"How old is she, dear?"

And I can't bring myself to say "Piss off, it's none of yours," because they're old wifies, aren't they? So all this wakes Mary up, and she does one of her amazing smiles again, which shoots all thoughts of stories or words right out of my head, and then she wants up so I sit her on my knee and the old wifies coo and say, "come on now" which she loves and I finish my coffee, and don't have enough money for another, then Mary gets fed up of the wifies and the café, so we ram our way out through the tables and go home.

"And JK wrote a whole book like that?"

"Seven," Caroline says, "she wrote seven I think."

"Bloody hell," I say, shaking my head, wondering too how she managed to get her brain out of 'baby world' and into Warthogs or whatever it is. And then I think that it's because I've got too old, not in age, but in my mind—I can't think like a kid anymore and I see through the fairy stuff, it's transparent like the pink flouncy dresses I used to love dressing up in.

I sometimes only see the grey, the real life showing through, and it's the colour of Edinburgh stone.

Detective Harkness stubbed out his fag end on the foot of Leith Walk; he looked up at the dying light of the winter afternoon as it sunk below the dusty grey rooftops. A familiar figure sloped up to him, a skinny man with arms like birds' legs, he smiled a toothy grin.

"Awright copper?"

"Hello Leon." Harkness didn't bother to hide his disgust, the man's breath was on him like a fog. Harkness lit another cigarette, puffing the smoke into Leon's face, who coughed and waved it away.

"Folk die fae passive smoking y' ken."

"S'awright, Leon," replied Harkness with a sneer, "your body's fucked as it is—bit 'o smoke won't do you any harm."

I stop writing as I hear Mary wake up with a burble and then it's another couple of hours before I can take a look back at my crabby handwriting on the page of the notebook. What the hell was I writing about? Trying to do an Ian Rankin with a dab of Irvine Welsh was the idea, but what was I thinking? I don't know about any of this, I don't know *anything*...I can't even remember what I had in my mind when I started.

My brain has just stopped—who knows if it'll ever come back, and as if on cue, Mary starts to wail.

"I don't know about anything though," I rant at Caroline when she asks if I've written anything. "I don't know about detectives or heroin or wizards or 'the dark underbelly of Edinburgh'," I say sarcastically wiggling two fingers as speech marks under Mary who's on my hip and staring at me like I'm mad—which I am.

Caroline rolls her eyes and looks smug, I want to hit her. "You don't have to write about any of that," she says.

"But that's what they want, isn't it?" I rally back, "that's what they want from Scotland, isn't it? All we do is drink and swear and have a laugh while we're doing it."

"Leanne–"

"This is all I'm good for now," my voice gets louder and Mary's bottom lip starts to quiver, so I jiggle her harder. There's tears starting to flood into my eyes and I try to wipe them away with my other hand.

Caroline takes a gamble and gently reaches for Mary who's getting ready to yell, not liking my rough effort for comfort. I let Mary go and sit down in the scratchy chair. Caroline gently sways Mary to and fro.

"This *is* what you're good for now, Leanne," she says in a voice that I've never heard her use before, it's not condescending or superior; it's a mother voice, a soother. "Write about what you know," she looks at Mary, "Write about this wee one." Mary looks at me, and smiles.

No-one tells you exactly what it's going be like.

Instinct doesn't cover it; I don't think even love cuts it either. What they don't tell you about is this storm of feeling—a rolling thunder that builds and builds until you almost can't take it. It rolls in like the sea, this feeling, and after all these weeks, I find myself soaked. And I now don't care if I sound like every gushing dewy-eyed mother that's ever lived, me and Mary are wrapped in with each other, part of the same, and words can't cover that. I can't write in Caroline's sodding leather notebook because I'm feeling too much. And I'll never go back to the bloody Elephant House.

There's a café round the corner that is much more, well, up my street. Coffee is 60p a cup and I can sit there as long as I like.

As I said, words don't cover Mary, so I draw her. It started with a doodle when I was in the Sea Breeze and Mary, for once, was asleep. I did a few pencil lines; the perfect shape of her eyelids with the tiny delicate lashes. Her hands, her wee curled fingers that can hold just one of mine. Then I couldn't stop, and I filled pages of the leather notebook with sketches of her. My Mary.

10

A bird had flown in through the window. That had been the start of the trouble for Mrs Lambert that day. She had always deemed the sight of a bird in the house as a bad omen; a thrush had hopped in the back door on the day her father had died—her mother had panicked about the newly scrubbed carpet while her father fed it breadcrumbs

That afternoon he had a heart attack.

Mrs Lambert herself had discovered a blackbird in the kitchen the morning the police had called to tell her about Michael, the WPC had come rushing through when she had shrieked in surprise, the bird was hopping along the work surface, upsetting the spoon in the sugar bowl. No, it was not a good thing, a bird in the house.

She was still been in bed when it happened, the bedroom window being open as it always was come mid-June to late September. Mrs Lambert's flat was three floors up and so she had never been worried that some-one might climb through it as she had been when they had lived in Lochend. (Her husband had always scoffed at her worry that they might be robbed in their beds;

"I think I'd wake up, Val."

"Not if we were drugged," she'd reply, having read of this happening in one of her magazines.)

This particular bird was only small, tiny in fact. It had brown feathers that started flapping hysterically, the wings fanning out as it hit against the windowpane. Mrs Lambert leapt out of bed, fearful that it might start dropping filth on the sheets. She winced as the pain in her side stabbed, a dogged reminder that she should, in the doctor's words, 'Take it easy'. The bird hit the glass again, making rapid fluttering noises, interspersed with taps as its beak and claws scrabbled against the hard surface. Mrs Lambert climbed onto the bed and drew down the top of the sash window.

"Shoo! Go on, get out," she cried, waving at the small bird with her hands. After a few seconds of their dance together the bird spied the gap in the glass and obediently flew through it. Mrs Lambert shut the window with a bang and there was silence in the room. She sat down on the bed to catch her breath and rubbed at the pain in her side. It wasn't getting any better as she hoped it would, if anything it was worse than the day before. Still, no matter—she would take one of the little blue pills and all would be better, for a few hours at least.

Her eyes surveyed the room that was steeped in grey. The half-drawn curtains revealed a long block of colourless sky, even and without shade or tone. From where she was she could just see the tops of the chimneys of the houses opposite. Their roofs made a narrow chorus line along the edge of the large sash window, their slate roofs poised in mid-kick.

It would be acceptable, this weather, she thought, if it were the end of November. If it was going to be the kind of day where the sun never managed to rise high in the sky and the light laid low like a criminal, and it was really too cold and too bare to go out. Days like that made her feel safe; a day to be indoors and wrapped up warm.

But it wasn't going to be that kind of day, she could see that now; even at this early hour. Because it was not the bleak mid-winter, but only the beginning of August, and if she were proved right, it would be another dull day in a long line of grey days that was a permanent reminder that the summer had neglected to arrive in Edinburgh that year.

The season had left the heating on as an afterthought, but all the balmy breezes brought to the city was confusion. Sunbathing was out of the question as the key ingredient was notably absent. Gardeners, walkers, holidaymakers and ice cream sellers were decidedly nonplussed. It had not been hot throughout June and July and people longed for the characteristic burning dry heat that made the veins pop up on the backs of their hands like inversed rivulets, heat that left them wilting and sighing and flapping the air with anything available to flap. But to everyone's dismay, skin remained pale chicken flesh when it really should have been deep burnished bronze (or at least burnt in red patches.) Tomatoes hung on the vine, stoically green. Barbeque skewers, charcoal and sausages choked up the supermarket shelves—unsold and going off.

You could get away with not doing a lot in the summer time, Mrs Lambert thought, you could sit in the garden, under a sun- shade with a cool drink—but it was too dull to sit outside, and without the excuse of the exhaustion that heat brought, she felt distinctly uneasy at the thought of doing nothing. And yet lately, she hadn't been able to bring herself to do anything, and she now realised that it was on days like these that she was wasting time, feeling so ill that it was only just possible to see out the light of the day. Her stomach now started up its daily churning, but her ears pricked at the sound of the tinny chimes of the clock in the kitchen, and they struck her with a new intensity. To waste this day, as so many others had been wasted, seemed blasphemous.

Again she frowned at the outside sky; again she resented the weather and the time of year—it was all wrong, she thought, she wouldn't be feeling this disgruntled if August actually *felt* like August. If the seasons would sort themselves out into the proper order, then there wouldn't be this *nothingness*, this unease. She was twitchy. She had, as her former husband would have put it, cabin fever.

She exhaled loudly and a wave of sickness hit her stomach causing her to sit up sharply. Swallowing a wave of dull pain that throbbed down in her guts, she lifted her chin; she had to do something.

Getting up off the bed Mrs Lambert reached for her house coat from its hook on the wall, shuffling her feet into the pair of slippers that sat under it, like small furry animals in wait. She drew back the duvet from her single bed for the sheets to air. Later she would make it up, the air from the window would freshen the room and it was only Friday so the covers wouldn't need washing for a few days yet.

Padding though to the tiny kitchen to fill the kettle for tea, she struck a match, and lit the gas on the hob. The blue flames smelled comforting, making the room feel cosy, the walls rounded; it was the smell of her child-hood kitchen when her mother would be baking and the stove lit.

'*Val*', she could hear her mother say, without look-ing from a saucepan or her knitting, '*Valarie, put the kettle on will you love*'. Suddenly, she could see her mother's face, clear as day in front of her, her forehead frowning in concentration, tongue slightly touching the side of her mouth as she carefully cut away the pastry around a pie dish or finished off a row of her knitting. But the moment passed so that all she could see was a patch of brown damp on the wall.

The kettle whistled mournfully, on its way to be-coming shrill. She turned it off, her stare still drawn to the place where her mother's face had shimmered on the wall.

"Three teabag Valarie, one for me, one for thee and one for the pot."

Mrs Lambert murmured under her breath, at the same time plopping the little bags into the stained pot, knowing that it would be too strong for her, but now it was too late to fish them out as they had already soaked up some water. The steam powdered her face as she put the lid on and looked at the small kitchen clock.

8.32 a.m. She lidded the teapot and shuffled over to the window. Down below her on Wellington Street, she could hear, but couldn't see, the clatter of bins, the morning sounds of singular traffic and footsteps on pavement, hurrying to work.

It had been years since her feet had rushed off down a street to an office, and she remembered looking

212

up at the windows above the street, seeing old people or young mothers at the windows, still wrapped in dressing gowns, staring down on the street of the working below them, cradling cups of tea.

"Blimey, I wish that was me," Jan would say, all lipstick, chipped nails and cigarette smoke. They had walked to work together for three years, but Valarie Lambert never felt that they had a real friendship. She was too *rapid* for Valarie. And when Jan would say this and look longingly at the housewives who had the day stretched out before them, unplanned and un-bossed, Valarie would always nod readily in agreement, but really she loved the hustle and bustle of the workplace. She loved the feeling of walking home having done something with the day, going home to Derek and their little home which was still in the warm welcome glow of the first years of marriage.

Then when the boys had come along, she had been one of those mothers who looked through the windows in the morning, gazing at the scurrying workers from behind the glass of another world, the world of motherhood. Racks of washing were a permanent household fixture, strings of nappies on the line, and a waft of baby oil pervading through the small walls of the house. Valarie Lambert loved it. She felt she had found her niche, her nook. Her lot in life were Derek Junior and Michael; their matching stripy t-shirts, ties on Sunday to church, and lunch at her mother's. Water pistols, grazed knees, Christmas mornings in a sea of wrapping paper and excited shouts. Valarie adored every minute of it and would have had more babies but Deek was adamant,

"Two's plenty enough Val, we can't afford anymore and I don't think my nerves could stand it."

She was to find out later that it wasn't Deek's nerves, but Deek's wandering eye that had already latched onto the woman he would leave her for, which had decided the size of the Lambert family.

Valarie's heart broke into two raw pieces when she turned around one evening and found it was only her shadow, cast by the streetlight, that stood in her living room. Her two sons having moved out, albeit still in Edinburgh and they sometimes came round for their tea, but how she missed a full house; cups in the sink, banging on the wall to the boys late at night when they made too much noise, scrubbing mud off trousers and Michael or Derek teasing her for tsking at their swearing. Derek was nearly thirty and Michael was twenty-eight now, and had stopped telling her anything anymore. When they put their arms round her she could not believe how once she had cradled them in her arms, sung them to sleep, and stroked the velvet nape of their baby necks.

She was surprised at how little sorrow she felt at Deek's departure. His sons leaving home had made him finally decide between the two women in his life. Valarie had never met Debbie, even after Deek had moved in with her, nor had she wished to. She had seen her from a distance once, in Princes Street gardens. Spotting Deek's loping walk from yards away, her eyes immediately strayed to the figure beside him; it was an easy figure; smudged at the edges, with a face she would have never looked twice at. And Valarie had felt no anger or upset, only a curiosity to see what sort of woman Deek was apparently now interested in. Debbie was obviously younger than herself, and she knew this must have been an attraction. But she was evidently not as tidy as Valarie, Debbie's clothes were looser, not as fitted, her hair blew long in the wind, flying in all directions, and Valarie imagined that she probably kept her house in the same condition. Deek had never been a neat man, he had fallen in with Valarie's orderliness out of habit, and Valarie now supposed that this was what he wanted all the time, a relaxed mess. Well, she had thought briskly, he could have it, and welcome.

And now she was one of the old women at the windows, warming her hands on the teapot in the morning, glued into her routine of shopping on Thursdays, changing the sheets every second Tuesday, a coffee with friends in the British Home Stores café, friends who were as much as a habit as doing the washing up, not real companions. Valarie Lambert longed to be a busy young girl again, caught up in a pencil skirt and rushing on her way to work in the chattering streets, to big stone buildings of rustling paper, the smell of coffee and raised eyebrows.

If only something would happen, she thought, and again her mind wandered to the boys, to a rosy glowing dream she had. A dream which had been growing slowly in the recent years, which was one of grandchildren and of picnics in the meadows again. She pictured herself pushing a pram, strolling alongside Michael or Derek and her future daughters-in-law, changing nappies and gurgling baby laughter. She would have something to *do* again, a purpose in life. She had all the time in the world nowadays (the days which were good that is, the days when she could move without wincing) and wouldn't it be better put to good use?

If Derek's girlfriend Sandra had a baby then Valarie could look after it as surely Sandra would want to get back to work, her career being so important to her after all. But Sandra just didn't seem the motherly kind. She was not of the women of Valarie's generation, who by the age of thirty would have been married by now with at least two kiddies under her belt. Valarie simply couldn't understand girls like Sandra, playing at being men in their sharply cut grey suits. She had met Sandra a few times, always at the house she shared with Derek, and she would be served tea in modern white cups, and eat expensive biscuits. Valarie had never dared to broach the subject of children in front of Sandra, but she had subtly hinted to Derek whether or not he and Sandra had considered marriage.

"For God's sake Mother, we've only been together three years," Derek had said, but with a smile on his face.

"Me and your dad were married after just a year of courting," Valarie had replied a little put out, Derek had a habit of reminding her that she was old fashioned, that she didn't understand how people operated today.

"Aye, and look what happened to you!" joked Derek, putting his arm around her, and Valarie had allowed herself a rueful smile.

She sighed and reached again for the teapot, unable to see even a start to her cosy imaginings being brought into reality.

Valarie Lambert was conscious of being alone in her small immaculate flat in the middle of a city where her family were around her (her boys who she had suffered pain for and loved, a husband she had shared happiness with, sisters, nephews, nieces) but they all felt very far away, these people were circling around her, but out of reach like moons around a planet. She sighed. *'This will not do, Valarie'* she thought, sitting upright in her chair, *'you can't mope around like this all day.'*

An idea struck her. She would make today different. It already felt a bit peculiar, what with the bird, the inconsiderate weather and seeing her mother on the wall, so she would make it even more unusual. She would break from her Friday routine of catching the bus to Portobello and doing her grocery shopping, she would have a holiday, a bank holiday all to herself.

Instead of pouring the remaining tea into a cup, she reached up to the high cupboard, frowning at her shaking hand and lifted down the old red thermos. The white screw cap was browned with the tea of ages; picnics, the sea side, family walks up Arthur's Seat when the children were small, and then later on came with her to hospital trips, taking her father out for the day. Prison visits. Mrs Lambert knew that it was probably unhygienic and not keeping the heat as it used to, but the faded red pattern was now so intrinsic with her memories of happy times that she couldn't bring herself to part with it, besides who knew? Perhaps she might be using it in future outings, she would lift it out of the bag and Derek or Michael would exclaim in surprise, "I remember that flask! Look kids, we used to have this when I was little."

The thick tea slopped in as she filled it halfway and added milk. All these actions were out of the ordinary for a morning, and it suddenly added an air of festivity about it. With this thought in mind she added a rare heaped teaspoon of sugar, and closed it, trapping in the steam with the lid.

Pottering through to her bedroom again, she untied her dressing gown and chose from the wardrobe a bright skirt in a rich leafy green instead of her usual uniform of fitted dark trousers, the waistband of which now hung loose and shapeless on her thinned hips. Although the air felt temperate, she knew the sun would not be there to warm her so she added a knitted purple cashmere jumper, given to her by Derek one Christmas. She had hardly worn it because of its rich colour and, in Michael's words 'made her look like she lived in Morningside'. But it seemed fitting today, and she spent a moment stroking the soft wool and between thumb and forefinger.

Mrs Lambert slipped on her light summer coat and tied a spotted headscarf round her chin, she knew this would make her look older, but her hair had grown so thin lately that even at this time of year she felt the chill on her scalp. She collected the thermos from the kitchen and slipped it into her black shopping bag, together with a packet of digestives. She thought of the small bottle of blue pills in the bathroom cupboard, normally she wouldn't leave the house without them, but today they could sit there and she didn't pause as she opened the front door, stepped carefully down the dark cold steps of the tenement, outside onto the pavement and into the day.

To her surprise and joy, a shaft of sunlight had wriggled its way through the heavy, leaden mass of cloud, causing it to break up. The renegade rays of light caught themselves on car windscreens and criss-crossed onto the cracked pavement. As she turned onto London road, the wind snatched at her breath, Valarie Lambert smiled to herself and turned her chin up to the sky, inhaling the morning air; ignoring the traffic fumes.

She strode on with as much strength as she could muster, ignoring the stab in her gut and the urge to walk with her newly acquired stoop (she'd stood aghast at her reflection in a shop window recently, bewildered at how old she looked). The breeze ruffled her thin whiffs of hair—baby curls almost, and her footsteps collected in their number. Valarie could feel them wanting to dance into a skip, she looked down and was surprised to still see her old legs; fully expecting to see a pair of girlish plump ones in embroidered white socks, with patent leather shoes and bows. Shoes that encased feet which had trotted all the paths of Edinburgh in their time—in and out of different houses, shops, fetching messages or to meet other small tripping feet that ran and scattered and leapt. Today, on this uncommonly warm and thick grey morning, she could been any age, sixteen or six and as she came to a crossroads, her head flicked back and forth to check for cars, her eyes suddenly quick and sure, but crossing over to the traffic island she stopped short. Where exactly was she going?

She looked down at the plump brass pigeons that lived there on the concrete, and were now motionlessly cooing round her ankles.

"Well?" she asked them aloud, "Where am I off to?"

It was out of character for Mrs Lambert to speak to the brass pigeons, or anything else which was inanimate for that matter, the pigeons themselves, said nothing, their solid blue-gold wings unruffled, their clawless feet locked into the pavement.

The rays of sun had multiplied while she had walked and she peered at them from under her hand, her clear blue eyes blinking against the glare. The sun would do, she thought, it wouldn't make it to a summers day, but it would do for now.

The line of her vision rose, above Blenheim Place, up past the flats on top of the pet shop and the restaurant on the corner, (presently in the incarnation of an American diner, doubtlessly closing in a few months time as none of the restaurants which opened there managed to stay open for long) and onto the mounded top of Calton Hill. Her eyes narrowed and danced. Yes, there would do nicely, she hadn't been up there for years. Once upon a time she would have hiked up the Crags and Arthur's seat in an afternoon, and all the way home in time for tea; but now, she had to admit—at her age, and with the type of pills she had in her bedside table—Arthur's smaller brother was more her size.

Decided, she left the pigeons and set off from the curb. The early bird cars had been joined by a few others, scuttling round the corners in the morning light, but they were still few enough to not cause her a nuisance.

She crossed the road and started up Royal Terrace, admiring the quiet dignity of the street, it seemed as though she had left the working side of the street, away from the dirty uncouth streets of Leith, up to the more civilised roads of her own area- and now she was entering the other end of the scale entirely—here were houses which were very grand to look at, but Valarie Lambert would have never felt comfortable living in. She inwardly sighed at a particularly large house, whose pale green curtains she thought so elegant, *'Yes, but think of the heating'*, she thought *'and the dusting would take forever.'*

She came to the fork in the road that led to the base of the wide steps up to Calton Hill. A large holly tree stood in front of her, its roots scattered with litter and Mrs Lambert tutted at the sight of it; beer cans, cigarette ends and to her absolute disgust, plastic puddles of contraceptives which lay like pink transparent snake skins, discarded by their temporary owners. *'Really,'* she thought indignantly, *'Why would anyone want to do it here?'* she shuddered at the sheer thought of it, young people; boys and girls really, fumbling, panting and shivering in the cold air, getting pricked by the holly thorns and if anyone in the grand houses happened to twitch open their curtains...but in this day and age, and how young people seemed to be these days they probably wouldn't care. She sighed to herself, teenagers seemed another race to her. She saw them huddled in their groups, around bins or outside the supermarkets and she couldn't help but feel nervous. There was a time when the boys were that age and she had felt motherly towards all of them, looking fondly at their strange clothes and still remembering what it was to be young. But now, with her body becoming slower and frailer, she felt intimidated by them, their fresh faces now looked cruel, they were the race who were replacing hers, and she couldn't feel any warmth towards them.

Mrs Lambert was now halfway up the wide shallow steps and although they were not steep, she had already stopped twice to catch her breath. The sun had come out properly now, chasing away the last of the clouds, and she could see patches of blue in between. How lovely, she thought, that on this day, a day out of the ordinary, the sun had come out after weeks of grey sweaty skies. It would be bright and clear when she reached the top and make the view all the more spectacular.

Thinking briefly that maybe it had been a bit silly to leave her bottle of blue pills in the house, Mrs Lambert slowed her pace, and steadily made her way to the top.

Emerging onto the path of the hill, the breeze welcomed her, warm and playful. She untied her headscarf and felt the air rush through her thin curls. She smiled to herself as she rounded the corner and took in the view—it really was a glorious sight—probably better than the one at the top of Arthur's seat, she thought, as you could make out more of the detail, all those windows and bricks. Edinburgh spread out below her like a toy town—an intricate hobby of a dedicated model maker. To the left was the New Town, rows of orderly houses laid out in semi-circles and rectangles, in the middle Leith Walk, leading down to high rises and industrial wasteland, in the distance lay the Firth, steely grey and almost hidden in the clouds that hung over it, the sunshine having not made it to Portobello and Mussleburgh yet.

Valarie Lambert drank all this in, so pleased to have come out here this morning instead of the familiar rounds of weighing up vegetables in her hands and seeing the same things in the win- dows of the shops that were there the week before.

"Now," she said aloud to herself (this was much unlike her, but she didn't much care as there was no one around) "let's have the rest of that tea before it gets cold." She spotted a bench not far off, and walked slowly towards it, the pain in her side throbbed angrily. "All right all right, I'm going to sit down now," she told it.

Settling herself down, she brought out the thermos and poured herself a cup, the tea was still hot, and she sipped it down, glad of the warmth it brought to her. She breathed in the sunshine again and shut her eyes so that the rays could beat down on her face.

"Mind if I sit here?" Mrs Lambert's eyes snapped open, she hadn't thought there was anyone else around and her heart leapt at the voice, had they heard her wittering away to herself? If they had they would think she was mad, an old mad lady who wandered the streets…

It was a girl looking down at her, the sun was behind her head so Mrs Lambert couldn't quite make out her features. She shielded her eyes from the glare, at the same time automatically gestured to the girl to sit down.

Now she could see that the girl was more of a woman and she wasn't dressed well—in tracksuit bottoms and an old anorak. Beside her was a pram, and Valarie Lambert couldn't resist a peek inside. The baby looked very young, wrapped up in blankets and one of those zip up cover things. She could see now that it must be a girl as she had a pink fleecy hat on which nearly covered her eyes.

The mother (for Valarie supposed this is who she must be) sat down on the bench with a sigh. She looked tired, and Valarie remembered that feeling well. The woman fumbled in her pockets and drew out a packet of cigarettes, taking one out and angling the pram away from her, cupped her hand around it and lit up. Valarie Lambert inwardly tutted, she had never liked smoking and although Michael, and the two Dereks had all smoked (although Derek Junior had since given up) she had always made her disapproval known. The sight of young mothers, and even expect- ant ones puffing away had always filled her with a irritation and a certain sadness. Of course it happened all the time when she was young—but no one had known about the dangers then, but she had always hated when people smoked around the kiddies. She could only hope that whoever the mother of her grandchildren turned out to be, she would have the good sense not to smoke. Still, she thought, such a shame to get worked up on such a lovely day, and ignoring the wafts of smoke which occasionally drifted over her, she once again turned her attention to the view.

224

"Marvellous, isn't it?" she said, feeling the need to share her contentment.

"Aye," said the girl a little ruefully, "nice and quiet at this time."

"Have you been up long?" Mrs Lambert asked, gesturing to the baby. The girl raised her eyebrows so as to stretch her tired eyes.

"Since about half-four."

Valarie chuckled, "Oh, I remember those times," she smiled indulgently, "the whole house awake by five—almost nodding off on the bus sometimes."

"Aye, well I'll be glad when these times come to an end to tell the truth," the girl replied, unsmiling, "sleep deprivation could be used as weapon like, you feel like you're going mad half the time." "Don't worry," Mrs Lambert said cheerily, "you're young, you'll get over it and when you get to my age you don't have the excuse of a baby when you start forgetting things and dropping off in the afternoons."

In spite of herself, and her worries, the girl smiled. She took another draw of her cigarette, Mrs Lambert looked at the smoking tip, the tiny coal fire smouldering its path towards the girl's mouth. It really was a strange habit, but there had to be something in it for people to take it up so much. She thought of all the glamorous film stars in her youth, blowing sexual smoke and allure into their co-stars' faces who didn't seem to mind. Without thinking what she was doing and asked, "I know you'll think this strange, but I'm having quite an odd day myself " she laughed " I wondered if I could possibly try a puff of your cigarette?"

This took the girl by surprise so much that she silently held out the burning stick towards Valarie, baffled into obliging. "Be my guest. I should give up as it is," she said as she watched Mrs Lambert take it in inexpert fingers which shook a little as she raised it to her mouth and took a minute puff. She coughed slightly and the smoke came out in short puffy clouds instead of a long plume. The girl laughed.

"Well, what do you think?"

"Absolutely disgusting," Mrs Lambert choked, handing the cigarette back and smiling, "why would you want to take it up?"

"I've no idea," shrugged the girl, "but you've got the right one by never starting."

"I'll stick to my tea, thank you—would you like some?"

"Aye, go on then," the girl took the small cup that acted as a lid for the thermos and sipped once, twice at the cooling liquid. They sat in silence for a while, sipping and smoking, the warm wind blowing around their faces as they surveyed the city in morning. There was a gurgle from the pram and the girl stubbed out her cigarette under her foot.

"Well, that's peace and quiet done with," she said and went over to take the baby out.

"Oh she's lovely," said Valarie, trying to catch a glimpse of the baby's face. The mother pulled the hat back on her head and she could see now that the baby had tufts of black hair escaping from under the pink fleece. Her eyes were dark too, and large as they took in the sight of Valarie on the bench. The girl sat down with her on her lap and the baby stared at Valarie.

"Hello," Valarie said, her heart -warming at the sight of the tiny hands that now rubbed the eyes as the baby let out a huge yawn. She loved babies, she really did, and this one was exceptionally beautiful. "Ah, she really is lovely," she said again. "Reminds me of my boys when they were small."

"Aye, well, she has her moments," said the mother, used as she was to her daughter stunning strangers.

"Don't they all though," agreed Mrs Lambert, "But they wouldn't be normal if they didn't, and you'll look back to cherish them," she smiled at the baby again who in turn stared at her, unblinking.

"Hello sweetheart—hello!" Valarie put out a finger at the baby's hand, the baby watched it suspiciously, and then suddenly looked up at Valarie and smiled. Both she and the mother laughed. "Well, you're honoured like," said the mother. "She won't do that to many people first off."

"What's her name?"

"Mary," said the mother, at the same time getting up from the bench and putting the baby down in the pram, "and we've got to get going, say bye-bye, Mary."

Valarie almost asked where they were going, and could she come along too, but she thought it might scare the girl off. But she would have so much liked if they could stay a little longer, Mary was still grinning at her from ear to ear.

"Well bye-bye Mary," she said sadly, "perhaps I'll see you up here again," and she waved a hand.

"Bye-bye," said the girl, answering for her daughter and bending over her as she started pushing the buggy. "You might well see us, we come up here quite a lot when I can manage that hill," and they turned and walked down the path. Mrs Lambert looked on as the buggy disappeared out of sight.

She sighed heavily to herself. That was a nice thing to have happened, and she was sure that she might see them again. Maybe she should come up here a lot more, it had been such a pleasant morning and what with seeing a beautiful baby who had smiled at her so naturally, it had really made her day. But then, she thought, maybe if she came up here frequently it wouldn't be as special...of course if there was a baby in her life on a regular basis, everyday would have this joyous feeling—because she could see now that it wasn't so much the sunshine or the novelty of being somewhere else, but the baby—Mary, who had really lifted her heart. Oh if only the boys would...

But they hadn't, and maybe they never would meet someone settle down and have children, and Mrs Lambert would always be looking at other people's children, building her dreams on them.

Mrs Lambert sat on the bench for another half-hour, until the remaining tea in the thermos had grown cold. Gradually the pain in her side wormed its way through the happiness in her head and completely blotted it out, forcing her to feel nothing else. She endured two more minutes of agony, the pain blinded her.

And then it was just Mrs Lambert's body that sat on the bench on top of Calton Hill. It sat there for until two strangers who had never met her when she was alive, approached her body to see if Mrs Valarie Lambert was still in there, but she had disappeared. The woman's grip on the small girl's hand tightened and the child knew she was witnessing something out of the ordinary. She licked the ice cream thoughtfully and looked at the woman who looked like she was sleeping, thin hair escaping from the silk headscarf.

"Is she sleeping, Debbie?" the girl asked the woman, her small face wrinkled into a frown as she contemplated the still figure on the bench. She licked the raspberry ripple cone again, the pink fairy wings strapped to her thin back flapping in the breeze.

The older woman looked carefully, "I think so," she said slowly, knowing at the same time it was a lie, but she felt couldn't tell the truth to this child, not yet.

"Come on, let's go, we don't want to wake her up," she said as casually as she could, at the same time cocking her head to one side and taking another look at the dead (yes, she was dead, there was no doubt about it, Debbie had seen a few dead people in her time, and the woman in front of her was definitely not of this world any more) but at the same time, there was something familiar about her face, maybe it was a trick of the wind. It was hard to tell how the features looked when pumped full of life, the eyes open, the mouth speaking…she pulled at the child's hand.

"Come on, there's plenty more to see."

And they walked off down the hill into the morning sunshine. Mrs Lambert's eyes were still looking over the multitude of houses, surveying the scurrying population of the city and the grey steely light reflected onto the Firth. Looking but not seeing.

11

Today, I'm awake before the buzzer. I silently praise myself; it feels obscene to be woken up by something so unnatural as that loud jarring BZZZZ. I've asked them to change it, or at least to turn it down, but they said, "But you might not hear it, Bob."

Of course I'll bloody hear it.

It's not like there's anyone else living here, making a noise.

I can't see the time but it can't be that early, as there's strong light coming in through the curtains, I can see the shadow of the ivy on the ledge, the leaves outlined clearly.

I might paint that.

I'll get her to take a photo—to get the light right… just as it is now.

Mind you, she'd have to be here earlier to get it at this time of day, the sun only comes through this room in the mornings, any later and the shadows won't be as sharp.

She wouldn't do it though, she wouldn't get here any earlier than she has to—and she'd make that face of hers—that confused yet patronising look she gets on, when I ask her something like that.

"Isn't there anything else you want to paint?"

Like the time I asked her to go out and get me some Cobalt Blue, and she came back with Royal Blue.

"It's pretty much the same, isn't it?" No Debbie, it's not. Don't get me wrong—the woman means well, but in another life we'd have never have crossed paths. Intellectually she's retarded. Her idea of sophistication is to go and see a film of *Pride and Prejudice*—

"How do you think they kept all their dresses so white? They always seem to be traipsing through mud."

Or to read a Dave Pelzer.

"Shocking Bob, but it had me gripped, truthfully it did."

I like to think I've educated her in some respects— shown her that wine varieties go beyond Chardonnay; that not all classical music 'sounds the same' and that there's more to life than *X Factor*. This is what I mean when I say to them that you can't just push two people together when they're so different, but then they put on that tone, and those eyes and say, "Now Bob, we all can't be from such an educated background as you." 'Educated' meaning 'middle class', which is what it all boils down to. I suppose they wonder how I ended up here; in sheltered housing, instead of a private place somewhere; and I would have, had not all my inheritance gone on medical bills instead of paying for a decent place.

I only wish I'd have stayed in Italy; they know how to respect their elders over there, keep everyone close… the sunshine, the food…the galleries. Everyone knows their history over there too, they know their culture, their artists—even the poorer folk can chat to you about Bellini or Caravaggio…at least they take an interest in it—there's a dignity in the lower classes; a culture all of their own, a finesse even. It's not like over here. Scotland's working classes are themselves an excuse for the state this whole nation is in...they seem to take *pride* in being messed up, living on the poverty line, breeding like rabbits...they think the world owes them a living... no self -respect.

And here I am, bang in the middle of the most 'deprived' areas of Edinburgh (for 'deprived', read destitute, uneducated and obnoxious) with no real money, no hope and not even a patch of green grass to look at or call my own. There isn't even a beauty in the rawness of the urban landscape...it's just ugly—the people, the place, the life.

There's no light in the eyes of the workers here, there's no love of anything—no excitement, no real *care* forthcoming (how I hate that word, sticky and glutinous as marshmallow).

I've never met a care worker who pronounces their 'aitches yet.

I wonder what the time is now. That ivy shadow is pretty much gone; it's blurred into the curtain.

Waiting for the buzzer to rupture the peace is actually worse than being woken by it. It's the first sound I'll hear; the first of the two curtains that frame the day.

BZZZZZZ.

And then we follow our stage directions.

Sometimes I'll picture her outside, stomping her feet if it's cold, hands dug deep inside the fraying pockets of her stained old coat. Fat cheeks puffing.

If it's summer, she'll be sweating, wearing one those strappy tops and I'll have to put up with the sight of the flapping rolls of fat at the tops of her arms and her trousers. Sometimes when she leans in close, to do up some buttons or hand me a cup, the smell of her turns my stomach—I can smell her cheap perfume or the faded mint of dying chewing gum to cover up stale fags or last night's dinner.

She'll ring the bell and there'll be an intervening minute while I get to the door, but in those few seconds I imagine us both having to compose ourselves for the inevitable meeting. I wonder how she feels in that short time, whether she's thinking the same things as me; that neither of us actually want to be here or see each other but I need her and she needs the money so here we are; and neither of us have a choice in the matter.

In my opinion, I don't think it's natural to be in another person's (especially the *same* person's) company every single day of your life. What I'd love is for a day when I could just stay in bed...watch a film; eating things that I can't afford. And be on my own.

All of which is impossible of course. *Someone* has to be here. They couldn't deal with it.

"No Bob."

Bob. It's never actually occurred to them to call me Robert, which is who I am. Was.

"No Bob," they'd say, "you have to look forward... you have to make the most of every day."

Well maybe I don't want to, maybe I'd like a day off, or at least a day off from her—it's always her, the woman just doesn't seem to get ill or take holidays—the only day she's taken off in the last three years was to go to have a tooth out…I don't think she has a social life, poor cow. Deep down I think I might be the only friend she's got, if you could call it a friendship, which I don't.

Just because you've known someone for years doesn't mean you have to be friends with them. Oh, we get on alright most of the time, but as I say, neither of us have a choice in the matter, I suppose if either of us had really objected to the other then she would have gone to someone else…but we didn't.

And now there's just a maintained indifference, and on the outside they probably think we now have a good rapport, but that doesn't make us close. She's not a friend, she's not family. I don't even pay her myself.

I don't know what she is.

I don't know where she is either…I'm sure it can't be that early.

We go through this pointless routine in the morning—when I eventually get to the door and press the intercom, and she says, "Hi-ya!" into it. Always the same. Never "Good Morning" or "Hello Robert, it's Debbie." No, it's always the cheery-don't-worry-I'm- here-now- "Hi-ya!" As if she's the cavalry, bounding up the hill.

She comes in, and there'll be a comment on the weather. "Ooh, it's cold again," or, "Ooh it's going to be another lovely day." I don't think she realises I have eyes, or windows.

And then, "How are you today?"

And I'll say, "Not bad, how are you, Debbie?"

And she'll say, "Still rocking and rolling Bob, still rocking and rolling."

Bloody idiotic, and she never says anything else. What I'd love is, for her one day to come out with, "Actually Robert, I'm bloody miserable and I'm sick of this job, I'm going to quit this week and move to Barbados," or something.

But she won't and she'll take her coat off and we'll go through to the living room, and then bang on cue it's...

"You had a cuppa yet?"

Of course I haven't, I've only just got out of bed, but this is my prompt to say, "No, not yet but I'd love one—would you like one yourself?"

"I wouldn't say no," she'll say, although usually she's halfway to the kettle already. And that's how the day (every day) begins.

We're governed by Boundaries. It's completely imbalanced. She's seen me in the most vulnerable states you can imagine—on the floor, trousers and pants round my ankles, piss trickling down one leg, or in the bath—with a bloody erection of all things (I don't even know what triggered that off, definitely nothing to do with her anyway) and she walked in and noticed at once, I had to stop myself from laughing as she blustered right out again mumbling something about leaving the cooker on...Maybe that was Boundaries again, and that's the point I suppose—she wasn't even allowed to laugh about it with me.

Then again maybe she was just embarrassed.

I have no doubt that the whole incident is written down on file somewhere, together with the Unspoken Rules of not discussing religion, politics or sex.

She knows my body better than any lover, but she got a nurse's touch, rough and practical; fingers that are used to skin, it's just another work material, like the mop or a J-cloth. We can't talk about bodies unless it's in a practical way; for instance I can mention that I've got a sore shoulder, but I can't say what would really help would be the firm yet soft warm massage from a pair of woman's hands. I can't say that because she'll think I mean hers (which I certainly don't), I would mean long slender fingers and a gentle assured touch, not plump clammy ones which spend half their time in a sink or with a lit Benson and Hedges in between them staining the skin jaundice yellow.

It would be *inappropriate*. That's what they'd tell me. I no longer know what this word really means.

Where the bloody hell is she?

I could get up I suppose…my dressing gown should be near the chair so I could get it…I'll want it on.

Oh, there's the clock, on the floor.

I can't hear it ticking. I think it's stopped.

So I wouldn't know the time even if I could see the face. What's today?

Thursday.

Oh God, it's Centre day.

With that prat…Dennis…Damien or Daniel or whatever his name is.

Tries to be 'matey'. Always asking me questions even when I'm not in a conversation, I just happen to be sitting there.

Has obviously got a degree in 'Helping The Needy' although 'Blind Leading The Blind' is probably more appropriate.

Of course, she loves it...blushes whenever he's around. Starts up her chummy act with me—laughing, joking and looking for all the world that we're more friends than client and care worker, which, in the happy-clappy world of Darren or Deirdre or whoever, is *how it should be.*

He's got that needs-mothering look. Never clean-shaven, clothes un-ironed. Thinner than he should be... Doesn't eat meat apparently...or cheese, or eggs.

Just eats happy souls.

Bloody Centre. Mind you if *she is* running late then we might miss the bus.

You just take your time, Debbie. I don't mind lying here a bit if it spares me that.

I don't know why I said I'd go...I thought they might have access to some decent oils...but it turns out they've got a few dried up watercolours and that's it. Still, I suppose it breaks up the week.

And there's Nancy; one of the workers there, she takes the floristry class, if you can call it that. Beautiful smile, hair you want to run your fingers through. I tell Debbie I don't really need her around when Nancy's in, and she clears off to the café. I don't want her sitting next to me like all the others—'Helping', i.e. 'doing it all'…my hands shake but they can still stick a rose in a brick of oasis.

She hasn't got a ring on her finger, Nancy. You'd think a stunning girl like that must have someone at home. Maybe she takes it off for work. I think it's because Nancy looks like her…the first *her*, not Debbie. (Nothing like Debbie). The one she took over from. Same kind of hair. She used to wear it up though, whereas Nancy wears it loose, so that it sweeps her face when she bends down.

Miranda.

I loved saying it. Miranda. The name rolling around your mouth like a good wine.

'Oh brave new world! That have such people in it!' *She* knew what I was on about, when I said that.

Didn't buy the bloody *Sun* for starters. She understood. She understood a lot of things. Good clothes, casual, but very well cut. Miranda kept herself nice, kept herself beautiful in fact. She was Italian, so you'd expect it. Studying Art History, so they thought of me apparently.

Could cook too, which doesn't happen a lot in this line of work; the limit being sloppy cottage pie or oven chips.

Said her grandmother taught her. I put on weight in the few months she was with me, I ate everything on the plate. Perfect Lasagne. Delectable Fish. Puddings to die for.

Nowadays most of the stuff comes from the freezer because Debbie Doesn't Have The Time. Miranda found the time.

She didn't run off the minute the clock strikes nine like bloody Cinderella.

Because that's the second sound. The sound that signals the closing of the theatre curtain and the end of that day's act is the'click' of the door when Debbie leaves. Sometimes it never seems to come. We both take turns in looking surreptitiously at the clock. Whole hours can go by without us barely speaking a word, but that's one thing I do appreciate Debbie for; she knows herself with something and by the time she's come back through, I've turned the TV on, and then we can talk through that; Television; the care worker's friend and ally. When a few hours have got to be killed, it's the perfect solution; it brings two strangers together through the medium of falsity…or fantasy.

Come about five to nine, she'll get up from the armchair stretch theatrically and look at her watch, (this is all for my benefit; I know she's been looking at the clock with squirrel-like glances for the last two hours).

"Right then Bob, that's about me, I should think," she'll say. Daft expression. What's about her?

Sometimes, if she's on the ball, she'll offer to get me a cup of tea before she goes, but mostly she'll want to be out as soon as that second hand hits the twelve. She'll make the I'm-going-now' movements and makes getting-ready-to leave noises. I know she's been taught to do this;

"Let them know that you're about to go," they'd have said to her, "Don't just leave abruptly, but make sure they know that you're going to leave soon."

Sometimes it will come as a surprise, because we're actually in mid-conversation about something. We can have a joke together I suppose—she affords me to poke fun at her sometimes, and I suppose this is us 'getting on', 'having a connection'.

The thing is that I forget the conversations as soon as she's gone. Small words that emerge from our mouths and then as quickly, get lost.

I wonder if she remembers them at all.

"I'll see you tomorrow Bob, bright and early," at which point

I'll groan and say,

"Not too early though!"

She'll laugh and exit the room and the house. The click of the door comes and at once the silence descends, even if the TV's blaring. Maybe it's because she takes up so much room that there's a void when she leaves. Her big grating laugh hangs in the air, and then melts into the furniture. Sometimes I heave a sigh of relief. I sink into myself and deflate. I feel so puffed up with superficiality that my skin feels tight with it.

I can never just be myself. If I'm anything but cheerful, someone will want to know why. She's not herself with me and I try to imagine what she is like, away from me. Away from work.

Maybe she's got someone. She never talks about anyone though and I don't know of any family nearby.

She's still not here. And I haven't heard the phone.

Thing is, she's never been off so I don't know if she'll ring. The last time this happened, it was Miranda who didn't show up, two hours I had to wait, before someone rang. Three hours before someone came. And yes, I can make a cup of tea for myself but that's not the point is it? They should be here at 8.30 and if they're not, someone else should be. They knew Miranda wasn't turning up though, but the girl who was supposed to come in instead had called in sick.

They didn't tell me Miranda wasn't coming in. But when they eventually did, that afternoon—after I'd shouted at the daft young one they'd got in when she messed up my breakfast, it was like an interrogation. Did I know why Miranda had suddenly handed in her notice? Did I know if anything had upset her? And I know what they were asking. Had I been *inappropriate* again?

I didn't say a word.

But that's what I could do with now. Bath time with Miranda. With her gentle, pitying eyes—no, 'pitying' is the wrong word, they were sorry for me, but also kind. She understood how I was a man, before the accident, and now.

Not like those other cretins.

She saw that I had *known* things...I had *known* women.

She was Mediterranean, that's the difference. Not like these podgy, frigid old women.

We never talked about it, it wasn't like that, and it was anything but sordid. She knew. It was more tender than anything I'd experienced when I was able-bodied and capable.

There's the phone.

They know I can't get to it quick enough. They'll leave a message. It'll be about Debbie not being able to come in.

Well, today will be different at any rate, but it's a long time until the *click* of the door closing tonight. A lot of hours to live through, and then I'll only be in the same position tonight.

When I'm lying in bed I see my wheelchair at the side of the bed, and the streetlights outside shaft through the curtains and hit the metal, making it gleam. The chair looks bereft without a body. It's a mask.

I wonder what's happened to Debbie. I hope she's alright.

12 (PART ONE)

She'd always said that she'd never *meant* to take the girl (besides, it wasn't technically *taking,* the girl had come with her quite willingly).

It wasn't something she'd set out to do that day, not something she'd *ever* meant to do come to that.

What *did* she set out to do in a day? Get through it mostly. Work through the hours, wish the clock to tick faster, the meals to be eaten quicker, wait for the sun to set, the shadows to grow, the light to fade…Days were simply lived through; tolerated. Where did Debbie's days go? Did they ever mean anything? Debbie had to admit that they didn't.

Debbie liked the telly. She knew it wasn't the in thing to enjoy television these days. She also knew she should be doing something slightly more useful with her time; like reading a book or a magazine even. But at the end of the day, she would come home, unlock the door, put on her slippers and the kettle, and slump onto the sofa in front of the ubiquitous box until Deek came in from work, which was when she'd get the tea on.

She told herself that in her line of work television was an important tool to be acquainted with; to know what was going on in the soaps or who had been kicked out of Big Brother could be a real conversation point. She watched a lot of it at work, depending on the client (was that the term she was to use now—Client? Or was it

Service User? She could never remember, it changed so regularly) and she usually had the TV on when she was at home, the glowing frame was a friend in the corner, it spoke to her more than Deek sometimes did anyway.

Television charted the seasons and this was especially what Debbie liked about it. It made her feel cosy and settled, watching the seasons drift in and out of the virtual world. Spring would bring in yellow and green continuity pictures, adverts for chocolate eggs and daffodil dresses, pictures of couples running about bare foot, as if it were ever warm enough in March for that. Richard and Judy would be chatting about the bright green in the trees and the warmth that they had felt on their way to work; how winter was properly over. Or when Autumn came, Judy would be wearing a nice thickly knitted jersey dress which looked soft and snug, and Phil would be making some chunky wintry stew. Debbie would return home in the dark, although it was only 4 o' clock, and look forward to settling down to a good detective drama; *Inspector Morse* or *Midsomer Murders*. There was something extremely comforting about a murder mystery; no real suspense, cardboard cut-out characters but the plot was all nicely sewn up at the end, leaving Debbie satisfied and entertained.

It was only the height of summer that took Debbie away from the small black box (although it had now progressed to a large silver flat screen, thanks to Deek's 'connections in the electrical business') and into the bright hot square of her small patio. There she would sit, slowly baking herself next to the dried and withered honeysuckle, shielding her eyes to read *TV Quick* (although it was too fine to stay indoors and watch television, Debbie would still catch up on her soaps, read the spoilers to see what would happen in a month's time and the reviews of programmes she had missed, imagining if they would have been worth watching).

But mostly, throughout the year, Debbie was there, a companion to the television and the avid viewer all the way. She agreed with the Expert Designers when they told her that this room was really *far* too small for this type of wallpaper. She felt all the excitement of the business plan really *working* and yes, it was the right idea to go with.

Christmas on television was a lavish affair, and it was then that Debbie wished she had a real log fire instead of the burning electric bars that either singed her knees or failed to give out any heat at all. She also wished it snowed properly in Edinburgh, snow was everywhere at Christmas in television land, it came down when lovers where reunited, when a case got solved, when the aliens left the planet. And the food too, recipes for Mince Pie With A Twist sprang competitively out of celebrity chef 's programmes, Nigella wore her rich red cashmere and licked her fingers delicately, a sprig of holly sparkled in the candlelight, and that—that *was* Christmas for Debbie. All her favourite films were on, and she thought wistfully that if she ever *had* had children, when they were grown up and she was dead and gone, they would see that *Mary Poppins* or *An Officer And A Gentleman* was on that Christmas and they would sigh sadly and watch it in memory of her, dabbing their eyes and explaining to their own children, "My mother used to love this film." The only trouble that Debbie had with television was that she wasn't part of it. Either in the tidy fictional worlds (although people did tend to get murdered, albeit in a safe, bloodless high-tea kind of a way) or presenting the shows that existed outside time and circumstance. She imagined the lives of the presenters as easy; surely they only worked a few hours a day, and what did that work consist of? Chatting cheerily to folk, nodding sympathetically with the public's tales of injustices and poking fun at celebrity's ordinariness. Debbie knew she couldn't have done it herself, but it did seem an easy life with lots of money involved. They probably had holidays all the time, had nice meals out and got their Christmas shopping done early because they didn't have to worry what it was costing them.

She didn't want excitement, that wasn't it, there was no way she would exchange lives with Tiffany out of *EastEnders* or a clever detective who used unconventional methods to get results. In her own way she'd probably had enough 'excitement' if that's what falling in love with a married man amounted to. If her and Deek's relationship were on television, there would be scenes of unbridled passion—they would have been unable to control themselves, up against grand pianos or wall-to-wall fitted kitchens, there would be long tearful scenes of them both looking into each other's eyes with yearning and Deek's wife would have been a cruel cold-hearted bitch.

In reality of course there was none of this—maybe a bit of lust when they first met (mainly in the office stock cupboard) but not really yearning—just a lot of pain and guilt for Debbie, because much as she liked to imagine that Deek's wife deserved to lose her husband (she obviously didn't care about Deek anymore and had stopped sleeping with him years ago) Debbie didn't particularly want to be the one who took him away. She hadn't been born to be the scarlet woman and she had hated all the secrecy and scurrying around. It seemed like a huge amount of energy for something which, after years of thinking she wanted, Debbie was now unsure of. But there was no way she and Deek could break up now, not after everything he had given up for her.

There was an instance in Debbie's life that had stayed with her for many years. It was not disturbing or sad, but it marked itself onto her memory as a signpost or at least a clue on a map that might lead to somewhere called 'X'.

She had been walking down the country lane down from the house where she had lived with her mother (this was when they still lived outside Carlisle) and a long blue shiny car pulled up beside her. An old-fashioned car—one that you might see on *Poirot*—or what Jeremy Clarkson would call 'a true classic.' It was a car for getting married in or winning a prize to sit in, not just for driving down a quiet road on a Tuesday morning. It stopped beside Debbie who immediately felt self-conscious; not just because of the shine on the car but the sight of her reflection in the window (hair dishevelled, mud spattered mack, peppered with dog hair). The window buzzed down (it didn't wind, it was too smooth for that) and a man with white hair and a

250

moustache poked his head out. He looked like a General, or what Debbie imagined a General to look like—like they did in the black and white films her father used to watch on a Sunday night. The hand that rested on the window wore leather driving gloves and gold cufflinks. The man's blazer matched the colour of the car.

"Can I give you a lift somewhere?" It was a voice from the *Antiques Roadshow*

It was beginning to spot with rain and Debbie felt a flick of cold on her cheek. She looked to the sky that was brooding over. "Erm…" she hesitated and glanced at the man in the car, he looked harmless enough, healthy and wholesome, well fed.

"I only ask as it's filthy weather, or soon will be!" he chuckled cheerfully, "you've still got a way to go before you get to town my dear," the man looked genuinely concerned for her. Debbie could see his age in his hands, a frailty in the thin skin. If he turned funny she could easily escape she thought, and the car probably didn't go that fast anyway. The rain increased in speed, speckling her mackintosh.

"Alright then, yes please," she smiled, but then glanced down at herself. "I'm a bit muddy though."

"Oh don't worry about that," the man flapped his hand at her dismissively,

"Come on, jump in."

She got in beside him. She could feel clods of mud fall from her boots onto the floor. She could see her face in the wooden dashboard, it was that polished. When they drove off, the engine purred like a contented cat.

"Where are you off to?" He had a confident voice, well-spoken as she'd expected and without a trace of the local accent. Even if Debbie had seen him without the car, she would have known that he was rich. He was relaxed and self-assured. It was Debbie's opinion that people who already had a built-in advantage such as money or good looks seemed to sail a lot smoother through life, they already had their Get Out Of Jail Free card.

As they glided down the winding lanes Debbie thought of *My Fair Lady*, and *Annie*, even *The Little Match Girl* and all the films where poor malnourished (well, at fifteen stone she couldn't really argue that) girls were picked up and swept away by richer older men. Maybe this was her Old Wealthy Gentleman.

She told him, "I've got to go the chemists for my mam." "Right you are," he replied peering at the road through the pelting droplets of rain. "I'm going into the centre so I'll drop you off there. We've run low on pears and cheese so I'm going to that new little deli on the corner, do you know it? Lovely little place—do some great stuff, my wife and I have a weakness for the goats cheese with peppercorns…We've got people coming round and she discovered this morning that we're completely out of the stilton and the one pear that's left is too soft, so I said I'd pootle down to the town…good excuse to get out I suppose, though I didn't count on this rain."

"Yes," she said, and smiled. Listening to him, she couldn't believe that people like this existed, and yet at the same time she knew that she desperately wanted to be like him—or to even *be* him. For the fifteen minutes she was in the car, she pretended to herself that she knew him, that she was his daughter or a friend, and they were just pootling down to the town to buy some pears and cheese because they had people coming round and the only pear left was too soft. Maybe they'd stop somewhere for a coffee and a pastry. She'd have a large cappuccino with lots of chocolate sprinkled on top, and an apricot Danish. They'd sit outside and the rain would stop to let the sun came out. They would sit there as long as they liked and watch the rest of the town stroll, hurry and walk on by. Debbie wanted so much to go home with him to wherever he lived, to have a nice lunch and eat pears and cheese with cloth napkins and heavy cutlery. To have a tablecloth, look out the huge garden through the French doors and drink wine, because they'd definitely have wine with their meal.

She wanted his life. She wanted her days to consist of a journey into town, of sitting in the garden, reading newspapers and books and looking at the sunset (even though she didn't read books and she very much doubted that this man would read either *The Sun* or *Bella*). But she wanted every day to be that simple, to be able to keep all her free time to herself, and not have to sell it to Scarborough House Retirement Home where she worked, or give it away for free when looking after her mother who was slowly dying of cancer in her small stuffy room. She didn't even know what she'd do with the time if she had it; squander it probably, but at least she would have the option of squandering it—pootling into town to pick up pears and cheese.

The man dropped her off at the chemists, and she watched him drive away as the rain came down even heavier, sticking her hair to her forehead and Debbie could feel it drip down the back of her neck, and soak in where her jacket was ripped at the elbow.

She never forgot him, or his car and his simple, wealthy life. She sometimes daydreamed that the man would end up at Scarborough House and she would become his main carer, because he remembered her from the time he had picked her up in his car. They would become good friends and then when he died he would leave his whole estate to her (his wife and all other family having disappeared of course). But as small as the area was, she never saw him or the sleek blue car again.

Years later and Debbie now found herself living in a small two-up two-down in the newer part of Niddrie Mains road in Craigmillar, on the outskirts of Edinburgh. From where she and Deek lived she could see a castle. Not *the* castle (Edinburgh Castle disappointed some tourists because it didn't really look like a castle, not with turrets, ramparts and a portcullis) but this castle—Craigmillar castle- actually looked more like a castle should do. When she looked out of the window at the view of the crumbling towers of another century, she imagined a life somewhere else. Not that she was *very* unhappy here, but it wasn't the life she had hoped for or dreamt of, she knew that much.

She'd come to Scotland on a whim. When her mother had finally died, Debbie had been left a small amount of money and the dilapidated wreck of the cottage. She promptly sold the house as she could still smell her mother's illness inside, wrapped around the very bricks. She recognised an opportunity to get out of Carlisle and had jumped out of it with both feet, although the jump was not to be very far as it turned out.

The Christmas after Mrs Bennett's death, Debbie had paid for herself and her cousin Michelle to go on a package trip to Edinburgh for New Year, or Hogmanay as the travel agent had termed it ("it's what they call it up there" she had explained to a baffled Debbie. 'Hogmanay' it sounded exotic—she could tell people that—a little fact she could come up with "oh yes, they don't say New Year, they say Hogmanay…").

The Travel Inn Debbie and Michelle stayed in on Pimlico Place, was nothing to write home about, and it rained for the majority of their stay but for Debbie, the city itself made up for it entirely. She felt like a little girl as she stared in wonder at the spectacle of Scotland's capital in all its finery; the Christmas lights draped around every vertical structure, the Salvation Army brass band; their instruments glinting, the castle lit up like a Disney film. There were lights strung up in the trees and from a distance the effect was a magical fairyland, outlines of branches spun out in sparkling dust.

They wandered round the German market on Princes Street, Debbie wished, not for the first time, that she had a small child in her life to buy some of the carved wooden toys for, the painted bright colours gleaming in the street lights. There were tiered candle carousels, decorated with scenes from fairy tales; Snow White chased the seven dwarves endlessly around a wooden roundabout, Red Riding Hood forever running from a wolf with wooden teeth. There were tin spinning tops like the type Debbie hadn't seen since childhood (and even then they had belonged to her mother), string puppets with real hair and wooden frogs which croaked when you rubbed their ridged back with a stick.

There were stalls of sticky toffee apples, slabs of German Stollen cake and large glistening gingerbread hearts, painted with white iced endearments to loved ones. The markets transported Debbie to another century of Christmas time, one of simple toys, candles on Christmas trees and children's faces glowing enchantingly.

She and Michelle drank over-priced hot mulled wine, not caring about how much it cost, wrapping their fingers cosily round the polystyrene cups. They watched the pink-cheeked ice skaters glide and spin down a temporary rink on Princes Street gardens, but neither Debbie or Michelle had the courage to try it for themselves.

Debbie was conscious that she was living a perfect day, one which wouldn't have looked out of place in a Christmas TV advert—it was exactly as television and magazines said it should be. In short, Debbie fell in love with Edinburgh, and come midnight, tipsy with wine and wedged in between a few other thousand people on Princes street, Debbie's heart swelled with excitement and she vowed to make this city her home—now that she could, she could live in this fairy-tale forever. The bells rang around her head and she found herself being lifted from the ground in a great bear hug by her large neighbour, a large ruddy Scotsman who shouted something incomprehensible at her, at the same time laughing heartily and kissing her wildly on both cheeks. Debbie flushed with pleasure, she didn't get attention like this a lot and it was the icing on the cake—everyone was so *happy* here, so welcoming; here she could make friends, maybe even find a special someone...

She and Michelle had caught the coach back home the next day, and the cloudy rosy vision of Edinburgh at midnight on New Years Eve stayed with Debbie the whole time she made preparations to move from Carlisle. She rang estate agents whose soft Scottish accents charmed her even more, before finally arriving off the train at Waverley Station with her family of luggage around her. She stepped onto the platform, caught a chill and an odd smell in the air and looked around excitedly.

The smell, which at first reminded Debbie of cat food, turned out to be the Caledonian Brewery. It was an odour which she never really grew used to; it was too rich, too savoury. And then there was the wind that permeated the city, whooping around the streets and hurtling across the bridges, it spun her down the streets, whipping her hair out of shape and giving her a permanent cold head. Her first weeks in the city were nerve-wracking, and more than once she casually wondered if she'd made the right decision to move.

But she pushed it to the back of her mind and got on with starting a new life for herself. She worked for two solid days on cleaning the tiny flat she had rented on Leith Walk; it was in a horrible state when she first got there; the only furniture being a stained mattress and a vast collection of cigarette butts. She only stopped to sip coffee and gaze out of the window to look down on the traffic and people below. Leith itself was another city entirely. The buildings, people shops and atmosphere were wholly different to the plush middle-class world of Edinburgh city centre. Leith was Edinburgh's poorer relative, one that sometimes embarrassed it at parties. Leith was unpredictable, it lacked the glossy sheen that Edinburgh liked to polish and show off to visitors—Leith didn't care what anyone thought, and it made Debbie nervous, she tended to turn left whenever she exited her flat, as to go right would mean a more prolonged experience of Leith Walk and its inhabitants, whereas left meant only a short sharp shock of Elm Row and its pubs until you met the civilised east end of Princes Street.

On the first night in her flat she lay in the darkness, eyes wide against the shouted foreign consonants in the street, the shattering splinters of broken glass, thuds in a nearby doorway. She looked out the next morning expecting to see a cracked road of chaos, but the street was quiet and docile and clear; the street cleaners having seen to the mess already like silent servants, so accustomed to papering over the parties of the nights before.

Slowly she got used to it, grew accustomed to city life and discovered, (as everyone did who moved somewhere new) that places become ordinary if lived in too long, they lose their shine and allure. Having woken up after five Hogmanays now, Debbie now saw Edinburgh as her home but had also stopped seeing the sights which had so seduced her on that first visit, ignoring the city sky- line, skipping over the castle—only stretching her eyes to see if it was her bus coming in the distance, or at the clouds to see if it was going to rain.

Work came about in the form of temping at the Scottish Widows' head office, covering a receptionist's maternity leave. Humdrum and unchallenging, but Debbie was glad of an income and a job where her workmates were quite willing to go to the pub after work, meaning she didn't have to find friends elsewhere; A social life and employment in one easy package.Shortly after Derek 'Deek' Lambert (Scottish Widows technician and handyman) had left his wife for her, Debbie had left the office, as she didn't think she could stand the gossip. She now worked as a Personal Assistant for a company who looked after disabled people in their own homes, it was a simple job really, and she liked most of the clients or service users or whatever they were. She got to drink a lot of tea, saunter around the shops and watch a lot of telly. The toilet and washing stuff, the 'personal care', didn't bother her as she had lost all her squeamishness while caring for her mother in her last weeks.

Scotland and the Scottish people were still a bit of a mystery to her, even though she had lived in a Scottish city for years, and was in a relationship with a born and bred Edinburgh man. If she was honest with herself she could admit that actually she was quite envious of the Scottish, with their generous drinking and patriotism. Whenever Hogmanay came round again (it never did match up to the first beguiling New Year which had so enticed Debbie) a small part of her felt like an intruder and that she wasn't supposed to be in Scotland, clinking dram glasses with Jackie Bird and the rest as the castle exploded into a shower of silver rain when the clock struck twelve.

When she had first arrived in Edinburgh, Debbie had imagined that she would start to go to the theatre, take in some art exhibitions and climb Arthur's Seat regularly on a Sunday afternoon before going home to a roast dinner and half a shandy at the local pub where everyone knew her name.

In reality, her only walk nowadays was the swift one from work back to her house, or from the chippy of an evening—striding quickly, not making eye contact with anyone until she got on a bus or to her front door. And she never did have the cosy afternoons of sitting on a tartan rug eating shortbread on a sunshined hill overlooking Auld Reekie. Deek preferred to either be in the pub on Sundays or sitting watching the football on one of the Sky channels. Debbie had given up trying to cook a roast lunch for him as she had wanted to do (she had visions of a *Darling Buds of May* type of meal with the extended family all about her; huge plates of glistening roast duck and chicken, mounds of steaming vegetables) the weather permanently glorious (in Scotland—who was she kidding, she would think grimly as she thudded a large potato into the microwave). Derek's sons never visited, and there didn't seem to be any other family around. Her old colleagues at the office—although cheery and ready for a drink after work, didn't seem to want to know her on the outside; real friendship apparently meant overtime for most of them.

For Debbie, Niddrie was worse than Leith. At least in Leith she had felt part of the city, part of the hustle and bustle and within reach of the aspiration of the New Town with its proper town houses. On buses she would catch glimpses through the large Georgian windows into rich red living rooms with open coal fires, walls of bookshelves and dimmed lampshades.

But Niddrie seemed disconnected with everything she loved about Edinburgh. There was no prettiness, no spectacular layering of buildings to gaze at on the sky-line. In Niddrie and Criagmillar you were thrust right into the twenty-first century street; a slum line of shops, half of which were boarded up, the other half you could bet in or eat chips. Debbie wouldn't have dared to go in any of the pubs, the most ramshackled of which had the ironic name of The White House.

She'd tried to live the Pears and Cheese cosy life. She'd made jam to no avail; the smart neat pots with their little gingham cloth tops stood in line in the cupboard, filled up with a slightly unset and untouched matter as Deek didn't like jam and Debbie herself only ate it at breakfast. She'd had a go at making her own patch- work quilt and it still lay unfinished and unravelling at the bottom of the bed. On her days off Debbie woke in the morning and tried to pretend that all her days were empty and her work days were something she did voluntarily, simply out of the goodness of her heart did she go and help Bob or Winnie or Pat—really she didn't have to work at all—it was just something to fill her days with.

But this morning Debbie had woken up with the sense that something wasn't quite right. Deek had snorted awake next to her and they both lay silently in bed, eyes open, listening to the traffic go this way and that, the local kids shouting their way to school, their mothers screaming and smoking after them. Deek looked over and seeing her eyes were open, crawled an exploratory hand onto and under her pyjama top.

"Awright, Debbie love…?"

Normally Debbie would have reached over and pressed her chest into him, but today this didn't feel right either. She ignored Deek and his hand, flung the duvet off her and sat up out of the bed. Deek tutted.

"Ahh, come on—be late for once in your life."

"It's not that," she said shortly and breathed deep, trying to figure out the strange make up of her mind. Deek pulled himself up.

"What's up then? Wrong time of the month?"

"Yeah, something like that," she muttered, pulling on a threadbare towelling dressing gown, and stomping down the hall- way to make a cup of tea.

Twenty minutes later, Deek had stumbled out of the house on his way to work, his first cigarette of the day trailing itself out after him, and Debbie was back on her bed, still in her dressing gown, wondering whether she could think of a good enough excuse not to go into work. It was Bob today, and the way she was feeling, she knew that if he was in one of his moods, she wouldn't be able to take it; she'd probably break down in tears or something and if she did that, she knew she'd never be able to look him in the eye again. If it were Winnie or Pat today, it might be different, she could plead PMT as Deek had suspected, or even make up something—a little white lie to get a bit of sympathy...

She never took days off, but today—could she make this one the first? Whatever she was doing, she ought to get dressed, she thought. Peering through the grey net curtains she could see that the sky hadn't varied in colour or clarity since yesterday. "Summer in Scotland", she snorted to herself, this was a good as it got—no rain at least, and no chilling wind, but grey, opaque and generally dull. She had known the sun to shine, the heat to burn; she could remember it clearly, the first year she came here when everything was still buoyant and full of potential. It hadn't happened since as far as she could tell; and she had now acquired what she saw as typical Scottish skin; pale to the point of translucence, pimpled and prone to sunburn the moment the sun's rays hit it.

She chose her green cut off trousers and her blue vest top; clean on and still smelling of her fabric conditioner 'Jasmine and Blue Velvet'. This made her feel vaguely better as she thought of the advert—a smiling mother whipping her radiant sheets out of the machine while a smiling angel of a daughter clapped her hands in glee at the emerging smell. *Smiling angel of a daughter...* Debbie's mind wandered briefly down the path of her imagination where she and a fantasy daughter snuggled up cosily on a sofa, reading a fairy story or something... she shook her head to uproot the dream—now wasn't the time to be going down that road...

Debbie checked her watch; there was still time to decide whether or not to phone in to work, it would annoy, she had been on-call more than enough times to know that it was hopeless to try and cover her shifts—no one was willing to come in on their days off, unless they were one of the foreign workers or a student. Another cup of tea then. And a slice of toast with Marmite.

Plodding back to the small kitchen, she could hear the radio still blaring out from the kitchen, Forth FM's inane morning presenter energetically pronouncing that the National Lottery winner had not been claimed yet.

"…And that's eight point six million big ones, folks—if they don't come forward this week, it'll be a rollover…what would you do with the money, hey? Remember to check those numbers now…"

Debbie's ears pricked up, frowning to remember where she put her ticket. As the kettle threw up steam and clicked itself off, Debbie fumbled in her black leather purse. Plucking out the crumpled pink slip, she flattened it out and scanned it—at the same time thinking how useless this was as she wouldn't know what the numbers were anyway…She closed her eyes, her heart suddenly heavy, but with no idea of what was weighing it down, she just felt *tired*. And a bit stupid. Was this life with Deek really as good as it got? The same meals. The same telly—telly was ok but by the age she was now, she'd seen a lot of it before. It was the same with sex, not just the fact that Deek, once sated, would roll over and start to snore almost immediately, but also his uncharacteristic firmness on the subject of contraception. Consequently, Debbie had come to resent it more and more.

"You've taken your pill haven't you, hen?" he would ask regularly, much to Debbie's annoyance. What would he do if she got pregnant? Leave her? But knowing Deek's predictability he'd probably stick around...Debbie sighed—were things really that bad with him? She didn't know.

Flicking on the television she prodded in the buttons for tele-text, waited until the Lottery numbers came up and plucked the pink slip up again. Casually she looked back and forth from the pixelated numbers on the screen to the pale grey paper numbers on the paper.

Back and forth.

Back and—forth and

OH. MY.GOD.

(Her heart thudded.)

CHRIST!

(Her sweating fingers shook and trembled.)

SHIT!

(She was going to be sick.)

Breathe. And breathe. And breathe. *FUCKING HELL.*

She ran to the sink and was sick. She'd won. She'd won, she'd only gone and won the bloody lottery–

No. let's check again...eyes to paper. *2* (2nd February, her birthday)...eyes to screen...*2*...eyes to paper...*16* (16th November, Deek's birthday)...eyes to screen...*16*...eyes to paper...*19* (19th April, Mam's birthday)...*19*...*26* (26 Niddrie Main Road, their house number)...*26*...*31* (31 days in the month they were in, August, this was the only number in the list which changed)...*31*...eyes to paper...*39* (Debbie's age) eyes to screen...*39*

Debbie's throat felt tight and sore, dry as if she'd swallowed chalk. She breathed heavily, could feel her chest heaving but she herself had no control over it.

That's that then.

She definitely wasn't going to work today.

12 (PART 2)

She'd always said that she'd never *meant* to take the girl (besides, it wasn't technically *taking,* the girl had come with her quite willingly).

Debbie staggered off the bus on Charlotte Square, realising just in time that if she didn't get off the bus now she'd end up in Haymarket. She didn't even know what she was doing there. She didn't remember getting on the bus, she didn't remember leaving the house. What she did know was that no one knew where she was. When her stomach had finally stopped lurching and she'd checked the lottery numbers for the eighteenth time, Debbie had realised that, in a series of a few simple actions, she didn't *have* to do *anything* for *anyone else.* Ever again.

That's what that slip of pink paper had done, it had bought her time, purchased her life back so she could– Well, what could she do now? Anything, that's what, but Debbie didn't know where to start. So she hadn't phoned into work, because she now didn't have to—although the usual prick of guilt did poke at her, she'd resolutely pulled on her old beige coat and went out of the door, and now, couldn't even remember if she'd locked it. What did it matter? She didn't have anything worth stealing anyway, and even if she did she could buy it back easily now, anything of value belonged to Deek–

Deek. Oh Yes. She'd forgotten him up until now. Funny that, how someone who could occupy your mind so much, once upon a time (and there had been a time, Debbie was sure of it, when she had thought of nothing but Deek) could now be lost on the peripheries, an after thought to all that had happened in the last hour. What would he say? Well, he'd be overjoyed, she knew that much. If she wanted, she could change his life forever as well. What power the pink slip of paper had—to change lives…But in this new life of Debbie Not Having To Do Anything For Anyone Else, she didn't know if Deek even registered.

She'd bought the ticket after all, in the newsagents on Niddrie Mains Road. And she hadn't even thought about it. It was just the same thing she had done every Friday morning on the way to work, along with a pint of semi-skimmed and a *Sun* for Pat. And now look what had happened.

The sun had burned through the clouds and she'd dumped her old coat in a bin in the gardens. And then she'd led a small girl away from her parents on the pretext of buying her an ice cream.

They'd been standing on one of the side streets off Princes Street which Debbie always used so as to get off the main drag. The mother and father were huddled together, studying a map. The two daughters were standing apart, one with her head buried in a book, the other—the fairy child, ethereal and perfect, was bouncing on and off the kerb-side.

Debbie had stopped and looked at her, smiling. The child, aware she had an audience put on a performance of dancing and chanting nonsense. Eventually Debbie stepped up to her, her head giddy with the thought of what she might do. If she had this child, this girl who spoke to her so easily and seemed capable of loving so effortlessly, Debbie thought, if she could have her in her life, (instead of Deek or anyone else- people who were always *wanting* something- either tea or sex or the toilet)—life could be complete. This small creature with bouncing dark ringlets and large dark eyes who slipped her small hand into Debbie's without a protest. Even the fairy wings she wore, although cheap and gaudy, were in Debbie's eyes, from fairyland itself. She was everything childhood should be, laughing, innocent, carefree. Fate was already set.

Debbie's old scrimping, saving life was already fading, and in front of her was a gleaming ball of spinning existence, ripe and ready for her to step into and for everything else to disappear.

The little girl wouldn't mind—she already looked like she could depart from her family—although they were all dark-haired, this beauty of a child was ready for something better, such looks could not go unnoticed. Debbie could give her a wonderful life, they could buy a real castle and live out fairy tales and in the end she, Debbie, would be known as Mummy…Debbie could do that, she could do anything…

"Hello," she'd said to her, "I love your wings, you look like a real fairy." The dark-haired mother looked up absently at the voice and smiled vaguely before pointing out to her husband where she thought they ought to go.

"I am a fairy," insisted the small china doll of a child, skin so flawless it made Debbie's eyes hurt, "I can do magic."

"But what were you thinking?" they had said. They being Deek, the police woman (Shirley, she had said her name was) Caroline The Social Worker (who had now been assigned to Debbie, or Debbie to her, she didn't know how it worked). "Surely," they said, "you knew you couldn't really take a child like that? You must have thought what it would do to her parents?

And of course she'd *known* that—deep down in the recesses of her mind, of course she'd *known* it. But the huge gap between the knowing and the doing was immense. She knew that she was on a cusp, on the precipice of money and wealth, the doorway to another world within peeking distance, and today would signify the end of work, of routine, of boredom and unhappiness. The pink slip of paper would give her a memorable day. A day to catch the light. A pinky perfect day.

When was the last time that she'd wished the day would never finish? Probably as a kid—thinking it wasn't fair that Christmases and birthdays took so long to come and when they did, sped by in the blink of an eye.

As a child she was too busy living in a day to contemplate it, but at the night, tucked up under her candlewick quilt, watching the shadows on the wall, she would think with pleasure of certain moments during the day; moments which were exquisitely made; every element was there. The sun had shone, her mother had smiled a lot, the birthday cake had been flawlessly iced or the smell in the air had entirely encapsulated Christmas; cinnamon, pine—everything that it should do. Maybe that *was* perfection—it was everything everyone else said it should be.

As an adult, Debbie had given up pausing to check for perfection, because as soon as she did, the bubble would burst, the moment gone—she would occasionally give it a sly look out of the corner of her eye, but even then, it was as if the world became self-conscious and stopped doing what it was doing—something cracked and halted, and was inevitably lost.

When she'd seen the little girl, dancing about on the kerb- side, waiting for her parents to decide a direction, Debbie had wanted her, wanted to be part of her life, or even be the child herself. The feeling was the same as when the old man had stopped for her in the car, she had seen a life she'd wanted so badly that she'd wanted to eat it, wanted to inhabit each and every part of it. Today, she could have it though, that's what the pink paper meant, that was the difference. Today was a special day after all.

"One, two, three, four, five—once I caught a fish alive…"

On and off the kerb, pink shoes in the dirt.

"Six, seven, eight, nine, ten—then I put him back again…"

Edinburgh dirt, that is—Scottish dirt—was it different to English dirt? Lily didn't know. "Why did you let him go? Because he bit my finger so…"

She sang it quietly, puffing the words out as she bounced on and off the pavement, the pink shoes shouldn't be in the road, she'd already argued with Mummy about wearing them. Babs didn't like this song, or she didn't like Lily singing it, and Lily sang it a lot. Lily now ran up to her sister and raised her voice suddenly, "WHICH FINGER DID HE BITE?" waggling her right hand in between Bab's face and the book she was reading, "THIS LITTLE FINGER ON M Y RIGHT!"

Ha! That had made her look up from her boring old book anyway, should she sing it again? She should sing it again, that would get to Barbara too- Barbara-Bar-Bar-a!

"Bar-bra, Bar-bra, Barbara, Barbara, Barbara, Lar-bra, Tar- bara, Carbara, Cobra!"

On and off, on and off, shoes sparkling...magic wand, Lily's magic wand, like Chantelle's one at school but better as it was pink and had *six* fairy stones instead of five because one of Chantelle's fell out...

"Mum and Dad, Mum and Dad,
Don't know which way to go. La la la la.
Here we are in Scotland with kilts and thistles and castles and..." She looked around "and Scottish dirt and Barbara and ladies with yellow hair looking at me HEL-LO!"

And she waved at her, the lady with the blonde hair who was still looking and smiling now.

Barbara turned away from her small shouting sister in disgust, it really was too much, her being expected to tolerate this kind of behaviour. It was bad enough having to put up with it at home, let alone in public, Lily really was *so* embarrassing sometimes. Barbara looked around nervously to see if anyone else could see how stupidly her little sister was acting *so* immature...She shut her book with a small *thump*—she couldn't concentrate with all this racket anyway. Her parents were still bent over the map, unable to make *any* decision of *any* kind. Oh my god they were so thick sometimes, Dad just couldn't find his way out of a paper bag...She'd never wanted to come to Edinburgh anyway—well maybe she did, it was cool to get days off school, and they might go on one of those open-topped buses—there was a cobbled street somewhere if they could find it—Dad had told her about this, and it would be like one of those drama's on telly which she liked where the women wore corsets and all the men raised their hats hat them and said things like, "you have undone me, Miss Williams," and gave them flowers...where she *really* wanted to go was St Andrews though—which was wasn't even in Edinburgh; but she wanted to go to the school there which *Malory Towers* was based on, she'd read about it and wanted to see if it was how she'd seen it, if she could really imagine Darrell and the rest running to the next lesson—wow, that would be brilliant–

"Don't be silly, I'm not a real fairy!" Lily's voice rang out through the traffic noise. Barbara rolled her eyes again, Lily was talking to the big blonde woman who had been smiling at her, she was *so* stupid, Lily would talk to anyone, Mum was always telling her off for talking to strangers. Lily just didn't care though, if someone was paying her attention she'd speak to anyone.

"That's my sister Barbara—she's always reading a book though and books are b-o-r-i-n-g."

Stupid, that's what she was, she never read any books unless it was about Barbie or something *imma-ture*...She was still wearing that *ridiculous* fairy outfit, she hadn't taken it off since she'd got it for her birthday last month, every morning Mum would try and get her to wear something else but Lily would scream until she got her own way...*honestly*...

Barbara opened her book again, Mum and Dad would be a while yet—she heard Dad mention something about going down some road or other.

"Well, just if we pass it," he was saying while still looking at the map. "*Sticks and Stones* is one of my favourite books."

Much as she'd hate to admit it, Barbara probably got her love of reading from her father. C Blackwood was one of his favourites—that's who he was talking about now. He had written *Sticks and Stones* and according to Dad, it was one of the best, Barbara wasn't allowed to read it yet, "maybe when you're a bit older love," which made Barbara want to read it even more. C Blackwood lived in Edinburgh too but Dad didn't know where.

"I know I know! Can we just find where we are first?" Mum's annoyed voice, rumpling the map, trying to see better. Dad searching in his bum-bag for a pen.

"Well I'm just going to circle it now, or else I'll forget where it is."

"Can we not just get a bus from here?" Barbara called out, her legs were starting to ache from standing for so long and it was only ten o' clock in the morning. She could read better on a bus too.

"That's just the point," Mum still had her angry voice, "if I knew where 'here' was we could," she spoke to Dad while still looking at the map. "I knew we shouldn't have turned up here."

"But I thought it was quicker, maybe we're just here—look, this road turns up onto this one."

Barbara rolled her eyes again—honestly, it was *always* like this, anywhere new they went, Mum and Dad just couldn't find their way round. It was the same in London that time when they were trying to find Madame Tussaud's (Barbara had been so annoyed, they had found it about four-thirty in the afternoon and it was going to shut at five, she hadn't seen *half* of what she'd wanted to, they'd only just got through the 'Kings and Queens' section) and it was going to be the same here, she could tell. Mum and Dad had promised her and Lily that they would go to the castle and down the Royal Mile but at the rate they were going they wouldn't even make that, Lily would complain about something and–

Where was Lily?

Barbara had looked up momentarily from her book and over to where Lily had been jumping up and down in the gutter. But she wasn't there.

"And then can we go up that hill over there? What's on top of it? It looks like it could be the front of a castle, well not a castle but something posh…And then can we go and get a drink? I like lemonade best but usually I don't have it unless it's a treat or a party or something."

"Do you want some Coke? I've got some Coke in my bag here, it might be a bit flat..."

"No thanks, I don't like Coke actually, my mum says that's a good thing as it rots you from the inside that stuff does."

At the mention of her mother Debbie felt her stomach flip and surge but the little girl, Lily she'd said her name was, passed by the word nonchalantly and seemed not to notice that they were so far away from her parents now.

How had she done it? How had she gotten away with it? This didn't happen in real life did it? Not really, you saw it on *The Bill* all the time of course, children snatched (...*snatched*...) but not in reality, in real life children screamed, they ran off from the ones who took their hands, or she guessed they would anyway. But this child was different. It was like it was *meant to be,* their being together. Lily had just come with her, as soon as Debbie had suggested that they get an ice cream and she'd show her around Edinburgh, Lily had followed her, unquestioning. Her black curls bounced on her shoulders as she flitted in front of Debbie down the street and Debbie allowed herself the indulgent thoughts again.

She *could* have the perfect times, without even thinking about them.

She could have the hugs, the smiles, the cut knees and tears and kissing better, the wide eyes wonderment, the unconditional love and, and, and–

They were now walking quickly down George Street, Debbie had got them off Princes Street as fast as she could, easy as it was to spot people down that long straight road. And they would be spotted, she could safely guarantee that; her with this beautiful child, so unblemished and flawless, Lily's skinny, agile frame contrasting with Debbie's loose figure (she sagged in her own skin, and this was highlighted by the amount of it on show, in the now warm bright day). Lily was not just any child; Debbie could see others taking in the sight of her and smiling; and it wasn't just the fairy wings or the grin on her face (was that smile because of Debbie? She almost didn't dare to hope) but simply the air around the girl was alive with a feverish infectious excitement.

Debbie had simply led her away. '*Taken*' the newspapers would say…she imagined the news, the press conferences; flashing bulbs reflected on the tear-stained cheeks of the mother who pleaded helplessly into the camera, replacing its lens with the eyes of her child's abductor—*kidnapper*…Debbie physically shook her head to rid herself of the thought.

"This is one of the luckiest days of my life," she said aloud, more to herself than the girl, and then finding her small face upturned towards her own she grinned down, "did you know that, Lily?"

"Why?"

"Well, have you heard of the National Lottery?"

D'uh! EVERYONE has heard of the lottery," Lily rolled her eyes

"Well I've just one won it."

The girl's open brown eyes with their paintbrush lashes went wide with incredulation.

"No. Way," she pronounced slowly, mimicking an American television programme. But then, aware that her leg might be being pulled, Lily put her hands on her hips theatrically, "How do I know you're telling the truth?"

"Well..." started Debbie uncertain how to go on, "you're the first person I've told," she drew out the pink slip from her handbag, and stared at it, frowning, "I should take it to a shop I suppose."

"Is that it? Is that the winning ticket?" The girl's face was alight with wonder, and reached out her hand to touch it, automatically Debbie held it out of her reach and carefully tucked it away in her bag again.

"Best not, hey?" she said blithely, her heart thudding loudly as she realised what a risk she had just taken, showing it to Lily and getting it out in public—what if it had blown away, or someone had simply snatched it—where would she be then?

"But you've got to take it somewhere!" Lily was jumping in and out of the gutter again "to a shop or a police station or something...how much money have you won? What are you going to do with it?"

"I don't know yet," she looked down and feeling more confident, took Lily's hand, who gave it up readily, "What would you do with it?"

There was no hesitation in Lily's answer. "I'd buy a million CurlyWurlys, a new fairy outfit 'cause this one is old and I want another one, I'd buy a plane so we could all go to Disney World, then I'd buy us a new house—a castle where we could all live, you could come too," she added to Debbie.

"That's nice of you," smiled Debbie, "What else would you have?"

They had come to St Andrew's Square at the end of George Street and Debbie wondered where they could go from here. No one seemed to be noticing their presence, everyone within their own thoughts on their own path, housewives and young mothers, a fair sprinkling of tourists already on their way out from their hotels; matching kagools and cameras, foreign languages reaching Debbie's ears, swirling around them in a haze.

They turned and Debbie could hear a shout behind her, Lily turned as well. On the corner of Rose Street there was a homeless man selling the Big Issue magazine. He shouted up and down, "Big is-SHOO. Big is-SHOO."

Debbie had seen him several times, but always ignored him. He didn't look particularly scruffy or dirty, just a heavily lined face and a voice full of gravel. Lily was several skips ahead, Debbie could see that she had her eyes fixed on the man, he drew her attention, magnetised her to him, just by the fact that he was shouting; she just *had* to see what he was shouting about. Lily ran, stretching the distance between her and Debbie. Debbie didn't like that pull, she trotted quicker, her chest jiggling, she could feel herself get- ting out of breath but she could predict the child's intentions—it wasn't a risk she could take; anything which involved Lily talking to anyone else, anything that might be memorable–

"Slow down will you?"

But before Debbie could stop her, Lily had ran up to the Big Issue vendor and asked, "Why are you selling a big shoe?" The vendor looked at her, puzzled, "What's that, hen?"

"I'm not a hen!" shouted Lily, laughing, and he laughed too. Debbie puffed up behind her.

"Stop it!" she cried, eyes close to tears she grabbed Lily's hand, "Lily shut up, come on!" and she pulled her away, her mind buzzing, stupid girl, stupid girl, stupid girl. Lily was not impressed. She wrenched her hand away from Debbie.

"What are you doing?"

"You shouldn't talk to strangers!" Debbie found herself saying breathlessly.

"You're a stranger," Lily shrugged.

"I know," gasped Debbie, "but I'm different."

"How?"

"I just am, now come on, shall we go and get an ice cream?" *Please,* Debbie thought, *please just forget…just pretend that didn't happen.*

"Where's my mum?"

"She's…she's…" (*Oh God. Oh God. What do I say? What do I do? What have I done?*) Debbie was frantic, "She's up there!" she cried, her finger pointing up to Calton Hill, like it was a distant planet, "She said she'd meet us up there."

"Ok," Lily had shrugged, intent on the thought of ice cream again. "Can I get raspberry ripple?"

"You can get whatever you like," Debbie breathed, her shoulders pumping. There was a muggy, stifling feel to the air, there seemed to be no freshness in it, as if it was all recycled and Debbie couldn't get her breath.

On the steps up to Calton Hill, Lily was still chattering away to herself when they passed a girl bumping her buggy down. Her face was strained in tight concentration, as she tried to stop jiggling the baby inside too much. Debbie glanced up at her and they exchanged a look; it conveyed two mothers feeling the same exasperation—the girl trying to struggle with a buggy down these bloody steps, and Debbie, slowly following her nattering 'daughter' up to a hill she probably didn't want to go up in the first place. The look said, 'the things we do for kids, hey?' And Debbie was warmed to the core that she could be mistaken for Lily's mother.

The sun had burnt through the clouds by the time they'd got to the top. Debbie came puffing up a good few yards behind Lily's light flitting steps. The wind made Lily's pink net skirt float and wave around her and she squealed with delight. She went running over the grass, waving her wand, up and down the sides of the verge off the path, apparently forgetful of Debbie's promise that her mother would meet them up here. The wind caught her breath and scream. Debbie, delighted, ran after her as fast as she was able. She was a child again, as she hadn't been or felt for many years. They bounded together over the slopes, the wind gushing and blasting them from all sides. Suddenly Lily stopped short, spotting something a few feet in front of them.

It was a woman sat on a bench and on seeing her, Debbie stopped too, suddenly feeling self-conscious and silly. She had thought they were the only people on the hill. The woman wasn't looking at them though, she didn't even seem to have noticed they were there. She was looking out to the distance, over to the stretch of Firth, which Debbie could just make out on the horizon.

Lily was staring at the woman, and then mouthing something to Debbie, who frowned as she tried to make out what she was saying. Lily was giggling at the same time and silently pointing at the woman, hiding a smile behind her hand.

As Debbie approached the figure from behind, she could make out that there was something not quite right about the way the woman was sitting. She had her feet stretched in front of her, but she was slumped, not fully sitting on the bench itself, with her head sat at an awkward angle. Lily had stepped up to the figure and was peering closely at her, her small face crinkled.

Debbie joined her in front of the woman and she saw in an instant that the stranger was dead. The woman's headscarf had slipped in the wind and uncovered thin wisps of hair. The cheek-bones poked the skin which was tissue-like in its thinness. *Probably cancer*, Debbie found herself thinking, having seen the remnants of the disease many times now. Strange, how once a person was dead, they were known as a different name; Cancer, Heart Attack or Car Crash, their names replaced by what had killed them, all other history seemingly having disappeared. Debbie's fingers went cold, what had she done, bringing a child up here, would Lily notice? Lily was staring, smirking at the woman.

"She's asleep...shhhh!" she said, holding her fingers up to her lips.

Thank God, Debbie thought and tugged at Lily's hand, "Yes she is, now come on, don't wake her."

Lily had stepped a little closer to the woman, the gaze on her face was that of a focused trance, her fore finger was near the woman's hand, ready to poke, ready to shake, Debbie caught hold of her wrist just in time.

"Come on then!" she said, her voice too high, too loud and she spun Lily away, running so she would chase after her, at the same time muttering, blinking, shaking her head to throw away the picture of the dead woman's face from her mind. "Come on come on, let's get going, going, going," she half-sang under her breath as they hurried over the grass to the wide shallow steps at the other side to the hill leading to Blenheim Place and the top of Leith Walk—to other people, alive ones, walking, talking—roads they could lose themselves down, blend into and disappear in...Leith was good for that; the roads were not so straight as the New Town, there were more corners to hide down.

By mid-afternoon the Haar had crept into the city like a blanket of snow on a crime scene. For Debbie it was so welcome that she began think she might believe in God. The cool sea mist drifted in and around the streets, covering her and Lily's footsteps. So far, Debbie had noticed no one following them. There were no surges of police cars, no fencing off of areas where they had last been seen, for what Debbie had just done, she thought, there seemed to be no reaction whatsoever.

And now, here was the fog enveloping them like a cloud. Hiding them from searching eyes, aiding and abetting their escape.

"I don't like it," Lily's voice wavered through the thickening mists, sounding small and frightened.

"Don't worry," Debbie's hand tightened around her small companion's, " just keep hold of my hand." It was if they were stepping into another world, or at least a space between worlds.

"I don't like it," Lily whimpered again, her voice growing louder and more shrill, "I want to go home now, I want to go home," she started saying. Although there were not a lot of other people about, Debbie could feel eyes upon them. She was every inch aware of Lily wriggling away from her now, her small body surprisingly strong, the young mind using all its will to force Debbie away.

"Come on Lily," Debbie said through nervous gritted teeth, unused to trying to negotiate with a child, "we're not far now."

"Not far from *where?*" Lily whined loudly, "I'm *tired,* I'm *hungry,* I want to go *home* and–"

"Shh Lily, come on now!" Debbie cajoled loudly with rubbery cheer.

"And–" Lily grew even louder.

"Lily–" Debbie said steadily, desperate to keep the peace. "AND I WANT M Y MUM!"

The sentence hung in the air, a weighty block on wire. Who had heard it? Who had it hit? The Haar was so thick now that Debbie couldn't even see the people who walked within a few feet, but they were close, she

knew that, she could hear breathing and talking and after Lily's battering ram of a statement, Debbie felt sure
she heard intakes of breath, tutting whispers. For all she
knew there was a pair of searching policeman's ear and
eyes a few inches away in the fog.

Debbie looked to the sky, the fog so thick that
she felt she could be in a cloud, suspended in mid-air.
What should she do, Lily, still wriggling in her grip, had
started making indeterminable whining noises, a bored
monkey.

"Want to go home, want to go back," she went on,
"I'm *hungry,* I'm *tired…*" every elongated syllable another
poke at Debbie, accentuating her innocence of motherhood or even babysitting, (her only past experience being a few hours watching television with her neighbour's
four year old daughter).

"*Ok,*" Debbie breathed hard trying her best to re-
main calm. This was not part of the dream, part of the
perfection. Children didn't whine and shout and pull
like this in dreams, they obeyed and looked up at you
with unconditional love…the pinky daydream shimmered and swelled, ready to pop.

Lily still dragged on her arm. If Debbie knew the
girl any better she would have recognised the rise in the
tone of her voice, the wobble at the back of her throat.
All of Lily's family knew these as sure signs that she was
gearing up for a full throttle tantrum.

"Let's go and get something to eat then, what do
you want?" Debbie's last stand, trying to console with
food, anything to quieten the child down, anything

to fight this reality which was quickly eating away her fantasy.

"I want to go *back* NOW!" Lily's voice rose up and down, from side to side, a verbal rollercoaster.

"We could go to McDonald's—how about that, hey?" Debbie knew that all stops must now be pulled, even if it placed them closer to being discovered. Her anxieties had touched the ceiling of the shell of her patience. She was out of her depth. She could feel herself sweating despite the cold fog that swirled around them. Any minute now, she thought, any minute there would be a heavy hand on her shoulder, a deep voice in her ear enquiring if this really was her child and where did she think she was going and what did she think she was doing?

And what would she say? What could she say? That she had walked off with Lily as you would a wild flower, illicitly picked from a hedgerow. Because she'd just won the lottery.

Had she? Had she really won?

And she'd taken Lily because she could, because she wasn't going into work that day, in fact she was never going back, and really she *could* take this flower, this Lily, this child and run away, into the sun of a perfect life...

But now, with the fading flower stuck in a vase on a window sill, it looked forlorn and not nearly as pretty as it did in the field, surrounded by grasses in the wind.

Lily was whining loudly now, winding herself up to screams. And then, piercing through the fog, Debbie heard the voice, disembodied and familiar, she knew then that the bubble had burst and life—with or without the pink slip of paper, would never be the same again.

"Debbie hen," Deek's voice swam through the thick air, "You ok?" Then another voice, a good round Edinburgh accent,

"Is that you Miss Bennett? Have you got the child with you?"

Other voices, younger, vaguely recognisable, "Has she *what?*"

"What? Dad, you didn't say anything about a kid–" "You just said she'd wandered off–"

"Look lads, let's just calm down, I'll explain everything later, Debbie love…" An outstretched hand, ghostly in the fog.

"Deek, I–" she began, wondering how he had got here, what was he thinking? This man who she now lived with, as though married to him. How to explain? How to get away?

"It's ok, it's ok," he used a gentle tone she was thoroughly unused to, it spoke right through to her heart.

Lily's small voice whispered, the whine having gone "Can I go home now?"

In St Leonard's police station, Lorna the assistant desk sergeant was bagging up Deborah Bennett's belongings; a cheap Gucci imitation handbag, faded and cracked with multiple holes in the lining, half an open pack of tissues, an empty tube of Mintos, keys; three Yales, two silver, one gold and what looked like a key for a mortis lock, a lighter, pink, a crumpled pack of Benson and Hedges with two broken cigarettes. A tiny brown teddy bear, faded and worn with one ear missing, well thumbed, his thread of a smile just hanging on.

Together with these items was a huge bundle of receipts and odd scraps of paper. Receipts for everything that Debbie Bennett bought it seemed—pints of milk, biscuits, baked beans, DVDs (*Steel Magnolias* and *Annie*) and Chinese takeaways. There were nearly fifteen bus tickets as well as old lottery tickets, torn and screwed.

Sighing to herself, Lorna wondered how some women ever found anything in handbags of these states. She placed a clutch of papers onto the desk, the small wisps and slips toppling on top of each other. At that moment the telephone rang and in her haste to answer it, Lorna's elbow caught the edge of the small tower of receipts that held ally to Deborah Bennett's recent comings and goings. The tower fell, like autumn leaves down to the scuffed linoleum. Lorna tutted into the receiver, making the unknown caller frown at the other end of the phone.

"Saint Leonard's police station," Lorna's voiced strained as she held the phone under her chin at the same time struggling to pick up the slips from the floor. To her eyes she had picked them all up, but into a corner of the heavy shadowy desk glided one pink slip with six numbers printed on it. By the time Maureen, the station cleaner spotted it and crumpled it, unchecked, into a clear plastic bag, Deborah Bennett had been released on bail.

Walking slowly out of the station, blinking in the pale daylight, Debbie left St Leonards wondering if the day of the lottery win and the fairy girl had all been just a dream. Needless to say, no one had believed her about the win,there was no evidence to say that she had even bought a ticket, let alone won the whole jackpot. When asked her numbers, she found to her horror that all her mind threw up was an empty blank space, the numbers she had used ever since she'd started doing the lottery simply disappeared into thin air.

Suspicion turned to pity in the WPC's face as the interrogation turned into a confession. Lily's parents didn't want to press charges, they had simply wanted to turn on their heels as quickly out of Edinburgh as possible. And Debbie had seen herself through the young police woman's eyes; a sad sack of a mad woman, who had just wanted to have a kid for the day and a few hours off work.

Debbie never mentioned the woman on the hill. Not even when news came to Deek about how his ex-wife had climbed to the top of Calton Hill and quietly died. Debbie had flushed scarlet when he had told her, she couldn't meet his eyes. It was incredible that the only time she had seen Valerie Lambert close up had been when she was dead. She couldn't tell Deek, she wouldn't have believed her anyway, already thinking she was unhinged, he treated her as he would an eccentric, fragile and elderly relative. They split up a few months later, when Deek found that he could no longer come back to a cold, dark house where Debbie would be sat in the dying light, glued to the television, no tea in the oven and no real conversation, or sex, or cups of tea. It was Deek who moved out, but Debbie who moved from the city.

EPILOGUE

*L*ily *looked out at the fluttering landscape. The hills had been becoming more prominent and rounded since they'd crossed the borders into Scotland. For the last half-hour there had been dramatic coastline on her right; the sea glinting with white waves crashing on the rocks far below her. The train ride had not been that long, but she felt like she'd travelled a great distance. Manchester seemed a long time ago, although it had only taken a few hours.*

The accents around her in the carriage had accentuated the feeling of being a stranger to Scotland. She reluctantly admitted to herself that she was indeed coming as a day-tripper, a tourist, but in her mind she knew every inch of Edinburgh, having re-visited it again and again in the past few months. She had been turning the views and the scenery of the city as she remembered it over in her mind. The map of Edinburgh had been sketched within her with the help of strangers; Lynn, Ellie and Michelle, the facilitator who had encouraged Lily to go back to Edinburgh in the first place.

"Just be careful," she'd warned, "Make sure you take someone else with you."

But Lily hadn't wanted to go with anyone else. John had offered but she didn't want him around, didn't want to have to explain her actions. Or if she was completely honest with herself she didn't want to become emotional in front of him. She couldn't rationalise it, it wasn't that she'd never cried in front of John, but this was a portion of her life that she'd never shared with anyone else and she didn't know how she was going to react when she encountered the scenery again. She didn't want to feel beholden to anyone; to have to make sure things weren't awkward for them. Besides, it had probably been about twenty-five years since she'd done something on her own. Over the years, she and John had become one single package, a unit who never did anything without the other. It was out of habit rather than any deep co-dependence, but it did feel odd booking a hotel room with a single bed and coming back from the buffet carriage with only one cup of coffee and a single Snakcake.

By six 'o clock in the evening she had arrived in Edinburgh Waverley. The strong summer light blanketing the city as Lily stepped out of the station and up the gentle slope to Waverley bridge, dragging her small suitcase on wheels behind her.

The moment she saw the outline of the toy city across the bridge, she could see that it was not how she remembered, but it had retained something that rang deep bells within her. Thirty-nine years it had been since she had stood on these streets—and technology was making its mark in the ancient city; a high-speed train that shot through Waverley like a whispering bullet. Trams instead of buses rattled around the streets, so it had an old fashioned feel even though the trams were modern slick white Crawlers which were now inhabiting most cities in the north of Britain.

Lily glanced around, nervous to make a move. She busied herself with checking the hotel reservation copied into her digital organiser.

Fifteen minutes later she had slid the key card into the lock of her hotel room and the door swung open. Lily went in, closing the door behind her and silence descended upon her. She sat on the narrow hard bed, her back straight, the street noise dimmed to hush behind the loose rattling window.

Her phone buzzed its way to her attention from the bottom of her handbag. She pressed the green call button, already knowing that it would be John.

"Hello?"

"Hello love, how are you?"

"Ok," she paused, "I'm at the hotel now."

"How is it? How was the journey?"

"Not bad." She was aware of how quiet and vague she was being, but she couldn't bring herself to be any more bright or enthusiastic. It was how she felt inside, still, quiet—almost at peace, like things were finally fitting into place.

Lily had caught Edinburgh's ancient smell; the breweries were still working, although all the manual labour had been replaced by machinery long ago. But the air was still filled with the scent she had smelled only once, when she was six years old and led by the hand, away from her parents.

But she had followed only too readily…was that what was pushing depression on her now? Maybe that was what highlighted her uneasiness about the episode; would all children have gone so willingly? Would her kids have gone too? And it was willingness, she remembered that now too, how she had been bored; Babs had her nose in a book, her parents were busy looking at the map and arguing, Lily had felt ignored, pushed to the side. When she had seen Debbie smiling at her she had felt like she was back in a familiar place. As a child, Lily had been comfortable in the limelight, she knew it led to a good place, to people smiling at you and telling you nice things. Lily had often been told how pretty she was, and how good at she was at singing and dancing. She had liked being told things like this, particularly when it was in front of her parents, who never seemed to praise her in the same way other people did.

In the same way Debbie had.

In her darkening hotel room, thirty-nine years later, Lily Maxwell remembered how a blonde woman, ordinary looking and slightly overweight, had led her away from her parents when she was six and told her how special she was.

"I didn't pick just anyone," Debbie had told her, later on in the day, "I saw you from miles away and I thought how pretty you were and how you were just like a fairy."

In the thin evening light, forty-five year old Lily let her thoughts wander. The memories became clarified in her mind; wondering if it was actually being in Edinburgh and amongst the same stones that made things clearer to her now. Or was it simply that she was allowing the memories to come at last? Vividly, calmly and without judgement. They had been waiting for more than four decades after all. Debbie had just won the lottery, or so she said. Lily remembered being unsure about whether to believe her. Her mother revealed, years later that Debbie's lottery 'winning ticket' had never been found. The press had had a field day.

Lily had felt privileged that Debbie had chosen her, although she didn't really know what she had been chosen for. Later that day was when the unease had set in, even as a child, Lily remembered that she had felt anxious; what were they doing walking around a city Lily didn't know and Debbie was unsure of? The woman hadn't been confident (as an adult Lily could see that now) she hadn't been sure of what she was doing or where she was going—Lily had dictated most of their move-

ments, where they should stop for a drink or something to eat, which streets they should turn onto.

There was only once when Debbie had firmly led her, and that was when they had come down from the hill.

'Calton Hill' Lily saw it must have been. She had looked at the 3D map online during the journey, and decided it couldn't have been Arthur's Seat they'd walked up, that looked too high. The hill she and Debbie had walked up had been quite a small one, although the view, she now thought, had been spectacular.

They had been the only people up there at half-past ten in the morning. It was early enough to miss most of the tourists who had been milling around the city; a group had been on their way up there as they came back down; a gaggle of Japanese tourists complete with huge cameras and blind smiles.

But there had been one other person on the hill. The woman on the bench. The young Lily had thought she was old, but now, in her mind's eye she saw that at most she would have been in her mid-fifties. The memory of the woman swam into her mind, it was because she had been asleep that six year old Lily had thought it odd; that someone should be asleep on top of a hill. People went to sleep in their beds at home, or on sofas in front of the television, not at mid-morning on a bench, on top of a hill where everyone could see…the woman was sat as if she was looking across the tops of the houses to the Firth, as if she was just sunbathing with her eyes shut (Lily had seen people do this, they closed their eyes and tilted their heads towards the sun, and they usually smiled as if it was the best thing in the world).

In the dim hotel room Lily Maxwell aged forty-five lay fully clothed on the bed. The faint din of the city fell in and out through the window. Something ticked in the back of her

*mind, something counted down expectantly, until suddenly she
sat bolt upright, the timer in her mind reading 0.00...*

*That woman had been dead. That had been it. That had
been why Debbie had flushed suddenly and had pulled at her to
"come along now" they had to get going. The woman had been
dead and Lily had never realised.*

*How should she react to that? How did she feel? Should
she—did she really have the right to feel anything at all? She felt
herself breathing hard in the dim twilight, and feeling slightly
sick. And guilty. Yes, there was definitely a guilt attached now,
as if she had danced on someone's grave or laughed at a funeral. It was if she had had no right to witness the woman's
body, or her last moments (if that had what they had been).
The woman had been a stranger, yes, but one who was newly
dead, her soul could have still been close and Lily had simply
twizzled around her dressed in her pink fairy wings and licked
a raspberry ripple.*

*Then again, how was she to know? What blame could a
six year old possibly have in the greater scheme of things? She
didn't know, but she imagined an inkling of this feeling lay in
the dark, cold lives of the women in the Survivors of Childhood
Abuse group. It was the same confusion, the same thought that
it could have been their faults in some way. The zig-zag reason-
ing of children's minds.*

*Lily didn't feel hungry and so for the rest of the evening
she lay on the bed, the television making welcome background
noise. She made herself tea with the small kettle that seemed to
have been resident in the hotel for years, the amount of lime
scale that carpeted the bottom. There were two packets of shortbread biscuits in tartan wrapping and Lily then remembered
the hotel that she, Babs and her parents had stayed in on that*

holiday. It had been decorated with tartan on every surface; carpets, wallpaper, chairs and tablecloths. It gave the whole place a dark, gloomy air, like that of a cartoon haunted house and Lily recalled that this had scared her. She'd made Babs keep the light on for as long as possible in their room when they'd lain under their scratchy tartan blankets.

The next morning she awoke to piercing sunlight shattering through the cheap worn curtains of the hotel. She turned over, feeling uncomfortable for having slept in her clothes. She got up slowly, feeling delicate and almost hung-over, her mouth dry and the folds of the pillow having made an imprint on her cheek.

She showered for a long time, and was relieved to be in possession of a slight appetite when she had finished.

"Sorry I'm late."

"You're ok, it's only just gone ten."

"Still, I meant to be here a bit earlier."

They were being overly polite with each other, Michael could feel it taught and strained between them. It was understandable he supposed. Given the circumstances.

It was like this every year though. They would meet at the foot of Calton Hill on the morning of the 16th of August, sometimes the sun would shine, sometimes it wouldn't. They could usually depend on the hill being deserted at this hour, there might be a few alcoholics sleeping off the night in the bushes or else some wide-eyed young men in tight jeans wandering down the steps holding hands.

They had started coming here on the year after their mother had died. Michael couldn't even remember who had suggest-

ed it. Derek probably. It had been round the time he had been trying to become more in touch with his feelings or however he put it...Michael gazed into the middle distance inhaling on his cigarette. Every year, usually on this day actually, he told himself he should stop. And he would, one day. He'd promised his daughter Mary as much, what with her mother dying of the bloody things, it was the least he could do; and he had cut down—a little, that's what he'd told Mary anyway.

Mary approved of this ritual he and Derek had; of remembering the dead when they had been forgotten by everyone else. After all if you weren't going to remember the woman who gave birth to you, who would you remember? That's what Mary had said anyway. Every year she would go to St Patrick's and light a candle for her own mother (Mary having converted to Catholism in the last ten years); it was her way of doing things, but Leanne would have hated it. Ironically, Michael had got to know Leanne better after he'd impregnated her. She'd finally told him that Mary was his two years after she was born, and even then, they'd kept their distance from each other, only meeting up for Mary's sake. As they grew older and mellowed a little, they'd began to talk more and even got to where they could call each other friends. Michael had more of an involvement with Mary's life although she never really thought of him as a father.

He and Derek started to slowly climb up the crumbling steps of Calton Hill. Within minutes, both of them were puffing.

"God!" Michael blew out, "What a couple of old fuckers!"

Derek smiled. It was true, he would be seventy this year and God did he feel it. If he was honest with himself he didn't really know why they still did this old routine every year. Their mother had been dead nearly forty years and here they were, still *traipsing up this bloody hill every year just to look at the spot where she popped her clogs.*

"Isn't this actually really morbid, Mikey?"

His brother stopped on his step and looked at him. "What?"

"Isn't this…" he gestured to the air which surrounded him, "…actually really fucking morbid? Trundling up this bloody hill every year to look at where Mum died? What's the use in it?"

"Ach Derek, don't get so het up about it," Michael shrugged airily, "it's nice, isn't it? We hardly see each other at all these days—especially since you've moved, and I think it's good to still think about Mum—I mean, she's been gone a hell of a long time but she was still our bloody mother wasn't she? No-one else remembers her, Dad's gone," he took a last pull on the fag, "and let's face it, we don't do something once a year for him do we?" Michael stubbed out his cigarette before moving quickly up the steps, although he had to stop quickly again and take the next few slowly.

"God this gets harder every year," Derek muttered to himself.

They finally reached the top. The sun was breaking through the smattering of clouds, just like it had on that morning when they had raced up here on the back of the phone call, and had found the body of Valerie Lambert slumped on the bench, gazing out to the Firth as if waiting for a ship to appear.

It was somewhat perverse to remember this particular day anyway, thought Derek. Surely it would be better to remember a happier day, her birthday or something, one where they could actually visualise her as happy, enjoying herself. Why would they commemorate a day where they could only remember her awkwardly thin body sat at a crooked angle, lifeless and empty? Coupled with this was the memory of when that woman Debbie had lost it and snatched a child...horrible business; the kid had been unharmed, but the whole situation had a real sinister shade to it. Derek thought, it could have been so much worse... Debbie was long gone now of course, well, he supposed she was. She'd disappeared under strange circumstances anyhow, now that he came to think about it...his grey memory was hazy over it, but afterwards it had come to light that she'd won a lot of money on that lottery thing that had been fashionable at the time and when she'd found out about it she'd flipped, went into town and snatched a little girl, who'd have thought it of her? It just went to show what money did to you, he'd been earning a fortune once upon a time and it hadn't made him happy—less so because of it probably.

Debbie had disappeared a few months after...no word to their father, who had been lost for a time...the two women gone from his life. He and their mother had not seen much of each other in the last years but Derek had always had the feeling he'd still loved her. Their father had cried openly at her funeral... his small neat little wife of seventeen years, those feelings don't just go away...And Debbie had left him as well, the poor sod, he'd had to make his own cups of tea...Derek now snorted at the thought.

He struggled to remember Debbie, but her face was blurred in his mind. He could remember a bulky frame, long blonde hair—nothing like his mother of course. She had been his father's last girlfriend, he never met anyone else after her; Derek Senior had cut a lonely figure up until the day he died, although he had his couple of mates who he drank with at the Castle. Derek and Michael would call round the house in Nid-

drie and it would always be in a worse state than when they saw it last...He'd died thirty years ago now, and neither Derek nor Michael had said that they'd missed him, he was just one of those fathers; practical, quiet and distant. They had known him only by coincidence really. Genetics and habit the keystones to their relationship.

The two brothers finally reached the peak of the hill and looked around for the bench, which although it had come in different guises over the years (painted and re-painted, wooden and iron) it still sat in the same position, looking out over and down Leith Walk, the houses and buildings fanning into Porto-bello and Mussleburgh. And out to the left there lay Newhaven, Leith docks, Granton and Cramond. Depending on how he felt each year, Derek had seen Edinburgh as huge and sprawling; an intricate mess of brick and strangers, or else tiny; a city of meaningless ants.

There was a woman on the bench. For a moment both he and Michael stood looking at her back, their hearts in their mouths. It wasn't that the woman looked like their mother, she wasn't even sat like their mother had been, or be mistaken for her from the back. But it had never happened before, there had never been anyone sat on this bench on the sixteenth of August, in all the years they had been walking up here. It gave them both a very odd feeling, as if they had come across a stranger wearing their mother's clothes.

At first it was awkward. The two elderly men had come over and just looked at her. "Am I in your seat?" Lily had asked, on the verge of getting up.

The taller of the two had stuttered, "Not our seat, no," but when Lily had gone to moved, the smaller man had said,

"Don't worry hen, it's just that there's never been anyone else sitting on this seat in all the years we've been coming up here."

And they'd told her. They'd explained that this was where their mother had breathed her last. And then Lily had explained that this was where she had been taken by a stranger, on her only visit to Edinburgh, aged six. Not exactly abducted, but Lily now felt that if she hadn't been such a precocious child—and a show off to boot, she might not have got in, or out of the situation.

And if she hadn't had such a fondness for raspberry ripple ice cream...And if she hadn't sought attention so much...

And if she hadn't been such a pretty child...And if...what if?

And it was their mother she'd seen. Not only that, the three united strangers discovered, but it was Debbie, their father's girlfriend (and well-regarded nut case within the family) who saw Mrs Valarie Lambert's newly deceased body before anyone else. She had never told anyone.

But it was also because she'd had Lily with her; Lily who she had led away from her parents not one hour ago. Lily Peters, aged six. Licking a raspberry ripple ice cream.

The three had sat on the bench for a good two hours. Who would have thought they had so much to talk about? Lily wondered. They had all only met each other once, forty years ago but the more she spoke to them the more she remembered how they had been on that day when they'd eventually caught up with her and Debbie.

At the time she'd thought how strange it was that three men had puffed up to them through the thick fog (it had been so thick that Lily had kept seeing her feet disappearing, caught up *in the opaque air) and asked what Debbie was doing and didn't she think she ought to go home? For Lily, it had come as a huge relief. The men had provided a halt in the mystery of the slow plodding through the fog, Lily becoming more exhausted and upset the more they went on.*

The men had kept looking at Lily and she had felt shy because of it; ordinarily she would have basked in this attention, but now they made her feel self-conscious, she'd wanted a familiar neck to hide in and she wished for her father.

There was a lot of shouting, Lily remembered that much, Debbie stuttering, her cheeks wet and red. She began hissing to the oldest man about the lottery ticket. The shorter man with the darker hair was winding his finger round his ear like Barbara did when she wanted to annoy their mother, it was a sign that he thought she was loopy—Lily knew that. It was the same man who had told Debbie to take Lily back to her parents, the other men nodding and agreeing.

"But they'll lock me away," Debbie had said, "What will they do to me? What will they do, Deek?"

By then it had been five o'clock in the evening and Lily's feet were heavy and sore. She wanted to be at home then with her mum and her dad and her white blanket which she still slept with, even though Babs said she was too old to have it…she even missed Barbara…Debbie had knelt down to her.

"Don't you want to stay with me, Lily I can buy you anything you want, you know."

Debbie was shaking, she gripped Lily's shoulders hard.

"Please can you take me back, please?" It was the first time in the day that Lily had been scared and her voice emerged as a tiny lost bird. Debbie's mouth crinkled up and started to wobble, she caught the small child up in a strong hug. Lily made the

woman's arms wet when she started to cry too, although it was mostly out of tiredness than anything else.

At the police station Debbie was marched off as soon as the double doors opened on St Leonard's reception. Lily ran to her parents' open arms.

Barbara scowled from behind her book. Deek hurried in after Debbie, feeling obliged to look after her. She would tell him to leave ten minutes after, not needing him anymore. This day had levered her out of her rut, and the rut had included Deek. With her pink slip in her pocket, her ticket to another life, she didn't need him. Seven minutes after this, Deborah Bennett was told to turn out her pockets, the pink slip included. As we know it was bound to its fate under the desk of Lorna, only to be swept away like leaves on the wind.

Derek and Michael stood outside of St Leonards, each puffing silently on a cigarette. They had witnessed the happy reunion, they had shaken their heads at their father's and Debbie's behavior. Michael looked to the sky and thought how mad the world had got since he'd been allowed back into it and wondered if that was simply a coincidence. Derek's mobile phone rang and he made Michael answer it.

The brothers' worlds imploded and expanded simultaneously as he listened to the voice on the other end. A voice belonging to a nurse who worked at the Royal Infirmary. Telling him that they'd just found out the identity of a woman who'd been found dead at the top of Calton Hill. A Mrs Valarie Lambert. They'd got this number from a small piece of torn paper found in Mrs Lambert's purse.

Thirty-nine years later the two elderly brothers took the middle-aged woman who their father's ex-girlfriend had taken *away from her parents when she was just six for a drink in Robbie's on Leith Walk. It was a pub of a dying breed, where the bar was still wooden, the walls still held peeling mirrors of a century ago and old men still in the corner and remembered when you could smoke, and smoke anywhere. Derek, Michael and Lily sat at a wobbling table and raised their glasses, to Mrs Valarie Lambert, to Lily and to the funny quirks of life. Was this what Gillian would have called closure? Lily wondered. A shaft of guilt hit her at the thought of her little 'episode' being tied up nicely like this, all neatly done up with a bow on top (although there was now a new sharp sourness with the thought of poor Valarie Lambert, sat dead and hunched all those years ago while Debbie and Lily leapt like butterflies around her) whereas the other members of the Survivors of Childhood Abuse would not get within spitting distance of any exit sign from their experience. They would be stuck in their limbo, tied to the dock, swaying this way and that; just about floating*

There is a street on a city, pavement ribboning the edges. The cars and buses rumble past, bicycles darting in between like insects. The pedestrians bob along, some looking at who goes past, some ignoring them; packed into their own worlds wrapped up in phones, in music or communicating in cyber space. Invisible to the naked eye; fine threads of gossamer connection, winding around lampposts, hooking onto railings, the delicate links stretching out all around the houses, webbing the inhabitants together. Further and further they extend, out into the countryside, across roads, in and out of towns, doors and windows. Who knows who? Which bodies and minds have met, kissed, conversed, argued or hit? Where are the connections?

Where are the hidden doors for those who are not even strangers yet?

That's what Lily Maxwell knows now, that within Edinburgh there is a door with her name written on it, and it's been opened for thirty-nine years. Propped open for her memories and anxieties to float down, but now it is firmly, and quietly, closed.

CPSIA information can be obtained at www.ICGtesting.com
Printed in the USA
LVOW041844140113

315672LV00001B/95/P

9 781469 931722